brutal
INTENTIONS

LILITH VINCENT

BRUTAL INTENTIONS by LILITH VINCENT

Copyright © 2022 Lilith Vincent

| All Rights Reserved |

Cover design by Untold Designs
Editing by Fox Proof Editing

No part of this book may be used or reproduced in any manner whatsoever without written permission from the publisher, except brief quotations for reviews. Thank you for respecting the author's work.

This book is a work of fiction. All characters, places, incidents and dialogue are drawn from the author's imagination and are not to be construed as real. Any similarities between persons living or dead are purely coincidental.

This book was made possible by Christian Locke's thirst traps. The world is wetter—I mean better—because of them.

BRUTAL INTENTIONS: AN ENEMIES TO LOVERS ROMANCE

He's devious. Corrupted. And his brutal heart wants me.

Lazzaro Rosetti just locked eyes with fresh prey: the virginal, high-school girl from a rival family. Me, Mia Bianchi.

He's screwed his way through half the city's female population and he's running wild—until his family finds a way to curb his behavior by forcing him to wed.

When he speaks his vows at the altar, he's holding Mom's hands, but his menacing green eyes are staring right at me.

From the moment he crosses our threshold, Lazzaro makes my life hell. I'm Mom's unprotected and despised youngest daughter and Lazzaro inhales my vulnerability like it's the finest perfume.

Someone's going to pay dearly for his bachelor wings being clipped, and I'm his perfect victim.

Author's note: *Brutal Intentions is a standalone MF romance with forbidden themes, breeding, an age gap, a possessive alphahole and a virgin. Laz is married, and not to the heroine. All characters are over eighteen. The story is dirty and delicious, so please read at your discretion.*

PLAYLIST

Black Out Days (Future Islands Remix) – Phantogram
shedontknowbutsheknows – Tove Lo
She Knows – J. Cole, Cults, Amber Coffman
Dark Angel – Provoker
Like a Villain – Bad Omens
Snakes on My Chest – Ilkan Gunuc, Oliver Cricket
One More Night – 4RR
Partition – Beyoncé
Watch Me Work – Tinashe
Into You – Ariana Grande
Criminal – Britney Spears
Papa Don't Preach – Kelly Osbourne
Him & I – G-Eazy, Halsey
Dakota – Stereophonics
All Night – Beyoncé

Search "Brutal Intentions by Lilith Vincent" on Spotify or go to
https://spoti.fi/3AA2e0f

A NOTE TO READERS

Dear readers, it's me, Lilith, and we know what Lilith loves, don't we? Lilith loves what starts with dub and ends with con, emphasis on the big fat D. Just one D this time, and it belongs to Laz. No harems, no sharing, and the heroine has her V-card. Birth control is merely a suggestion to this man.

Laz is—and I cannot stress this enough—so fucking married. He's cheating on his wife with Mia. There are no two ways about it. Whether he deserves to be castrated for that is up to you to decide, but I hope you stick around to find out.

If we're just meeting for the first time, hello, I love you for being here. This book has forced orgasms and an alphahole stepfather. Don't come for me if you don't like taboo books. Come for yourself or your partner/s instead. It's much more fun that way.

Chapter One

MIA

I open my eyes, and a scream rises up my throat. Every muscle in my body goes rigid and terror claws at my heart. Please let this be a dream. *A nightmare.*

Directly in front of me is the floor-to-ceiling mirror on the front of my wardrobe, and I stare into my own wide-eyed, terror-stricken reflection. My cheek is pressed into the pillow and the white ruffled strap of my pajama top has tumbled down. A shaft of silver moonlight falls across my comforter, and the clock on my bedside table ticks out every agonizing second. It's nearly one in the morning. The witching hour?

More like the devil's hour.

And the devil's in my bed.

A large, muscular figure cloaked in darkness. He shifts with a sleepy murmur and the sheer size of him rocks my whole body. His head is behind mine on the pillow, and I can see little of him except for the dark, silky hair falling across his forehead and the sleeve of his black T-shirt tight around his muscular bicep.

This man is huge. Tall, and built like a linebacker. The first time I laid eyes on him, I thought that he was uncomfortably, aggressively large, and I still think that every time he walks into a room. I feel like I'm sharing this usually generous bed with a nine-foot demon from hell. His body heat is scorching the backs of my bare legs and my normally sweet-smelling bedroom is filled with an invasive masculine scent.

I hate this man in the daylight, and I fear him at night. I can't stand him looking at me or even breathing near me, and I absolutely loathe the sensation of his body brushing against mine. Every second of every day, I'm trying to avoid his massive body in the kitchen or ignore the way he glares at me across the dining table. The last place he should be is in my bed. We're not lovers.

We're not even friends.

Lazzaro Rosetti is Mom's twenty-nine-year-old husband, a grade-A asshole, and my new stepfather.

I angle my chin up and sniff the air, trying to catch the scent of alcohol, which might explain why the hell Lazzaro has mistaken my bedroom for the one he shares with Mom, but there's nothing but the aroma of his cologne. I say "shares," but my new stepfather is unpredictable, coming in and out of the house at all hours of the day and night. He's more like a restless animal than a man. Sometimes I catch him sleeping on the sofa or on a deck chair out by the pool. One morning last week, he was sleeping on the living room floor, and I stepped over him on my way to the kitchen. Lazzaro came suddenly alive, grabbing my ankle and refusing to let go as I squealed and tried to shake him off. His grip was an iron manacle, and his green eyes flashed with malice. All the while, he was grinning like this was a game to him.

I managed to kick him in the ribs with my sneakers and he grunted in pain. Still grinning, he yanked me closer so he could take his revenge by looking up my skirt.

Lazzaro gazed up at me from the floor. "Mm, white lace. My favorite."

Cheeks burning with humiliation, I shoved my skirt between my legs. "You asshole."

Mom's footsteps could be heard coming down the sweeping marble stairs, and Lazzaro let go of me so fast that I stumbled. By the time she came into the kitchen with a crimson-and-gold silk robe hanging from her elegant shoulders, he was leaning against the kitchen counter waiting for the coffee machine to finish dispensing a double shot of Colombian roast.

I found my voice a few seconds later. "Mom, Lazzaro just grabbed me, and he wouldn't let go."

Lazzaro passed the coffee to Mom, no cream or sugar, just how she likes it. She stared in confusion at his out-of-character thoughtful gesture, but then accepted the cup.

"Mia stumbled and I didn't want her to fall and hurt herself," he explained mildly.

"That's not what—"

Mom winced and pinched her brow. "Mia, please keep your voice down. I just woke up. And next time, look where you're going."

Lazzaro folded his arms across his enormous chest and smirked at me behind his wife's back.

Mom pushed out through the double doors to drink her coffee in the garden. She didn't look at me once. Mom almost never looks at me.

After all these years, you'd think I'd be used to it, but it still hurts being the Bianchi family's shame. Mom's face falls or her eyes skim over me whenever I walk into a room. Grandmother flinches whenever I speak at the dinner table. My three uncles give me stony glares before kissing my older sisters hello warmly.

There was a vicious whisper in my ear. "So, it's true. No one believes a single word out of your mouth."

Lazzaro was standing right behind me. He was so close that I could see every detail of the scar that cuts vertically through his lips on the left-hand side. It gives him a dangerous, roguish appearance, especially when he smiles and bares his strong white teeth.

His vindictive mouth whispered, "Or maybe it's just that they don't give a fuck what you have to say, and never have."

Now he's in my bed, and I don't know if it's a mistake or on purpose. But I'm not sticking around to find out. I grasp the edge of the mattress and wriggle my way toward it, staring at our reflections in the mirror and hoping I don't wake him.

Lazzaro's eyes pop open. I catch the feral gleam of his green gaze in the darkness, and my stomach swoops. A slow, nasty smile spreads over his face.

He's not confused.

He knows exactly whose bed he's in.

I want to scream, but I don't, because eighteen years on this earth has taught me that no matter what goes wrong, it's always my fault. If Mom runs in here, Lazzaro will protest that he made an honest mistake. Mom will tell me I'm attention-seeking, and I'll end up being forced to apologize for causing drama in the middle of the night. I'd rather gargle hot sauce and toilet cleaner than say sorry to this man.

"What are you doing in my room?" I hiss, holding tight to the blankets.

"Your mom's pissing me off."

When are they not pissing each other off? Every time they fight, I'm the one who pays for it. Mom walks around slamming doors and shouting. Lazzaro finds me and destroys whatever peace I've found watching TV, swimming in the pool, or reading in the garden.

"Then go and sleep on the sofa."

"But I like your bed."

"Then I'll go sleep on the sofa."

But Lazzaro grabs the back of my pajama top as I try to get out of my bed. "Running off? So fucking rude when I'm being nice to you."

"How is this nice?" I exclaim in an outraged whisper.

"Did anyone else talk to you today?"

Tonight, Uncle Tomaso and Aunt Sofia came to dinner with their children, two cousins who are older than me and another who is younger. At one point I asked one of my cousins how school was going. Aunt Sofia immediately talked over me and changed the subject.

"Screw you," I whisper, shuddering with anger and humiliation.

Lazzaro slides an arm beneath me and drags me back against his chest. "Cold? I'll warm you up."

His burning hot flesh presses against my back, scorching me from the nape of my neck to my heels. I struggle to get out of his grip, but both of his arms come around me. One of his hands is on my waist and the other is on my bare inner thigh. He's wearing sweats, but as his hips press into me, I feel the telltale ridge of something hard and thick against my ass.

Panicked words fall from my lips. "What the . . . is that your . . . Oh, my God."

"What's what?" Lazzaro speaks directly into my ear, his deep voice rumbly and tinged with lust and amusement. I dig my nails into his muscular forearms and grit my teeth against the restless, fluttering feeling low in my belly. He gets off on tormenting me, and he's made that clear from day one. The moment he crossed the threshold into this house after their honeymoon, his expression dark with anger and every muscle bunched beneath his black T-shirt, he zeroed in on me. Someone was going to suffer for what he'd been forced to do, and I'm his perfect victim.

No, it started before that day. Our eyes met at the church altar and his gaze fell to my nipples, which were pebbled into points and painfully obvious through my pink satin bridesmaid gown. It was so cold in the church, they were practically visible from space.

The priest prompted him to say his vows, and he lifted his eyes to mine as he spoke the words, *I do.*

Like a curse.

Like a *threat*.

"Why are you torturing me like this? What did I ever do to you?"

In our reflections, Lazzaro's eyes narrow with spite. "It's nothing personal, Mia. I just hate your fucking family."

He didn't want to marry Mom, and Mom didn't want to marry him, but it was arranged by our families like something out of the Middle Ages. The Rosetti family wants to force Lazzaro to settle down, and Mom wants some of the power and money that the Rosetti men wield like weapons in this city. Absolutely nothing about their marriage has to do with love. It's pure business.

I lie still for a moment, letting Lazzaro think he's won whatever sick game he's playing. He reaches up and palms one of my breasts like he owns it. My nipple hardens against the friction of his hand, and pleasure courses through me.

I ram my elbow into Lazzaro's stomach and fling myself off the bed. I manage to get to the edge of the mattress before he snatches me back against his hard chest.

"Ah-ah, Mia," he taunts. "Can't have you roaming the house in the middle of the night. Good girls stay in bed."

I growl with frustration as loud as I dare. "I hate you," I seethe, wrenching myself back and forth in his iron-like grip.

"I hate you more."

I buck in his arms until his hand lands on my pussy and his fingers curl to cup my sex over my pajama shorts. I inhale sharply. "What are you doing?"

"Ride my fingers."

"Go to hell," I say through my gritted teeth. My whole body is rigid as I wait for him to continue my humiliation. Grow bolder. Become an even worse man by invading my clothing. But Lazzaro doesn't move. Instead, he laughs softly, and I see in our reflection that he closes his eyes and relaxes.

"Whatever. They're there if you need them."

And Lazzaro goes to sleep, leaving his fingers right where they are, tucked against my sex. My heart pounds, and my chest feels like it's about to explode. I take as deep a breath as I can, locked in the cage of Lazzaro's arms. I'll wait until he's asleep and then get the hell out of here.

My eyes focus on our reflection. I'm flat-chested and straight-waisted, and I have never felt sexy. But I look different in Lazzaro's big arms with his muscular forearm draped around my middle, and I feel a little bit precious with his sleep-softened face pressed into the side of my neck. He looks as rough and scary as always, but the way he's curled around me seems . . . protective. Possessive.

Like I'm wanted for a change.

My gaze sweeps down his body, from the hard planes of his face and jaw to his shoulder looming over mine. The bumps of his ribs beneath his T-shirt and the inch of warm, tanned skin where his top has ridden up his belly. Lazzaro always looks too big to be allowed, but right now his bigness seems just right. My heart pounds and my stomach is alive with fluttering. I shift slightly in his arms and feel the unmistakable sensation of wetness between my legs and against his fingers through my thin cotton shorts.

And because I'm wet and slippery, the pressure of his fingers against my clit feels *amazing*. Lazzaro is the biggest asshole I've ever met, but he's also stupidly hot, and I hate him even more because of it. Every time he smirks at me, I can tell he's thinking how great he is.

Barely realizing I'm doing it, I rotate my hips in slow circles. My eyes drift closed as the tiny movements cause a tidal wave of sensation to crash through me. I've masturbated plenty of times before, and the results have been swift but unsatisfying. Mechanically, everything works as it's supposed to, but something was always missing.

Someone to fantasize about.

My eyes snap open and fasten on Lazzaro's sleeping face. Mom's husband is *not* the object of my desires. That's just sick. But he is aggressively masculine and smells like sin, two things I crave, apparently, because my hips are still moving on their own. Back and forth on Lazzaro's fingers. I let out a soft pant as the sensations kick up a notch.

I'll stop.

I will.

This is so fucked up and wrong.

But so is he for coming in here.

Lazzaro's arms are painfully tight around me, and his hard-on is wedged tight in my ass. The room is dark, and my core is so molten hot that reality starts to slide out of my grasp. There's just pleasure and a man's strong fingers against my pussy, and the memory of his sultry voice breathing in my ear, *Ride my fingers.*

I let out the tiniest of whimpers, but Lazzaro's breathing stays deep and even. He has no idea what's happening, and I'm close—*so close*—and I can't make myself stop. It's never felt this good before, and I have to discover what's waiting for me on the other side of this delicious feeling. Just a little more . . . just a little more . . . I want . . . I *need* . . .

Heat and pleasure rise up and crash over me. My body flexes in Lazzaro's strong arms as I hurtle beyond all conscious thought and straight into pure pleasure.

That was better than anything I've felt in my entire life.

I suck in a deep breath and open my eyes.

Lazzaro is awake and staring at me, his expression absolutely feral.

Fear lashes through me, and I yelp, grabbing hold of his taut forearms and clinging to him, even though he's the one I'm afraid of.

"I wasn't . . ." I start to say in a high-pitched, panicked voice.

With a growl, Lazzaro rolls on top of me. His bulk pins me face first to the mattress and his hot breath seethes in my ear. "Again."

My eyes open wide. Lazzaro's fingers are still tight against my clit. With his feet, he forces my legs open and thrusts his hips down, pushing my pussy against his fingers.

"What? No—"

My clit rolls against his hand, and I moan as pure pleasure builds inside me again. He keeps rhythmically thrusting himself against my ass while he moves his fingers in a *come here* motion.

"Stop that," I buzz angrily into the mattress. I try to buck him off, but he's too heavy, and I only succeed in working myself harder against his fingers. I can't possibly come again. Not so soon. Surely bodies aren't built that way, but to my horror, heat and pleasure are mounting within me. I feel him through layers of fabric like we're completely naked. His cock against my ass. His fingers on my clit. He's breathing hard in my ear like we really are screwing.

"Come on, Mia. Show me how bad girls get off in the middle of the night."

"I'm going to kill . . . *ahh*." To my shame, everything down there suddenly tightens up and bursts gloriously apart.

"*Again*," he orders, before I can even draw breath back into my burning lungs. A threat. A brutal demand.

A third time? I couldn't. My sex is oversensitized and his touch sends bolts of pleasure-pain coursing through me. I writhe against his hand, practically crying. Wishing it would stop but needing it to go on. I can't think, can't breathe. There's only me and him and I've never felt so gloriously out of control.

"Do as you're told, Mia. I'm not letting you up until you come again."

Lazzaro thrusts hard against my ass through his sweats and his hot breath is on the back of my neck. The hottest man I've ever laid eyes on has me pinned in place, and my body craves to give him what he wants. His brutal assault on my senses forces a third orgasm from me.

I press my face into the pillow and moan, wishing it didn't feel so good to be so thoroughly humiliated.

My stepfather raggedly breathes into my ear, "Good fucking girl."

I whimper as I come down and open my eyes to see his hand covering mine on the mattress. Slowly, his fingers curve around mine until he's holding me tight. Lazzaro's erection is still pressed so tight into my ass that he's practically inside me. Maybe he's going to pull my shorts to one side and impale me with what feels like a goddamn weapon.

Lazzaro lifts his weight off me, and he rolls onto his side, taking me with him. He stretches luxuriously, pressing his cock into the fleshy part of my ass.

"You can ride me if you like. Screwing your mom is so boring." He draws the perverted syllables lovingly over his tongue. "She doesn't squeal and wriggle around like you do."

My nerve endings are raw, and I feel more exposed than if I were to be stark naked in front of the whole school. He's sick, talking about having sex with Mom after forcing me to come. I didn't think it was possible for a man as disgusting as him to exist in real life.

Lazzaro lifts a dark, sardonic brow. "Three orgasms usually earns me a thank-you. You get three from the idiot boys at your school?"

My ex-boyfriend couldn't find my clit with a map and compass. "You've had your fun. Now get out."

"Oh, I'm still having fun." Lazzaro pushes his hand through his hair and grins down at me, taking in my flushed face, my disheveled hair and clothes. He's actually proud of himself, the goddamn psycho. He hooks a finger into my pajama top, teasing along the neckline.

"Pull your shorts down and beg me to fuck you. You're so wet, I'll glide right in and be balls deep before you can moan my name."

A swift, hot pang passes through me. The mental image of his naked body braced over me while my legs wrap around his hips explodes in my mind. It's not hard to imagine because his cock is jutting forward in his sweats, the ridged head straining against the fabric. His black T-shirt has ridden up, exposing the taut muscles of his stomach and the line of dark hair from his belly button trailing down beneath his waistband. Our legs are tangled together, and this tight space created by our bodies smells like his warm skin and my pussy.

Down the hall, I hear a bathroom door close. My mom is the only other person in this house. My *mom*. And I'm in bed with her husband.

I'm just as sick as Lazzaro.

I reel back and slap his hand away. "I will cut your balls off if you ever touch me again. Don't you dare creep into my bedroom. Don't even look at me from now on. Get. Out."

But Lazzaro isn't going. He just lays there grinning at me with his hard-on right there between us. I slide away from him and practically fall out of bed. This time he doesn't stop me, and I grab the robe from the back of my door. The last thing I see before I run out of the room is Lazzaro settling down beneath my comforter and closing his eyes.

The house is dark and silent apart from my wild breathing. I head for the farthest corner of the house from Lazzaro, the living room downstairs, and curl up on the sofa beneath my robe.

What the hell just happened? That was ten kinds of fucked up and I should be screaming this house down. Instead, I'm lying on the couch with a drenched pussy and a heavy feeling on my tongue, like I already know the shape of my stepfather's cock in my mouth.

I cover my head with fluffy white fabric and moan in horror. I'm going to sleep, and when I wake up, this will all have been a dream.

A nightmare.

And morning sunshine will make the memory fade away.

"Mia? *Mia.*"

I'm shaken roughly awake, and someone is digging their nails into my shoulder. I open my eyes and blink in confusion at Mom's beautiful face, perfect with makeup and lush with beauty creams, frowning down at me. Mom never comes into my room unless she's angry with me. First thing in the morning and I've already done something wrong?

"What are you doing down here?"

"Huh?" I sit up and look around, my gaze landing on the cream sofas, the vase of white peonies, and the spotless glass coffee table. Last night comes flooding back to me in a shameful rush. Waking up in my untidy but cozy bedroom with Lazzaro in my bed, barely putting up a fight while he ravaged my fully clothed body. Grinding against his fingers like a cat in heat.

Mom's eyes narrow. "What's that expression on your face?"

I drop my head into my hands and pretend I'm rubbing sleep from my eyes. My face is flaming hot, and I can imagine the horrified and embarrassed expression I'm wearing.

Someone's in the kitchen humming to himself and making coffee. A deep hum in cheerful tones, as if he's had a wonderful sleep and he's excited to greet the day.

"I couldn't sleep. I had a stomachache." It's barely a lie because right now my stomach is churning like I'm going to throw up. If I come face to face with my stepfather at this moment, then Mom's going to know what happened just by looking at us. She's scarily perceptive, especially when it comes to me. I pull on my robe, push past Mom, and hurry for the stairs.

Once inside my bedroom, I slam the door, and my eyes drop to the mattress. Lazzaro has left my bed in a disheveled state with the comforter pulled back. There's a messy white stain on the sheets.

I step closer, wondering what the hell it is because it wasn't there when I went to bed last night. I realize with dawning horror that there's something strange about the stain. There's one large puddle, and then off to one side are some marks. The scent of him washes over me, and I finally realize what it is.

Lazzaro has painted a heart in cum on my sheets. A filthy little love note, from him to me.

Chapter Two

LAZ

I drop the six-pack of beer onto the counter among the boxes of vegan cookies and paleo protein balls. Artisanal fucking beer. I just want a cold one to take my mind off things, and I have to wade past shelves of quinoa and kale chips.

A freckled young man in a linen apron glances at my tattooed arms and ripped jeans in a way that tells me he's not loving my presence here. "Anything else, sir?"

I wave a hand at him. "Please. I'm only sir in the bedroom."

The cashier's eyes bulge.

I glance at the goods crowded around the register. "I'll take some gum and the phone number of a blonde who's great at giving head."

I get my beer and some gum in a paper bag along with a dirty look. "That will be twenty-four dollars and thirty cents, sir—cents. Thirty cents."

Twenty-four dollars for some gum and beer? God, I hate it here. I give him a fake grin as I hand over my cash. "No phone number? I guess it's not my lucky day."

When I turn around, I run smack bang into a milfy type with dark roots, winged eyeliner, and a lot of gold jewelry. I smile down at her. "Or maybe it is."

The blonde's eyes widen, and she pushes out her definitely fake tits. I love fake tits. I love real tits. I don't really care as long as the woman attached to them enjoys being fucked into the mattress.

Her husband, a man wearing a pastel shirt, loafers, and a sweater knotted around his shoulders, actually steps forward like he's going to fight me. I nearly burst out laughing because I could flatten this guy with one punch.

I hold up a hand in mock surrender. "Please. I have children." I flash a smile at his wife. "Or I will by morning. Want to party?"

The husband bristles like a wet cat. "I will call the police!"

For what, hitting on his wife? No one can take a joke on this side of the city. I pull my sunglasses down over my eyes, make my thumb and forefinger into a phone, and hold it to my ear as I take one last look at the blonde. "Call me if you like a big dick, baby. Looks like you could use one."

The preppy man yells after me, "You're wearing a wedding ring, asshole."

I stare at my hand in genuine surprise. There is indeed a titanium band around my ring finger. I keep forgetting it's there. Giulia chose it, and it's etched with fussy decoration.

"Thanks for the reminder," I mutter, shouldering through the door and out of the store. My black Chevrolet Camaro ZL1 is haphazardly parked among the minivans, and when I slide in and gun the engine, heads turn.

The longer I spend in the suburbs, the more I feel I'm going to go postal.

In Giulia's perfect, white marble kitchen, I crack open the beer bottle on the edge of the counter. The bottle top goes skittering into a corner and I leave it there while I take a swig. The beer tastes like shit, and I stare dispassionately out the window and across the garden.

Someone's laying on a deck chair by the swimming pool wearing a blue bikini. Mia, my shiny new stepdaughter. A smile spreads over my face.

Speaking of girls who like being fucked into the mattress.

What the hell was that the other night? I mean, I know what it was, at first. I was bored and angry, so I decided I'd go take it out on the one person in the Bianchi family who no one gives a shit about. We've got a lot in common, me and her. What I don't understand is what Mia could possibly have done in her short life to earn everyone's loathing. Her mom walks around acting like she doesn't exist. Her uncles never kiss her hello or even smile at her. Everyone talks over her at the dinner table. I get the same treatment from my family but as a confirmed and constant asshole, I definitely deserve it.

I wanted to have a really good, messy fight with Giulia, so

I thought I'd go into Mia's bedroom and make her scream for her mom, but damn if Mia didn't look cute in her tiny white PJs and feel even better wriggling in my arms. She didn't scream, no matter how much I manhandled her, and then she went and masturbated on my fingers while she thought I was asleep like some delicious, slutty wet dream. My stepdaughter is as filthy as I am, and that blew my goddamn mind, so I blew hers by forcing a few more orgasms from her.

As she stared at my dick, I thought she was going to beg me to fuck her, but then she ran from me like a scared rabbit. Not very far, though. She can't get far from me while we're living under the same roof. The thought makes me smile as I lift my beer to my lips.

My phone rings in my pocket and the smile is wiped from my face as I see who it is. I keep my gaze fixed on Mia's ass in the sunshine as I lift the phone to my ear. "What?"

"Hello, Lazzaro." Faber, my eldest brother.

"It's Laz, you fuck. How many times do I have to tell you that?"

Faber has always called me Laz, but since our father died, he's started calling me Lazzaro. I know why he's doing it. To put me in my place. Next, he's going to demand I call him Fabrizio. I get this shit enough from my wife. Every time Giulia calls me Lazzaro it grates on me like nails down a chalkboard.

He's Faber and I'm Laz. Why is that so hard for him to understand?

Faber ignores my question. "How are you and Giulia?"

I take an angry swig of my beer. "Why don't you ask what you're really calling about?"

"Well, is she?"

Pregnant. That's my duty, to knock up Giulia Bianchi, because Faber's got the idea that me becoming a family man will persuade me to settle down. "My brother is calling me to ask if I'm regularly screwing my wife. What a sicko."

"Believe me, I don't enjoy this any more than you do."

My temper bursts apart like a volcano exploding. "Then give me what I'm fucking owed, and we don't have to do this!"

My brothers are holding my inheritance hostage. My fair share of the family business that Dad started and that I've spent twelve years of my life sweating and bleeding for. Faber gets his money. My other brother Firenze gets his. But does Laz? No, they're keeping their baby brother's share from him because they don't like how a twenty-nine-year-old man chooses to spend his leisure time. If I want to screw my way through every beautiful woman in this city, then I damn well will. I don't care if my bedmates are strippers, waitresses, heiresses, or assassins. I just want to have some fun before I wind up with my blood and brains spattered across the sidewalk. That's what happened to Dad, a bullet in his head as he was walking back to his car after a spaghetti dinner. His brother was gunned down in the street, too, and so was their father. Rosetti men have short life expectancies.

I can't sue my brothers because our money is dirty, so it's either murder them or play along, though if I have to silently screw Giulia's dry pussy one more time, I might just load a gun. My wife doesn't move when I fuck her and doesn't make a sound. Ice-cold skin. Ice-cold heart. Ice-cold pussy.

"You can have your inheritance when you do what's required of you."

My lip curls. "Screwing that bitch is like fucking an ice block and you want me to keep going until she's pregnant?"

Faber makes an impatient noise. "Spare me the details, Lazzaro. Just be a man and get the job done. You've never had any problem screwing anything before now."

Like hell. I don't fuck just anyone. I have sex with enthusiastic women who get so wet and hot it's like I'm screwing a living, gushing furnace.

"It's Laz," I say through my teeth. "And you fuck her if it's so easy."

Faber sighs, and I picture him pinching the bridge of his nose. "You are my constant headache. Giulia has been calling me, Lazzaro. You need to put more effort into settling into your new family."

His pompous tone ratchets my temper up to a thirteen. Giulia has been calling Faber to complain about me? That's a fight I look forward to starting later.

"Oh, yeah? You put some effort into pulling that stick out of your ass. Go fuck yourself." I hang up and toss my phone across the counter. The beer has turned sour in my mouth, so I grab a bottle of water from the fridge and neck half of it.

Marrying Giulia was the biggest mistake of my life because I can see what will happen next. Marrying her? Not enough for Faber. Moving in and playing husband? Not enough for Faber. Knocking that cold bitch up? Not enough for Faber. This was his idea, and I want my perfect, control freak brother to just admit it was a terrible one and give me my money.

If Giulia is already calling Faber to complain about me, then it won't be long until he's being driven up the wall. Faber hates complaining.

Maybe I can get Giulia's three equally cold and ruthless brothers to start calling him as well. With them all breathing down Faber's neck, he'll crack up and admit his idea was the worst he's ever had.

I smile to myself. Not a bad plan, Laz. Not bad at all. In the meantime, I'll step it up a notch.

And I know who I'm going to torment first.

As I head out into the garden, warm afternoon sunshine washes over me. Heat radiates off the white tiles and the swimming pool is a stunning shade of blue. Mia is laying on her stomach reading on her phone. Her legs are slightly parted, and I can see the outline of her plump pussy lips through her bikini. My mouth waters. Pussy that hates your guts and still gushes on your fingers? That's my new favorite flavor. Pussy I have to steal a touch or a taste of in the middle of the night behind her mother's back?

Fucking delicious.

Mia has no idea I'm standing over her. I tilt my bottle and trickle a thin stream of water over her pussy, delivering a cold shock to her sensitive flesh.

She gasps and turns over. "What the hell? What are you doing?"

"Making you wet." I pause, letting my grin grow wider. "Again."

I'm rewarded with a red blush that flames her cheeks. She grabs her towel and covers herself. "Leave me alone, Lazzaro. I've got nothing to say to you."

"It's Laz. How was school?"

"Like you care. Go do burnouts in a parking lot or something."

"That reminds me. I was driving around all last week, and you know what? I didn't see you with any friends, not even once."

Her mouth falls open. "You were stalking me?"

I roll my eyes. "Please. So dramatic. Avoiding your mom is my number one priority, so driving is what I do. I passed your skinny ass purely by coincidence. So, what's the story?"

"The story is mind your own business."

There are photos of her with friends in her bedroom. Happy photos taken recently. I sit down on the pool chair next to hers and take a swig of water. "Let me guess. Your psycho uncles chased them off?"

Mia fights to hold on to her anger, but as her restraint collapses, her shoulders slump. "Just leave me alone, please. I've already lost my boyfriend and my friends. You can't make me any more miserable than I already am."

One of my eyebrows lifts. She had a boyfriend? What boyfriend?

She scrubs her hand over her face and sighs. "I hate it here. As soon as I can, I'm leaving."

"I get it, kid. Family's the pits."

Mia sits up and glares at me. She has long brown hair and big brown eyes. Bambi eyes.

"Don't call me *kid*, Lazzaro. We're not bonding. We're not going to be friends."

I kick her deck chair. "I swear to God, if you call me Lazzaro again, I will throw you into this pool."

Her eyes widen in surprise. "What am I supposed to call you? Dad?"

My mouth twitches, and I want to smile for the first time all day. A real smile, not a sarcastic one to piss someone off. "Kinky. But I told you. Call me Laz."

Mia lays down and turns back to her phone. "Whatever, Laz."

I stare at the long, slender line of her back and the curves of her waist and hips. She whatevered me, but I don't even care because she called me Laz.

Breathing comes a little easier. As I cross the threshold back into the kitchen, I stop dead as I come face to face with Giulia dressing an enormous salad. Something is heating in the oven. There are discarded food packets all over the counter.

I walk to the fridge and grab myself another beer. It might be disgusting, but at least it's alcoholic.

Giulia glances at the drink in my hand and her mouth tightens. "I see you're working hard."

I pick up an empty packet that lays discarded at her elbow and read the label. Beef stroganoff, one of those pre-prepared meals from a fancy catering company. "Darling. You cooked."

Giulia shoots me a poisonous look. "Tomaso, Roberto, and Marzio are coming to dinner. Make sure you're dressed appropriately."

How wonderful, an evening with my wife and her brothers, men who get on my nerves even more than Faber does. I take an angry mouthful of beer and swallow it down. "I had an interesting talk with Faber earlier. Nothing makes a man feel more at home than his wife bitching to his brother."

My wife picks up a pair of tongs and starts tossing the salad. "I talk business with Fabrizio. I'm glad someone in the Rosetti family has a head for figures."

I grab the tongs out of her hand. My wife is forty-one and beautiful. Practically a ten. I've rarely screwed women more attractive than her, but Giulia never smiles. Never laughs. Has never once tried to make me feel welcome in this house or in her bed. The only time we talk is when we fight. "If you have anything to say to me, say it to my face."

Giulia considers me, her head tilted to one side. "You're a pathetic excuse for a man. You don't hold a candle to your brothers, and everyone hates you wherever you go. You'll be dead by the time you're thirty." She raises one beautifully drawn-on eyebrow. "Is that honest enough for you, darling?"

My hand clenches around the tongs. Giulia knows that my family tree is littered with Rosetti men dead before their time. She just cocked a gun with her words and fired it. Straight into my heart.

"Perfect," I tell her, my jaw grit tight. "I like my snakes where I can see them."

I toss the tongs down, grab a piece of cucumber from the salad, and stride out of the room. What I really want to do is put a fist through the wall and go out and get blind drunk. I bite savagely into the cucumber and notice there are bottles of red wine lined up on a side table in the dining room.

Or maybe I'll just get drunk here and make myself everyone else's problem.

Twenty minutes later, Mia appears in the dining room wearing a blue dress, pacing back and forth as she sets the table, ignoring me as I'm perched on a windowsill drinking a glass of wine. Giulia directs her with sharp words and pointed fingers.

Tomaso, Roberto, and Marzio arrive, and the thug-like men greet their sister with kisses and friendly words. I'm given a few baleful stares. Mia is totally passed over, but she doesn't seem to be surprised by this and does her best to blend in with the wallpaper.

As we sit down, Giulia gives me an up-and-down look, and her mouth twists in disapproval when she sees I haven't changed out of my ripped jeans and T-shirt.

I spread my hands and shrug. "What? You said be appropriate. My dick's not out."

My wife gives me a dirty look and then turns away.

The four siblings do all of the talking throughout the salad course. I'm sat opposite Mia at the far end of the table, and everyone pretends we're not here. I have to snatch at the wine bottle every time it comes close; otherwise, I wouldn't be offered a drop. Mia tries to take a piece of bread, but it all ends up on Roberto's side plate.

I toast her ironically with my red wine glass. She gives me an angry little shrug, as if to say she didn't really want bread anyway.

"We need someone to manage those imports, but who?" Roberto is saying to Giulia. "Have you got any ideas?"

My wife's gaze rests on me for a moment. "No, I can't think of anyone responsible enough."

I lift my wine glass and knock the rest back. I'm wasting months of my life with this woman. Once I knock her up I could fuck off, but that means leaving my kid to be raised by an ice bitch who can't stomach her own daughter. Faber thinks I have no scruples, but that doesn't sit right with me. It shouldn't sit right with any man.

I drink steadily as the meal progresses. For a while, I try to play footsies beneath the table with Mia, but she kicks me so hard in the shin that I go cross-eyed for a moment.

As we're eating our beef stroganoff, Marzio is telling his siblings an obnoxious story about getting a waiter fired for spilling wine in his lap at a restaurant.

"I can't wait to have a son and for him to turn out like you lot." I jerk my chin at my wife's brothers.

Giulia's lip curls. "Lazzaro, you're drunk."

I reach for the wine bottle and top my glass up nearly to the rim. "Not drunk enough. And it's not Lazzaro. It's Laz."

"It's piece of shit," Marzio mutters. Mia is reaching for the dish of buttered beans at his elbow, but instead of passing it to her like the gentleman he thinks he is, he picks it up, serves himself, and then puts it down out of her reach. He didn't do it by accident, either. It was only for a split second, but he looked her in the eye as he took the dish away.

My gaze swings from Mia to him and back again. No one else at the table noticed the exchange. I open my mouth, and Mia anticipates what I'm about to do.

"Laz," she whispers with a shake of her head, her huge Bambi eyes begging me not to say anything.

But I never was any good at shutting up.

Loudly and to the table in general, I ask, "Why do you all treat Mia like shit?" Everyone goes on eating and talking, but I know they heard me.

I slam my fist on the table and every glass and plate jumps. "*I said*, why do you all treat Mia like shit?"

Silence falls. The brothers exchange dark glances that say, *This fucking guy again.*

Giulia glances from her daughter to me. "What are you talking about? My daughter can speak for herself if she has something to say."

Yeah. Except she doesn't, and now I'm angry enough to do it for her. I give Mia one last chance to speak up, holding out a hand to her and raising my eyebrows. "Well?"

Mia's lips are tightly closed as she stares at her plate. There's no trace of the young woman who talked back to me out by the pool. Why is she so scared around these people?

Giulia gives me a small, sardonic smile, and turns back to her brothers.

But I'm not done yet.

"Didn't I hear a rumor about Mia once?" I say loudly, tapping my chin and pretending I don't know the reason why all the Bianchis hate an eighteen-year-old girl.

Because I do. I know every last excruciating detail.

Mia is staring at me with huge, pain-filled eyes. Tears are collecting on her lashes, and she gives another shake of her head. She wants me to shut up, but I'm not going to. I've had a gutful of family bullshit today, and every Bianchi is going to feel my wrath.

I lift my glass and take an enormous mouthful of wine, pretending to think. As I put it down, I nod as if I just remembered something. "Oh, I know. It's because of that family scandal my precious, prissy wife caused by screwing around behind her late husband's back. Giulia got knocked up by a . . . kitchenhand, wasn't it?" I swing my gaze to my wife.

Actually, it was the owner of her husband's favorite restaurant, but I say kitchenhand just to get on her nerves. Giulia shoots me a look full of hatred and clasps her wine glass so hard that it might shatter at any moment.

I turn my nasty grin on my stepdaughter. "Mia's not a real Bianchi. Oh, Mia. How could you do this to your family?"

Not technically true, but it's how her family treats her. Bianchi is my wife's maiden name and the one she passed onto her daughters. The Bianchis are a far more prominent family than Giulia's ex-husband's and she didn't want to let her name go.

Mia breathes in sharply, trying to suck those tears back in and pretend like nothing's wrong. I wait for someone, anyone, to leap to their feet and rip me to shreds for laying the blame of Giulia's infidelity at Mia's feet.

No one speaks.

No one moves.

No one even looks at Mia.

Tomaso turns to his sister and resumes their conversation.

I shake my head and take another mouthful of wine. I had to piss people off day after day for ten years in order to receive this sort of treatment at home. All Mia has to do is exist.

She and I stare at each other across the table. She's breathing fast, but quietly, like she terrified of drawing the tiniest bit of attention to herself.

I pick up my fork and stab it through some green beans. "Pathetic."

I pass the rest of the meal in silence and so does Mia. She doesn't touch her food, and no one asks her if she's feeling all right or if she'd like anything else. When one of her uncles gets up to smoke a cigarette on the terrace, she mumbles something about wanting to be excused and hurries out of the room. No one gives her a second glance.

I get up and follow her.

She's half running to her bedroom, but I catch up to her in the hall upstairs, grabbing her by the arm and spinning her around to face me. "Wasn't that interesting? What an *interesting* dinner."

She rips her arm out of my grasp, her face creased with emotion. "Screw you, Laz."

Anger races through me. I grab both her shoulders and push her against the wall. "Oh, you can say it to me, but you can't say it to them? They won't lift a finger to defend you, Mia. Not one of them. Some family you've got."

"How dare you bring up that scandal at the dinner table? Their silence wasn't about me. They were appalled by you."

I scour her face with narrowed eyes, wondering if she really believes that. Maybe she just desperately wants to. I'll be doing her a favor by helping her realize that no one gives a damn about her.

"You're all alone, Mia. No one cares about you. The sooner you accept that, the better."

Chapter Three

MIA

*I*t's just a photo. It doesn't matter. These people are nothing and soon you'll have left this nightmare forever.

I repeat this mantra over and over as I walk home. I'm a Bianchi, and everyone in this city knows that crossing a Bianchi is dangerous for your longevity, except high school doesn't follow normal rules. High school is its own ecosystem with different in-crowds, out-crowds, and pecking orders. Lately, I reek of vulnerability. I'm the limping gazelle on the savanna, and the predators are closing in around me.

It's just a photo, Mia.

But it's not just a photo. It's evidence of me doing something that gets my stomach churning every time. I need two shots of vodka just to walk through that door.

I clench my backpack strap, and then whimper as my bruised and reddened knuckles blaze with pain. I think I hurt myself more throwing that punch than the person who received it.

A noisy, souped-up car approaches behind me, but my stomach is revolving a hundred times a minute. I don't recognize the sound until it's far too late to duck down a side street or into a store.

A black Camaro pulls up next to me, the engine throbbing, and dismay tumbles through me.

The driver rolls the windows down and thumping bass spills out. A mocking voice asks, "Alone again? Where are your friends, high-school girl?"

I can't deal with my stepfather right now on top of everything else. I keep walking and staring straight ahead.

The engine cuts, a car door slams, and Laz steps onto the sidewalk in front of me. Sunlight dapples his broad shoulders, and the wind ruffles his dark hair. Behind his sunglasses, his brows are drawn tightly together.

There's genuine concern on his face. "What's happened?"

"Who says anything's happened?"

"Your face, Bambi. You look like someone ran over your kitten."

I give him the finger and step around him. "Don't call me Bambi. I'm fine."

Laz grabs my wrist, and my middle finger is right in his face. "I don't believe you. Get in the car."

I try to twist out of his hold, but his hand is like steel. "Piss off, Laz!"

Laz's eyes flash. "Get in the car or I'll put you over my knee and spank you right here in the street."

I wince as a couple walking their dog nearby turns to look at us. "Don't be so crude."

"I can be cruder if you don't do as I say," he says in a threatening voice. "How about I start describing the way you ground your wet pussy all over my fingers? Loudly."

My eyes narrow. He wouldn't dare.

Laz takes a deep breath and opens his mouth.

"Okay, I'm going. Keep your voice down." I yank open the passenger door and get into the front seat. I've been ignoring him since he humiliated me at dinner four nights ago. He hates it in our house, but why does he have to take his bad temper out on me?

Stupid question. I know why.

It's fun for him, and he thinks I'm pathetic.

If only he knew the real reason I keep my mouth shut. That I'm biding my time and saving my pennies, and the second I graduate high school, I'll be gone like a shot. Mom and my uncles will never have to look at the Bianchi family shame ever again.

The interior of Laz's car is gleaming and perfect and smells like leather and him. When he gets in and starts the engine, I glance at his large, tattooed hands on the steering wheel. There's something captivating about the way he manhandles the stick shift into place as he guns the engine and turns the wheel. It's a totally ordinary thing that he must have done a thousand times before, and yet the churning in my belly suddenly settles and is replaced by a fluttering sensation.

Laz isn't special. Men just look attractive when they're driving, and any man driving this car would look hot. Connor, my ex-boyfriend, could be counted in the top three hottest guys in school, and to prove the point to myself, I picture him in Laz's place.

I scrunch my nose as I imagine it. Or not.

Laz glances at me as he steps on the gas, and we roar down the street. "What's that face for, Bambi? You don't like my car?"

I love his stupid car. "You do realize Bambi was a boy?"

We drive in tense, uncomfortable silence. I can feel the anger radiating off Laz's body in waves.

"I'm getting fucking sick of you," he says through clenched teeth. "If someone's hurt you, then go do something about it."

I push my fingers so hard into my palms that my nails feel like they're going to cut right through flesh. That's easy for him to say when he's six-foot-four, ripped, and a man. An intimidating man. Even if I had a black belt in karate, I still have these stupid big brown eyes. No one takes your threats seriously when you resemble a terrified woodland creature.

I shake my head and stare out the window. "You have no idea what it's like to be me."

"You're right. I have no idea what it's like to be a scared piece of shit."

Fuming, I reach into my school bag and thrust a letter at him. He takes it with a frown and opens the envelope against the steering wheel one-handed. Still driving, he glances between the road and the letter.

"To Mia Bianchi's parent or guardian, blah blah blah . . .

suspended for *fighting*?" A delighted grin breaks over Laz's face. "That's more like it. Who did you flatten?"

I snatch the letter back. Of course he would think it's funny. "None of your business."

"Come on. Who pissed you off? Tell me, and I'll finish the job off for you if you didn't give them a black eye yet."

I picture him sinking his fist into Kaleb's face, and the idea is enthralling. But then I'd owe my stepfather. "If I have a problem, I'll tell Mom, not you."

Laz bursts out laughing. "Why, because you think she'll care?"

His words feel like a slap across my face. Who told him about the man who fathered me? Did they ridicule me and Mom? Did Laz think it was the funniest thing he'd ever heard and laugh like he's laughing now?

"You've been in my family for five minutes, and you think you know us? You don't know shit, asshole."

Laz turns to me with a smirk and rumbles lazily, "Damn, I knew you had a dirty mouth. What else that mouth do?"

He's relaxed in his seat as he drives, knees spread and wearing his usual black jeans. They hug his hips and muscular thighs, and before I can help myself, I've glanced at his zipper.

Not his zipper. His dick. I felt him thrusting against my ass the other night when he was hard, and he was huge. He's not hard now, but there's a sizable package in his jeans. I can vividly imagine Laz cupping the nape of my neck as I lean over his lap and take him in my mouth. A little hiss of pleasure and then his low, breathy, *Good girl* as he raises his hips to fuck my mouth.

I look away quickly and glare out the passenger window, but not before I catch his shit-eating grin. He knows exactly where my mind went.

He's married to Mom, I remind myself. *He screws Mom. Remember how you heard them that time?* Not moaning and panting, but the unmistakable rhythmic noise of a headboard hitting a wall. Otherwise, dead silence.

Revulsion skitters through my body at the memory. Finally, a normal reaction to my stepfather.

When Laz pulls into the driveway at home, I get out of the car, expecting him to speed away again, but he follows me inside. In the hall, he overtakes me, looking into every room until he finds Mom in the kitchen. She's sitting at the counter answering emails on her phone.

"Your daughter has something to tell you," Laz announces, and then he stands back and folds his arms.

Mom looks past me as if she expects to see Rieta or Isabel standing in the doorway.

He means me. I'm your daughter, too.

Mom turns back to her phone and her acrylic nail taps the screen. "What do you have to tell me, Mia? You're not failing school, are you?"

The pain in my chest doubles. She assumes that if I've got something to say, it must be because I did something wrong.

Tap tap tap.

"Nothing. Never mind."

Laz glares daggers at me as I turn on my heel and sweep past him. "Pathetic."

I keep walking while images of revenge flash through my mind. Heaping all his fashionably ripped jeans into a pile and torching them in the back garden. Scraping a key along every panel of his beloved car. I want to scream at him. I want to rake my nails down his chest. But I also know that it won't make me feel any better when the person I truly wish to scream at is Mom. I want to crack that frosty, aloof demeanor of hers and make her see me. Even if I wanted to hurt her, I wouldn't know how. If I acted out, she'd flick me a haughty glance and return to whatever she's doing, because I'm less worthy of her attention than a mosquito buzzing around her head.

I lock myself in the bathroom and splash handful after handful of cold water over my face. I'm so sick of this place. The school year ends in four months, and I haven't saved up enough money yet. Maybe just one more month will do it, and I could sell the handbag Mom gave me for my birthday. A crummy little apartment would be better than living under this roof.

I turn the tap off by slamming it with the heel of my hand and gaze at my dripping face.

Or I could stop being a scared little bitch and actually face Mom like a grown up. Stand up for myself, for once.

Once I've dried my face, I head back to the kitchen and approach Mom. In a calm voice, I say, "Mom. One of the boys at school took a picture of me."

Not a lie. But not the whole truth, either.

"What picture, darling?" she murmurs, tapping on her phone screen. A large gin and tonic rests at her elbow.

I take a deep breath, and then falter. Is this the time to come clean? But if I do, all hell is going to break loose. "Up . . . up my T-shirt. I wasn't wearing a bra."

Mom raises her head and stares straight ahead. Then she puts down her phone and gets to her feet. Relief washes over me. I knew it was the right idea to talk to Mom like an adult. She's never had time for whining and complaining.

Without warning, anger flashes in Mom's eyes, and she slaps me hard across the face. "You disgusting girl."

Pain bursts through my face, and I cry out, covering my cheek with my hand.

"How did this happen?" she seethes.

Now is definitely not the time. It never will be the time. "G-gym class," I stammer, my eyes burning with tears of pain. "I forgot my sports bra." The truth is I don't need a sports bra. My boobs are barely there.

"You come to me with this story and expect me to believe it? You're whoring around in this town again, aren't you? It makes me sick to hear about your shameless behavior."

I flush red to the roots of my hair as I remember the face peering in Connor's steamy car window. Anyone else would have turned and walked away or minded their own business in the first place, but not my family. Uncle Tomaso yanked open the door and dragged me out of the car by my hair and threw me to the ground. He was yelling horrible names at me at the top of his lungs. Connor couldn't drive away fast enough.

"Which boy?" says a dangerous voice from the doorway. "What

photo? Where is it?"

I stiffen. I didn't realize Laz was still in the house.

"Why, do you want a copy?" I snarl over my shoulder, and his expression darkens.

I turn back to Mom, but a strong hand grasps my upper arm and drags me from the kitchen. I fight Laz every step of the way, but his bruising fingers don't let go. He hustles me out the front door and toward his car parked down the street.

"Let me *go*."

Laz pushes me into his vehicle and slams the door behind me. With a squeal of tire rubber, we race down the street.

My cheek is still stinging from Mom's slap, and worse is probably waiting for me when I get home. I haven't even told her I'm suspended yet.

Laz pulls up and parks by a bridge next to the river. It's a narrow street with the bridge towering over us and sheltered by trees. Absolutely no one is around. He turns to me with a savage glare.

Before he can accuse me of anything, I say, "I didn't send anyone a picture of my tits."

"All right. You didn't."

He doesn't even sneer the words. My eyebrows shoot up in surprise. I wonder why he believes me, and then I realize why with a dismal feeling.

"What's that face for?" he asks.

"You only believe me because you'd think it was hilarious if I wanted to show these off to anyone." I wave my hand at my chest.

A smile hooks the corner of his mouth as he glances at my top.

"I like your tiny tits."

I shove his shoulder with the heel of my palm. "Screw you."

Laz hooks a finger into the neck of my T-shirt. "Don't believe me? Show 'em to me."

I swat his hands away. "What? No."

"Some little shit who's bald as a baby bird down there has seen your tits and I haven't. I'll tell you what you've got."

"The guys at school are eighteen, not twelve."

His eyes flash. "You mean they're men? Now I'm jealous. That's it. Lift up your top."

He grasps my waist with both hands and slides his thumbs beneath my T-shirt.

"Stop that," I mutter, wriggling back against the car door. There's barely an inch of space to move. My heart is battering against my ribs. I could jab him in the eyes with my fingernails, but the intensity of his green gaze has me holding on to his forearms instead. I don't want him to stop looking at me exactly the way he is right now.

Like he really is jealous.

My eyes fasten on the scar that bisects his lips at the corner of his mouth. "How did you get that?"

"Fighting." Staring right in my eyes and moving so slow it's agony, Laz starts to pull my top up. I have eons of time to stop him, and he's not holding the cotton so hard that I couldn't shove it down. He pushes it high so that it's tight under my arms, totally exposing my breasts. As usual, I'm not wearing a bra.

He drops his eyes and I stare at his face, terrified he's going to laugh at me. I hate that Laz is good-looking. I hate that he has a long, straight nose, dark brows, and inky black lashes that are too goddamn lush for a man. A hard jaw, and those scarred, teasing lips. Only, they're not teasing now. They're full and soft. His eyes are soft, too, drinking me in like I'm a work of art.

Laz plucks my tender nipple between his forefinger and thumb, and it aches so good I moan softly. My waist arches involuntarily in his hands and I suck in a shaky breath.

"Fuck, you're sexy," he says in a roughened voice.

Mia Bianchi, whoring around in a car again, except this time I'm not misbehaving with a boyfriend from school, I'm showing my tits to a man who's nearly thirty, and who happens to be my stepfather.

Laz wraps his arms around my back and pulls me closer to him. As he dips his head, his dark hair falls into his eyes. He runs his tongue slowly up one of my breasts, and then pinches my nipple with his teeth.

I moan in his arms and heat floods my pussy. Heat, and a sharp, sweet ache. I brace one hand on the dashboard and another on the roof of the car as I breathe unsteadily. I want to touch Laz and find out whether his muscles feel as good as they look, but I don't dare touch him because I *know* he will. He'll feel better than anything I've ever felt before, and I won't be able to let go of him.

He's not yours, I remind myself frantically.

Don't touch him because he's *not yours*.

"What's this guy's name?" he murmurs coaxingly, running his soft tongue over my nipples. "The one who took the picture. I won't do anything crazy. I'll just make him delete the photo. You want that, don't you, Bambi?"

My God, I might come from just his tongue on my tits. My pulse is racing wildly, and I push my sweaty hand against the dash, trying to think. Will he really not do anything crazy? But everything Laz does is crazy, including what he's doing to me right now. "I don't trust you."

He takes a nipple in his mouth and sucks me. Hard. "Who, me?"

Oh, *fuck*. "You married my mom four weeks ago, and now you're . . . now you're . . ."

I feel him smile against my sensitized flesh. "Now I'm having the most fun I've had in years. I'm living under the same roof as a horny little bitch who's been hungry for my cock the moment I met her. She's got the prettiest fuck-me eyes I ever saw, and the sound of her moaning my name while I pound her sweet pussy is all I want for Christmas."

He plants slow kisses up my neck, and like the horny little bitch he says I am, I bare my throat for him. I didn't want him the first moment I saw him. I was just hyperaware of him the moment he stepped in the room with his smirk and those muscles. I was picking up on that big dick energy like my pussy was suddenly a goddamn radar. The more I tried to ignore him, the more violently he intruded in my thoughts.

Now we're in his car and my tits are in his big, warm hands while he kisses my throat. How the hell did this happen?

Laz pulls back and our faces are inches away from each other's. The scar across the corner of his mouth beckons me to kiss him, while the rest of the world feels very far away.

"Tell me, Bambi," Laz murmurs, teasing my lips by not quite

touching them with his. "Tell me who hurt you, and you'll never have to worry about him again."

"You care that some boy is tormenting me when tormenting me is your favorite thing to do?"

A wicked smile touches his lips. "I'm not tormenting you. This is foreplay." He glances above our heads at my palm pressed tight against the roof of his car. "Why aren't you touching me?"

I don't want to know what he feels like. I don't want to replay the feel of him beneath my hands over and over again as I lay in my bed in the dark, furiously rubbing my clit.

Laz tucks a lock of my hair behind my ear. "Bambi, don't look so terrified. I'm a mouthy bastard, but I'm not going to run off and tell anyone about this. You think I want to draw the wrath of the Bianchis down on my head by telling them I'm messing around with my stepdaughter?" He smiles wider, his white, shiny canines glinting. "So touch me."

Nope. It's a trap. He touches my body. I touch his. He kisses me. Next thing I know, I'm in the back seat of his car while he pounds the living daylights out of me. Yet another terrible decision.

I swallow, hard. "Let's just go home."

Laz takes a fistful of my T-shirt and drags it down and settles it carefully back into place over my ribs. He sits back, and finally I can breathe again. "Not until you give me that name."

The world rushes back. Holy shit. How does he command one hundred and ten percent of my attention like that? "Don't worry about it. I don't care anymore."

Laz's expression darkens. "There's a red mark on your cheek,

Bambi. I'm fucking furious. Either we go home and I give your mom hell for putting it there, or you let me unleash it all on the bastard who caused this shit in the first place."

My heart convulses with longing. Suddenly, I don't care if he's sincere or not. Laz wants to defend me. I crave to know what that feels like for the first time in my life.

I lift my fist and show him the red bruise on my knuckles. "But I got him good already."

Laz takes my hand and kisses the mark. "You got him so good. But let me finish him off for you. Don't worry, I won't kill him. I'll only punch him hard enough to give him a black eye. Flattening high school wasters isn't much fun."

"He's six feet tall, works out, and has an older brother and a mean father."

He shrugs. "So?"

"They're all into wrestling."

Laz's eyes flash with delight. "You mean it will be a proper fight? Now you're talking. Name and address. Now."

I sigh and stare straight ahead through the windshield. Maybe I'll regret this, but I tell him the address.

"Good girl," he says, his eyes lighting up as he starts the car.

When we pull up outside Kaleb's house, he and his brother Michael are playing basketball in the driveway. Both of them have stripped off their T-shirts and a good two inches of designer underwear is showing above their belted jeans. They're almost as tall as Laz, and Michael clearly works out just as much as he does.

Laz turns to me, his eyebrows lifting. "Jesus. I'm fighting these guys? You couldn't be bullied by Napoleon Dynamite?"

"No one's making you," I tell him, but bitter disappointment creeps into my voice. For a while there, it felt good that someone was going up to bat for me, even if it is my strange, weirdly sexy, and definitely deranged stepdad.

Laz gives me a lazy grin. "You think I can't take them? Bambi, they're toast."

We stare into each other's eyes and my heart batters against my ribs.

He steps out of the car and calls out, "Which one of you bitches wants to dance?"

I pass a hand over my face. Oh, my God.

Kaleb and Michael exchange glances and a puzzled frown. They seem to get the message that we're not here to sell Girl Scout cookies, though, as Michael throws the basketball aside and the pair stalk menacingly toward the car.

Laz slams the door and leans down to speak through the window. "Stay there, baby. I'll be right back."

He turns around to face the two boys, still smiling.

All of them are sizing each other up, Kaleb and Michael seem unwilling to get too close until they've figured out who's bigger, meaner, and crazier.

Laz has no problem stepping up and getting in their faces. "Let's play twenty questions. I'll go first. Who's the prick who took a photo of Mia?"

Kaleb looks past Laz and sees me. With a smirk for his brother, he says, "Hey, it's Miss Tiny Tits." He turns back to Laz. "Who's asking? You her pimp?"

Laz's smile vanishes. Without warning, he pulls his fist back and slams it into Kaleb's jaw.

Kaleb staggers away with a hand to his face and falls down.

I clamp both my hands over my mouth. Oh, fuck. This was a mistake. Kaleb is a boy and Laz is a grown man. This is not a fair—

Michael grabs Laz by the back of his T-shirt, swings him around, and knees him in the nuts. Laz's eyes bulge and he doubles over with a groan. Then Michael's knee hits him in the face, and blood pours from Laz's nose and drips onto the concrete.

I take my hands away from my mouth and wince. Okay, maybe it's fair.

Kaleb recovers and gets to his feet, ready to lay into Laz, but Laz straightens up, and sweeps his feet out from beneath him. While Kaleb is down again, he throws a punch at Michael. Michael might be big, but he's slow, and he doesn't see Laz coming and gets a split lip for his carelessness.

Laz pushes Michael back against the house and points a finger in his face. "Stay out of this. I'm not going to hurt your brother. I want his phone and then I'm leaving."

He goes back to Kaleb who's just started to sit up. Laz stands over him with his hand outstretched. There's blood all over his lips and chin. "Your phone. Then I'm leaving."

"Why? Who the hell are you?" Kaleb snivels like a ten-year-old boy, dabbing at his bleeding nose with his fingers.

"Mia's stepdad," Laz seethes. "And you know why. That picture you have on your phone of my girl."

With a sulky expression on his bloody face, Kaleb reaches into his pocket and pulls his phone out.

Just then, a truck comes roaring down the street. Kaleb and Michael both turn around to look, their faces lighting up. The driver parks behind me and gets out, and he's freaking huge. He's older than Kaleb and Michael, and he's six-foot-something of seasoned, angry muscle in a trucker cap and wife beater. This must be Kaleb's dad, and he's *pissed*.

He surveys the scene before him, reaches into the back of his truck, and pulls out a baseball bat.

"What the hell is going on?" He walks straight past the Camaro toward Laz without seeing me, brandishing the bat like he can't wait to beat someone to death with it. Michael, energized by the sight of his dad, starts closing in on Laz. Even Kaleb is grinning.

Laz's expression goes slack. "Oh, fuck."

Oh fuck, indeed. Without thinking twice, I scooch over the handbrake into the driver's seat and start the car. It squeals as I rev the engine and struggle to remember how to put it in gear. Stick shifts. I can't drive goddamn stick shifts.

After a moment of fumbling, the car shoots forward past Kaleb's dad, and I slam the brakes next to Laz. "Get in!"

He doesn't need to be told twice. He snatches Kaleb's phone from him, pulls the door open, and jumps in the car.

"Don't stall, please don't stall," I beg the laboring engine. In the side mirror, Kaleb's dad is getting closer and closer with that baseball bat. Michael has run into the garage, and he's come out with a bat of his own.

"What are you playing at, Bambi? *Go*."

I move my foot on the clutch and the engine sputters into life. Gasping in relief, I pull away from the curb and slam my foot on the accelerator. The car whines in protest. I forgot to put it in second gear and we're only going ten miles an hour.

Laz is twisted around in the passenger seat so he can look out the back window. I see in the rearview mirror that the truck swings out onto the street and races after us, three people sitting inside it.

"Oh, my God. Oh, my God," I say over and over as my blood roars in my ears. I change up through second to third gear and there's an excruciating grinding sound.

Laz stares at the stick shift and then up at me. "What the hell are you doing?"

I'm panicking, that's what. We're going to be caught and have our heads caved in with a baseball bat. "I can't drive your stupid car! I only took three lessons in a manual."

"Clutch," Laz orders, and I push with my foot. He puts his hand over mine, yanks the stick down into fourth and we slam into gear. The powerful engine roars and we shoot forward. For a second, my heart lifts.

But the truck is gaining on us.

The street ends, and I change down to second before taking the corner at speed. The back end skids out in a squeal of rubber and we nearly hit a tree. I wait for Laz to shout at me to be more careful with his precious car.

He pats my shoulder, hard, still staring behind us. "Yes! You've got this, Bambi. Leave them in the dust."

The road is clear ahead. I take a deep breath.

And floor it.

The gears change smoothly. Laz whoops in delight as we race ahead.

But the truck isn't giving up. Kaleb is leaning out of the passenger window, hollering something indistinguishable but threatening. He gets louder and louder as the truck surges up on our ass.

This is my neighborhood, and I happen to know there's a slip road down to the river that appears almost out of nowhere on the crest of a hill. I accelerate like I'm determined to get us up and over the bridge to the main road on the other side. The truck changes lanes to our left, preparing to overtake us and cut us off. They haven't noticed the slip road. We're driving past it. We're almost past it.

With my heart in my throat, I wrench the wheel to the right. Horns blare, and my stomach seems to vanish completely from my body. The Camaro grips the road and stays on course. The truck shoots past us over the bridge, and I hear a roar of frustration from the three men in the car.

I let out a scream of triumph and step on the gas, and we head down the side road and along the river.

Laz slams the dashboard with his fist and grins. "You lost them. Fuck yeah, Bambi."

I'm laughing too hard to catch my breath. The truck will be lost in a tangle of red lights and traffic by now. I take a right-hand turn and head for home.

"That was crazy. First I thought you were going to kill them. Then I thought they were going to kill you."

Laz waves away my concern. "Please, I had the upper hand the entire time."

"Yeah, you had the upper hand with your nuts when Michael slammed them with his knee."

He winces. "Be nice about my nuts." He pulls the phone out of his pocket and holds it up. "Are you going to tell me what this photo is and how they really got it?"

The smile dies on my face. Laz doesn't believe my lie about not wearing a sports bra during gym class. When I don't answer, he rolls down his window and throws the phone out. It sails away behind us and falls into the river.

I glance over my shoulder in surprise. "You're not going to look at it? You're not even going to bug me about it?"

He smirks at me, relaxing back in his seat, looking too damn sexy for a man with blood all over his face. "The memory of your soft tits in my mouth is going to be better than any photo. Nice driving, Bambi."

I find myself relaxing, too, enjoying the breeze in my hair and the thrum of the powerful engine. "Your car made it easy."

"Modded her myself." He lovingly pats the dash. "But you still drove like a hot bitch."

My mouth twitches as a warm glow spreads through me. The road opens up before us, and it feels like freedom. It causes a physical ache in my chest to head for home.

When we walk through the front door, Mom looks with distaste upon Laz's bloody face and my wild hair and flushed cheeks.

"We sorted out the prick who took that photo of Mia. You're welcome," Laz tells her.

Mom gives him an overly sweet smile. "Thank you for defending my daughter's honor, husband darling."

The smile drops from her face, and she shakes her head like she's disgusted with both of us.

He points a finger in her face and looms over her. "Don't lay a hand on your daughter ever again."

Mom gazes up at him with a bored expression. "One afternoon of beating up some teenagers and you think you're the man of the house? Go and get cleaned up. You're a disgrace." She turns back to her phone, muttering, "Both of you."

Blood is still dripping from Laz's nose. I grab an ice pack from the freezer and push at his shoulder. The last thing we need is another explosive fight in this house. "Come on. Let's go upstairs."

In the bathroom, he perches on the edge of the tub while I wipe the blood from his face with a damp washcloth.

"In all my fighting days, I was never tended to by such a pretty girl."

I shrug, gently dabbing around his nose like it doesn't matter to me one drop that Laz just called me pretty. "This doesn't look broken, but I think you're going to be sore."

He smiles up at me, his eyes sparkling. "It was worth it."

With a jolt, I realize I'm standing between his spread knees. He has his hands braced on the edge of the tub like he's inviting me to get closer.

I should move away.

I don't move away.

Instead, I reach behind me for the ice pack and press it gently over his nose. He hisses in pain, and reaches up to take it from me, holding it in place.

"That boy might still have that photo of you," Laz tells me. "He could have sent it to a friend or backed it up."

"Maybe," I murmur. I don't know if I care much anymore. That photo was all about power, and Laz and I just went and took a good chunk of it away from Kaleb. "Let them enjoy my tiny tits if they're so obsessed with me."

A smile spreads over Laz's face. "You're a fucking badass."

"Who, me?" I step to the side to grab a clean washcloth and wet it. When I step back, his knee is between my thighs, and I squeeze him, pretending to be intent on wiping the last of the blood from his jaw and throat.

Laz groans and his hand with the ice pack drops away from his nose. His face is on the same level as my torso, and he gazes at my bare waist and hips like he's wondering what I taste like.

"Do you want me to fuck you, Bambi?" he murmurs huskily.

I give a choking sort of laugh like I'm not vividly imagining straddling his thighs.

"Turn around and pull your panties to one side for me. A quick fuck before we go downstairs for dinner with your mom."

My heart races, and then trips up and goes flying on one of the words he's spoken. *Mom.*

What the hell am I doing? Laz is married to my mother, and she's downstairs right this second waiting for us. They snipe at each other, but a lot of couples do that when they care for each other. I'm sure Mom cares about Laz in her own way. She doesn't deserve a husband who cheats on her with her own daughter.

And there's something else. I've been giving Laz the impression that I'm a lot more experienced than I really am. I'm not a saint, but I am a virgin. Laz seems like his type is women who know what they're doing. Once I tell him that I don't, he'll lose interest.

Cheeks burning, I mutter, "What an enticing first time."

"We're in a hurry, but I won't leave you wanting. This dick is magic, Bambi. Hop on and give it a try."

Revulsion bursts through me at his callous words. He's so depraved that he can talk about deflowering his stepdaughter like it's nothing. Like *I'm* nothing.

I'm so tired of feeling like I'm nothing.

I take the ice pack out of his hand and slap it back on his face. Hard, so that he winces. Laz doesn't want me. He just wants the twisted clout of saying he fucked his stepdaughter.

I step away from him. "You're a pig. Thank you for an evening of cheap thrills and mindless violence, but keep your hands to yourself from now on."

Chapter Four

MIA

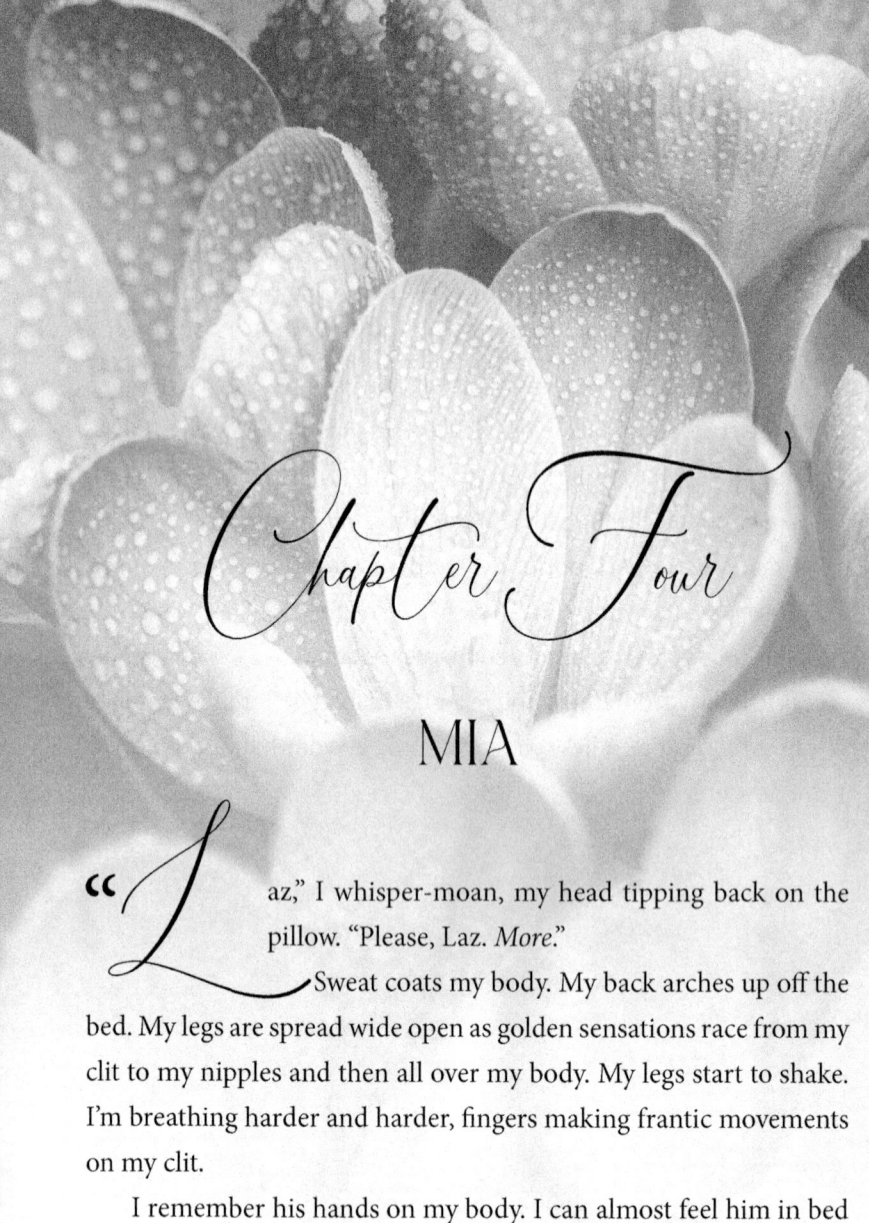

"Laz," I whisper-moan, my head tipping back on the pillow. "Please, Laz. *More*."

Sweat coats my body. My back arches up off the bed. My legs are spread wide open as golden sensations race from my clit to my nipples and then all over my body. My legs start to shake. I'm breathing harder and harder, fingers making frantic movements on my clit.

I remember his hands on my body. I can almost feel him in bed with me. His weight on me and the exact pitch of his deep voice in my ear. The achingly slow way he dragged his tongue over my tender nipples. The thrust of his hips, only this time we're naked, and the cock that I've only felt through his clothes is jammed deep inside me, and he's barely able to thrust because he's so thick and I'm so tight and—

I cry out as my climax rocks my whole body. I come hard, my inner muscles clenching on nothing, aching for *something*.

Aching for Laz.

My stepfather who's currently just down the hall and in bed with my mother.

Fuck.

What am I doing?

I snap my legs closed and lift my head, struck with a sudden, guilty impulse that someone's watching me. Listening to me. For a moment, I'm sure that I'll see Laz standing at the end of my bed, leering at me because he's just witnessed me making myself come while whimpering his name. Thinking about his body, his cock, his lips on mine, and his tongue deep inside my mouth.

I fall back with a moan, shame licking over me but wanting to go again. Morning light is peeking around my curtain, and it's nearly time to get up and go to school. Thank the stars my suspension is over, and I can finally get out of this house. My pussy is drenched, and the middle finger of my right hand is beginning to prune because I've been at this an hour and come six times. Rubbing my clit isn't enough. I want more, but I don't know how to give it to myself. When I shove my fingers inside myself, they're at an awkward angle and so shallow they do nothing for me.

I need Laz's thick fingers and his body braced over mine, a cruel smile on his face as he slams them deep inside me, watching me writhe helplessly beneath him.

From down the hall I hear Mom's voice, muffled through the closed doors. They're both in the master bedroom. Mom and Laz. What if they're screwing while I'm in here wishing he was dragging his fingers through my slippery pussy and getting his teeth into my nipples?

An even worse thought occurs to me, and I sit up, breaking into a cold sweat. What if he's telling Mom what we did together in his car? Or how I got myself off on his fingers the night he crept into my bed? The idea of Laz being overly bothered by his conscience seems unlikely, but he could pretend he has to unburden himself just to fuck with this family. I don't trust him one little bit.

Or someone might have spotted him sucking on my tits in his car the other day. We were down by the river, but we weren't exactly aware of our surroundings.

I grab either side of my head and moan in horror at the thought of that gossip getting back to Mom. I'm being flayed alive by my shame. I feel even worse than I did when my uncle dragged me half naked out of Connor's car.

"So why are you still fantasizing about him?" I whisper-shriek at myself.

But I know why. It's because Laz is so sexy it's obnoxious. Or he's so obnoxious that he's sexy. Either way, I want to punch him, scratch him, hurt him, and then have him overpower me, pin me down, and screw me senseless. The way I've been acting around him, he's heard that loud and clear, and shame burns me afresh.

"I wish he didn't know," I moan, falling back onto the pillows. He's been making my life hell these past few days, smirking at me and swaggering around. Making insinuations when no one else is within earshot. I wish I were someone else, anyone else, so I could just sleep with him and get him out of my system. It wouldn't be hard because from what I've heard, Laz is a total manwhore. I overheard his brother lecturing him about it at the wedding. Fabrizio Rosetti told Laz he needs to man up, be a proper husband, and get Mom pregnant.

Jealously floods me from head to toe at the thought of them having that little project together. Having loads of knock-me-up sex. Taking her temperature together and doing pregnancy tests. The hope. The anticipation. Planning it all out.

I fall into a daydream, wondering what it would be like to do all that with Laz. Especially the sex. I picture my hands pressed against Laz's bare chest while he fucks me, every thrust punctuated with a deep groan. Filling me up with his cum and then holding me like I'm the precious, soon-to-be mother of his child. Heat floods me in a great rush.

And then turns cold as reality rushes back.

Laz and Mom.

Mom and Laz.

Frankly, they're a terrible couple. They have nothing in common. She doesn't make him laugh. She doesn't call him Laz. She's never driven his—

I pinch myself, hard. What am I thinking? I'm not jealous about Laz. I hate Laz, and that hasn't changed because he did one nice thing for me.

I kick the blankets off my legs and stalk to the shower, a hot mess of anger, frustration, and self-disgust. I never thought I would, but I can't wait to be at school again. Mom grounded me for getting suspended, no phone, no pool, no TV, and I've had nothing to do but homework and reading and bumping into Laz every time I leave my room.

Literally bumping into him. I swear he positions himself around corners so that I collide with his body. Suddenly off-balance, I automatically put up my hands and grab hold of whatever's closest for support. Every time he smirks down at my hands on his chest, I want to slap his face and then go up on my toes to kiss him.

I bet he knows how to use that tongue for a really good, slow—

I make a strangled noise in the back of my throat, turn just the cold tap on, and step under the freezing spray.

School is a welcome distraction, and I bury myself in the work. I can feel rather than hear the other students talking about me, and they grow bolder as the day wears on.

After lunch, people start making comments directly to my face. Boys, mostly. They pretend to be afraid of me, backing away and laughing like I'm going to attack them.

"Bianchi, I thought you were suspended for fighting, not attempted murder."

"Watch out, boys, the kitten has claws."

"More like fists of steel."

I don't know what they're talking about until I catch sight of Kaleb just before the end of the day. His face is purple and yellow with bruises. He can't have told anyone that me and Laz showed up at his house and Laz kicked the shit out of him and his brother. I suppose that doesn't go with the pro-wrestler image the two of them are trying to cultivate. Better that everyone thinks he let me hit him.

Whatever he needs to get through the day.

Suddenly, I'm the bad girl at school. I find myself walking with a spring in my step, my ponytail swinging, and a smile on my face. My good mood only gets better when I find my sister, Rieta, waiting for me at the school gates in her red convertible.

I get into the passenger seat and give her a kiss. "Rieta, what are you doing here?"

Rieta is beautiful, with dark, coppery hair that flashes red in the sunlight and bright, tawny eyes. She smiles, and dimples appear in her cheeks. "I thought I'd take the family black sheep out for ice cream now that she's free."

"Mom told you I was grounded," I grumble.

"Oh, she told me all about it, in long and lingering detail. I hope you gave that boy a black eye." Rieta's still smiling as she pulls away from the curb and into traffic, and I can't help but grin as well. We both have to deal with having a type A overbearing mother, though Rieta's had it easier than me because she's always been a good daughter and married a successful and well-connected man.

"You and Isabel are so lucky to have me to take the heat off you."

Rieta peers at me over her sunglasses. "You think? How many times has Mom told you you'd be pregnant by now if only you tried harder?"

I wince. Rieta and Nero have been married for a year and a half, and no baby yet. "I'm sorry it's so hard. How are you feeling?"

Rieta sighs gustily as she turns onto the main street where all the cafés and shops are. "Frustrated. I'm doing all the right things. Taking my temperature. Sticking my legs in the air after."

I burst out laughing. "What?"

My sister smiles at the road ahead. "To keep the you-know-what inside you after he's finished. I feel so silly, but people swear by it. And yet, it's not working for me. At this rate, Mom's going to be pregnant before I am."

And now I'm thinking about Laz and Mom again. "Gross."

Rieta turns to me. "What's gross?"

"Them having a baby."

"They're married. It's only natural. Mia, why do you look so freaked out?"

I quickly rearrange my face and pretend to be bored by the conversation. "I'm not freaked out. I'm just . . ."

Freaked out.

Angry.

Jealous.

"Don't you think she's too old to have a baby?"

Rieta shrugs. "She's only forty-one, and she told me she's excited by the idea. Plus, everyone's keen for Bianchi-Rosetti family ties to be solidified. What better way than with a baby?"

"Yes, what better way," I agree, and yet my stomach is roiling and twisting like an angry snake in a bag.

Rieta pulls up outside the ice cream shop and smiles brightly. "Here we are. I'm going to have a cone the size of my head to make me feel better about not being pregnant. After being grounded, you must need one twice the size of your head."

I'm staring blankly at the dashboard, lost in my own world. Mom will get pregnant. Rieta will get pregnant. Everything will be baby talk at home. Laz and Nero will fawn over their wives and newborns, two big, strong men gone all soft. A sick, envious feeling spreads through my belly.

"Mia?"

"What? Oh, I don't really feel like any ice cream."

Rieta's face falls. "But you always liked ice cream after school."

Normally I do, especially when it's with the only person in this family who actually cares about me. I take a deep breath and smile through my nausea. "You're right, I do want some. But can we take it home and eat it by the pool? I've been banned from the pool for days."

My sister relaxes into a smile. "Absolutely. Go choose your flavors, my treat."

Fifteen minutes later, we have our shoes off and we're dangling our feet in the cool water as we eat our ice cream. I have a small cup with scoops of watermelon and peach sorbet. Rieta has a waffled cone stuffed with cookies and cream, death by chocolate, and raspberry ripple.

Mom emerges from the house and surveys us with a sharp expression. When she can find nothing to reprimand me with, she turns to Rieta.

"Don't you think that's too much ice cream for one person?"

"Dairy is important for women trying to get pregnant. And for women with pushy mothers." Rieta nudges me conspiratorially and winks.

I duck my head to hide my smile. I couldn't get away with talking to Mom like that, but she merely makes a *tsk* sound at Rieta.

"If I get pregnant before you do, I'll be having words with your husband. Nero can't work all the time and expect to magically father a child."

Rieta takes a dismal lick of her ice cream. "You probably will be pregnant before me. You're still in the honeymoon period where it's sex night and morning."

Mom smiles at her, her lips plump and self-satisfied. "Yes, he's a handful, my husband. So demanding."

I nearly gag on my sorbet. My mother never talks this way, and it's doubly disturbing when I remember how her husband has been trying to screw me.

"Throw the rest of that ice cream in the trash, darling. It won't encourage your husband in the bedroom if you put on a few pounds."

Rieta rolls her eyes at Mom's retreating back and returns to eating her ice cream. "Throw it out? This ice cream is way too good to throw out."

I make a vague sound in response, too preoccupied wondering if Laz has been having clandestine quickies with Mom all over this house, just out of sight. He's never touching me again. Never ever. Who the hell is he, thinking he can screw every woman in this house?

A moment later, the man himself walks out of the kitchen, grease stains on his fingers and muscular forearms. When we arrived, he had the garage door open while he worked on his Camaro.

"Hello, Lazzaro, how are you?" Rieta asks with a polite smile.

I expect him to correct her and tell her to call him Laz, but his expression merely flashes with annoyance before it wanders over to me. He takes in my bare legs and school skirt rucked up around my thighs away from the water. "I'm peachy. You girls look like you're having fun."

Rieta swings her legs back and forth in the pool. "Just finding ways to deal with the weight of Mom's expectations. I hope your baby-making efforts are going better than mine."

I'm dawdling my little spoon through the ice cream, but my gaze is fixed on Laz, and I see his jaw clench.

He's annoyed. What does that mean? He hates his private business being talked about? He didn't want me to know he's trying to knock my mother up because it will gross me out when he's trying to fuck me?

I shove my spoon angrily into the ice cream. Too late. I'm grossed out.

"Good luck, or whatever people say," he tells Rieta flatly. I can feel him staring at me, but I refuse to look up. Awkward silence stretches while I pretend to be absorbed in my ice cream.

Finally, he turns around and goes into the house.

"He's not the chatty type, is he?" Rieta observes.

"Oh, he talks plenty when he's causing trouble."

Rieta pulls a sympathetic face. "Is it really hard living here these days? If you ever need a place to escape, you can always come to mine."

It's always hard living under the same roof as Mom. It's kind of Rieta to offer her place as somewhere I can crash, but living with Nero isn't a better prospect. He and Mom are cut from the same cloth. Both serious, standoffish people, and they agree about disliking me.

"Thanks. I'll be okay." Especially since I have a plan. I wish I could confide in my sister, but I can't risk anything getting back to Mom.

"I need some water. Want some?" I get up from the pool and head for the kitchen.

"No, thanks, I'm happy with my ice cream," Rieta calls after me.

I smile to myself as I pad barefoot into the kitchen. With a waffle cone that huge, I bet she is.

The smile dies on my lips as I turn a corner and run straight into Laz.

"Nice chat with your sister?" he asks nonchalantly, leaning against the wall and blocking my way to the refrigerator.

"We haven't finished, and yes, thank you. Now move."

But Laz stays right where he is. "Don't let the gossip flow too freely."

My expression hardens. "Meaning?"

"You know what it means."

What does he think I'm going to do? Brag to my sister that my stepdad got me half naked in his car? That's not girl talk. That's self-immolation through pure shame.

"I had no idea you were dying to be a family man," I say.

His eyes flick up and down my body. "Want to help me with that?"

My lip curls. "You're disgusting."

Laz's eyes flash, and he growls. "I don't like your tone, Bambi. Be polite to your stepfather."

"Or what?"

"Or I'll have a little chat with your mom about the way you've been throwing yourself at me." He smirks like he's remembering all the times we've been pressed up against each other in inappropriate ways.

"You . . ." I start to explode at the top of my lungs, before I remember what I'm fighting with him about, and where, and I lower my voice. "You asshole. Me throwing myself at you? You know it's the other way around."

"Who do you think she'll believe?"

An angry flush stains my cheeks. "Emotional blackmail? Really?"

"Whatever gets me what I want."

"And that is?"

A smile slides across his handsome face. "The sweet pleasure of tormenting you."

So much for the other day when we almost felt like friends. I guess what he really wanted was to beat someone up. "Stay classy, asshole."

He grabs my arm and yanks me back to him. I practically fall against his muscled chest, and I have to pull my palms back from his rock-hard abs. Jesus Christ, the man is stacked. When I'm at school, all he must do is work out.

"Now, now, Bambi," he says with a menacing smile. "You wouldn't want your mother finding out about how you shoved your tits at me in my car and begged me to screw you."

A cold fist grips my heart. As much as Mom seems to dislike Laz, she'd believe him, not me. "I hate you."

"I hate you harder." The way he growls *harder* in my ear has my toes curling against the cold tiles.

Laz finally lets go of me and walks away, and I take deep breaths as I stare at his broad back, trying to calm my fury.

I'll only be here a few months. Just a few more months, but I might not make it that long. I might murder my stepfather in his sleep.

"Mia?" Rieta has come in from the pool and she frowns at the expression on my face. "Is everything okay?"

Nothing in my life is okay, but I force a smile for my sister. "I'm fine. Just chatting with Laz."

"Do you want to come over to my house and watch TV?"

Normally I would love that. Rieta's place is just a few streets away, and her husband won't be home for hours. He works late all the time. "Thanks, but I have to get ready for work."

"Are you sure you should be working these shifts? Mom says some nights you don't get home until two in the morning. It's a weird coffee bar that makes you work so late."

I glance guiltily at my sister, but she's digging in her purse for her car keys. It's not a suspicious question, just an idle remark.

With a shrug, I say, "It's near a college. Lots of students studying late and they need frappés."

"Oh. Okay then, have fun. I'll talk to you soon." Rieta kisses me goodbye and then heads for the front door, calling, "Bye, Mom. Bye, Lazzaro."

Neither of them answers her.

I take a swig of water directly from the jug in the fridge and wipe my mouth with the back of my wrist, reliving the latest hate-filled moments with Laz.

Don't store the way he growled *harder* in your spank bank.

But as I climb the stairs to my room to take a shower, I'm already mentally filling out a card with every detail about Laz's pitch and the expression on his face to file away in a shimmering cabinet under *Sick Bitch Daughter Gets Pounded By Her Stepdad*.

Chapter Five

LAZ

*I*t's perfect.

Everything about it is perfect. The shop. The palatial showroom. The six bays for servicing cars. The huge storage area. The staffrooms. The huge shady trees out front that would keep the heat off on hot days.

I can picture the sign that would hang in pride on the front of the building. *Rosetti Motors and Servicing*. The life I want is so close I can touch it. Taste it. Smell the engine grease.

This place could be mine.

It *should* be mine.

But my brothers are ruining my dreams. I earned good money for the family over the years, but like an idiot, it didn't go into my bank account, it went into the family account that my father and now Faber controls. It must add up to hundreds of thousands of dollars, shifting their suspect imports, overseeing so many illegal clubs. I busted my guts for the Rosetti family, and when I asked for what's rightfully mine, they've turned their backs on me. I'm a loose cannon, the unreliable one, but the irony is I don't even want to be a criminal. I'd be happier up to my elbows in car engines every day, buying, selling, and fixing up motors. I worked hard for the family. Now I want something that's mine.

My wife has enough money to buy this place fifty times over, but I'll tie a bungee cord to my balls and jump of a cliff before I go begging to her. I know just how Giulia would act if she bankrolled this place for me.

Lazzaro just loves tinkering with his little cars.

You're going there? Again? Didn't you go there yesterday?

Please, Lazzaro, stop pretending your silly hobby is anything close to real work.

I'd rather not have this place than have it under those conditions.

I stand up from the hood of my car with a groan. So, I guess I'm not having it.

I need a drink to drown my misery. Or ten, in a place where the other drinkers have never even heard of kale and quinoa.

I head across town to a place where the streets are comfortably run-down, the men wear ripped jeans and faded T-shirts, and the girls sport the best winged eyeliner in the city. I'm about to head into a bar when I spot my favorite strip club, Peppers. Your feet stick to the carpet, but the girls are gorgeous.

Treat yourself, Laz.

But when I get inside, I can barely concentrate on my beer, let alone the bartender with great tits or the dancer on stage with even better tits and an ass so tight you could bounce a coin off it. A few girls put a hand on my shoulder and ask me if I want a private dance. I thought I did, but now it doesn't seem so appealing, so I shake my head.

I'll finish my beer and go. Tonight's a bust.

"Please welcome to the stage, Tasha."

I glance up, more to show some respect to the girl who's performing than from interest. I'm about to drop my gaze when something about the slender, lilac-haired girl snares my interest.

First of all, she's so pretty and petite that my hands ache to get around that little waist of hers. The lilac hair makes her seem ethereal, and there's a flirty, knowing curve to her lips. She's got the tiniest pair of tits I've ever seen. Almost no tits, but adorable, raspberry pink nipples that have my tongue moving against the roof of my mouth. The way she's dancing is incredibly sexy, swaying that cute little ass and taking languorous swings around the pole.

Suddenly my dick is standing to attention. I can't tear my eyes away from her, and from what I can tell in my peripheral vision, every other man in this joint is staring at the pixie on stage as well.

She's a full minute into her dance before I realize with a jolt that I know this girl. I leap to my feet, my chair shooting out behind me and clattering to the floor.

"*Mia.*"

The girl calling herself Tasha has been smiling from one man to the next, and finally her gaze lands on me. Those brown eyes of hers widen momentarily as they meet mine. But then they're moving on to the next man, that languid fuck-me expression being bestowed on someone else.

My stepdaughter's a stripper? I've just caught her, and she's going to keep dancing like nothing's happened?

No way. No fucking *way*. I grasp the edge of the stage, preparing to leap up and drag her off it.

"Hey, what do you think you're doing?" A bouncer grabs me by the shoulders and pulls me back.

I round on him and point at Mia with a furious forefinger. "That's my stepdaughter."

The bouncer glances from me to Mia and back again. The anger melts from his face, but he compels me back to my seat and rights it for me. "Sorry, man. She's chosen to be up there, so you need to suck it up or get out."

I can't sit down, so I death-grip the back of my chair for the rest of Mia's dance. Guys keep holding out bills to her, and she lets them slide the money into the waistband of her G-string, and their fingers accidentally-on-purpose graze her flesh. Every time one of these lowlifes touch her, I want to drag them out of here by their hair, but the bouncer has his arms folded and his narrowed gaze directed right at me. One wrong move, and I'll be outside where I can't get to Mia.

When she finishes her dance, she has enough bills tucked into her panties to wallpaper a house.

I open my mouth to call her down off the stage, but she ignores me, gives a flirty little wave to the room, and disappears back the way she came.

Un-fucking-believable.

I step into the path of one of the dancers who's dressed in a spangled purple G-string, a white feather boa, and nothing else. "Tell her to come out and talk to me."

The woman gives me an up-and-down. "Who?"

"Mia." She stares at me blankly, and I growl through my teeth, "*Tasha*."

Purple G-string gives me a sarcastic smirk and places a hand on her hip. "We don't follow your orders here, honey. If you want to see Tasha, you'll need to pay for a private dance."

I pull my wallet out of the back of my jeans. "Then I'll pay for a private dance."

She points where I need to go, and after I hand over the money I'm shown into a small room and told to wait.

A few minutes later, Mia comes through the door wearing a ruffled white G-string.

Clear plastic high heels.

The curly lilac wig.

A flirty smile on her glossy lips directed right at me.

And absolutely nothing else.

She looks like jailbait. Mouthwatering, innocent jailbait. Not usually my type, the barely legal girl who probably doesn't know her way around her own clit, but I happen to know this petite angel has a pussy of molten gold and can grind herself to orgasm on my fingers.

I open my mouth to ask her what the hell she's doing here, but she puts her hands on my shoulders and pushes me back against my seat. A song starts playing, something sexy and slow, and Mia straddles my lap.

As she slinks closer to me, and I catch the scent and heat of her perfect body, my dick stands to attention again.

I grip the sides of my chair. Oh, Jesus. I wasn't expecting this. I planned to yell at Mia to explain herself, but she's dragging her pussy along my erection and suddenly I'm seeing stars.

"What the hell are you doing?"

"What do you think, baby?" she murmurs in the horniest voice I've ever heard. "I'm giving you a dance."

She's not acting like she even recognizes me. The crazy thought occurs to me that Mia has a twin, but I recognize the small mole on the side of her throat. I kissed that mole the other day in my car. It's definitely her.

"You do know who I am, right?"

Maybe she's high as a kite and she doesn't realize the man she's writhing against is her stepfather.

"Sure I do. What are you doing here, Laz?"

Mia holds on to my shoulders and arches all the way back, moving her body in a slow semi-circle. The colored lights overhead play across her flawless skin.

"Mia—"

"It's Tasha." She meets my gaze and gives me a wink. "But you can call me Bambi if you like. Shall I take this off?"

She runs a teasing finger under the waistband of her ruffled G-string.

I swallow. Hard.

The right answer would be to shove her from my lap and lecture her about how inappropriate it is for either of us to be in here, especially together, when I'm married, she's in high school, and I'm her fucking stepfather.

But I never was much good at making the appropriate decision.

She edges the strap of her G-string down, giving me a flash of her waxed-bare pussy. "I won't tell. As you can probably guess, I'm very good at keeping secrets."

No kidding. I would never have guessed in a million years that this was where she spent her hours as a "barista." She not acting like the Mia I know at all. Tense. Vulnerable. Mouthy. Tasha is bold and sexy and she's on a mission to show me a good time.

Anger is still simmering beneath the surface, but I couldn't push Mia from my lap if my life depended on it. She takes hold of my shoulders and eases me back against the chair, and I let her. I settle back with my knees spread and my hands gripping the seat.

I can barely breathe as Mia edges down the waistband of her underwear, first on one side, then the other. Her white nails and the ruffled white G-string glow in the black lights.

We're both watching her undress herself for me, our heads bent closely together. The whole world slips into the background and the music fades away.

Slowly, Mia edges herself back on my thighs, stands up, and turns around. She teases the G-string lower, lower, until I can see all of her glorious ass. Then she bends double and drags the underwear down her legs and steps out of them.

Still bent over, Mia reaches back and drags her nails slowly over her pussy, across her ruffled inner lips and spreading herself open for me. It takes all my self-control not to reach out, pull her against my face and thrust my tongue deep inside of her.

Straightening up, Mia turns around and drops spread-eagled back into my lap, hugging my thighs with her knees. She makes a rolling motion with her hips, back and forth, until she finds the thick rod of my cock in my jeans, and a smile spreads over her lips.

"Laz," she whispers, wrapping her arms around my neck.

I swallow, struggling for control. "Yes, Bambi?"

"You can't tell my mom you saw me here," Mia tells me, dragging her bare snatch up my erection. "You can't tell my uncles." She slides back down my cock, arching her back and making my balls ache. "It has to be our secret."

I groan and my eyes nearly flutter closed. Damn, she's so good at this. How many men have seen her like this and felt their cocks grinding against her pussy? My blood is boiling, half from jealousy and half from the need to take Mia in my arms and raw her senseless.

"You look mad," she murmurs, keeping up that insanely good pressure up and down my dick. "Or are you just horny?"

"I'm furious," I tell her, lifting my hands to her waist and pulling her tight against my cock. I buck my hips slowly, aching to be balls deep inside of her.

"You're not supposed to put your hands on me," she moans, her eyes fluttering closed.

"You going to stop me?"

"I am. Let's go, buddy."

I look up and see the bouncer from earlier heading toward us with a stony expression on his face.

He's really starting to piss me off.

Mia smiles up at him. "It's all right, Jimmy. We know each other."

"Rules are rules, Tasha."

Mia puts her hand out to stop Jimmy just as he reaches to drag me out of the room. "I understand. He'll follow the rules. Won't you, Laz?"

I don't want to let go of Mia, but I can't be thrown out of here. My hands slide from her waist and hit the chair. I grip it hard, my whole body feverish with need.

The bouncer seems satisfied and steps back. "Have a nice time. Stepfather."

I flick a glare at him as he leaves us alone again. "I hate that he's watching you."

"Don't think about him," she tells me, resuming the glorious motions of her pussy.

My head tips back with a groan. "Mia, I should be dragging you out of here, but I don't want you to stop."

"I told you, I'm not Mia here. I'm Tasha."

I open my eyes and gaze at her beautiful face. She's not acting like Mia. She barely looks like Mia with all that makeup on her face and that lilac wig, but it's the way she's holding herself too, spine straight and proud. She's enjoying not being herself for a while, and who can blame her? Her life is filled with pain and loneliness. Tasha gets to be anyone she wants. When I kissed Mia's tits in my car she was so self-conscious about them. But Tasha knows they're special in a bar filled with women with enormous implants.

"You didn't believe me last time when I told you you're sexy," I murmur, watching her through half-lidded eyes. She has her hands pressed against my chest while she moves to the music. "Will Tasha believe me if I tell her?"

She flicks her gaze up at me and then down to my dick. Her lips are curved into a smile as if my hard-on is the best thing she's ever seen. "I don't know. Try her."

I grip my seat even harder. "You're so hot. It's all I can do not to explode in my jeans, you've got my dick that hard. You always get me so hard."

"Thank you, baby. You're not so bad yourself. I've always had a thing for bad boys with tattoos."

But it's Tasha speaking, not Mia, a practiced line she's probably used dozens of times before and it sounds flat. Is that who usually pays for her lap dances, men with tattoos? With her sweet looks, she must attract the worst kind of creeps.

Mia strokes her hand beneath my jaw. "I can feel you getting angry again. Just relax and try to enjoy yourself."

"Stop being Tasha. Just be you."

She goes still, a line forming between her brows and her eyes growing huge with worry. "I don't want to be Mia right now."

My hands lift to touch her, reassure her, but I have to drop them again, and I growl in frustration. "Mia's who I want."

There. I said it. I'm married to her mom and my life is a mess, but I want Mia.

Mia gazes at me with those huge eyes of hers, and I see past the makeup and stripper attitude to the vulnerable girl within. "I'm not supposed to want you, Laz."

"I'm not supposed to want you, either. But I can't stop thinking about you. Everywhere I go in that house I can feel you. I can taste you. It's driving me crazy."

Mia throws me a challenging look. "I thought you just wanted to make me miserable for fun."

I do.

I did.

I didn't know what the fuck I was doing.

"I was angry. I was taking it out on you."

"Now you want to take it out on me in a different way?"

My gaze slips down her body and I breathe, "Fuck, do I ever."

"You're so mad at Mom and your brothers so you want to screw me as a big fuck you to them," she says.

"Yes. No. I don't know."

Mia scratches her nails through the short hairs at the nape of my neck. "I hate them too, Laz. So maybe I'll let you fuck me because a big fuck you to them would feel pretty good. But if anyone finds out, we're going to get in so much trouble."

No shit. I'll probably get beaten to death by her uncles. "I will. Not you. I won't let anything happen to you."

She strokes her fingers through my hair. "No one's ever wanted to protect me before. Sometimes it feels like my family would be happier if I were dead."

An icy hand grips my heart, and I wish I could tell her that's not true, but she wouldn't believe me, and I won't lie to her. "Then keep on living out of sheer spite. Or just live because you're beautiful, inside and out, and the world needs people like you."

I need people like you.

I need *you*.

She smiles, a real, beautiful smile that lights up her eyes.

I take a ragged breath. "Bambi, I want to kiss you so much."

Mia leans close and runs her fingers over my lower lip, murmuring, "I bet you kiss real good." She leans even closer and licks the scar at the corner of my mouth, and then runs her lower lip through her teeth like I'm delicious. "Mm. I've been aching to do that."

I will lose my mind in a minute.

"Remember when you came on my fingers? Do that on my dick. Show me how beautiful you are."

She changes her pace and the angle of her hips, and her lips part with pleasure as she rubs her clit across the head of my cock.

Her soft moans fill the air around us and her cheeks are flushing pink. "You know I can come like this. How about you?"

I never cared much for lap dances. If you're going to have a girl in your lap, what's the point of wearing clothes and not being able to touch her? It's more frustrating than fulfilling.

But not today. I'm transfixed by the sight of Mia moving against me, and her peachy ass rubbing against my dick just right. The way she's sliding up and down has me riding closer and closer to my peak. "Bambi, I've been craving to blow with you in my arms ever since I laid eyes on you. This wasn't what I imagined . . ." I break off with a groan. "But I'm not complaining."

I struggle to control myself because she's not quite there yet. Her small hands are clenching on my shoulders and her moans are getting higher and higher in pitch.

"Tell me that you've never got yourself off in another man's lap like this. Swear it." My voice is guttural and demanding.

Lie to me if you have to.

"Never." Mia shakes her head but doesn't break eye contact, and I groan as I realize she's telling the truth.

Her movements are needy and desperate now. She's on the downward slope to her orgasm and her mouth is open as she breathes hard. She rubs once, twice more, and then her breath catches and she clamps her arms and knees tight around me as she comes.

The frantic movements of her hips send me over the edge. I haven't come in my pants since I was a teenager, but that's how I feel with Mia in my lap. I wrap my arms tight around her and bury my face in her hair. We haven't even had sex, and I feel closer to this woman than I have to any other woman who's been in my life.

"Laz. The bouncer," she reminds me.

Shit. I drop my arms and sit back. Another song starts to play, and God knows how much money I'm being charged for this, but I don't care as long as Mia doesn't go anywhere.

I gaze at her as she pushes her lilac hair back from her face. She can't raise her eyes for a moment, as if she's suddenly shy.

"Mia, baby, that was crazy, and I loved every second."

Mia hesitates, and then nods.

I frown at her. "You didn't enjoy that?"

"No—I mean. Of course. It felt . . . We sure got carried away." Mia closes her eyes and takes a few deep breaths.

When she opens them, she's Tasha again, and the flirty smile is back on those perfect lips. My heart plummets in disappointment and the world rushes back in. Where we are. The fact that the bouncer just watched everything that happened between us.

"I could sit here all night with you." Mia wriggles against me, and a familiar scent washes over me as she exhales.

"Have you been drinking?"

Her smile vanishes. "I'm not drunk."

"That's not what I asked. I can see you're not drunk, but you're drinking at work?"

Mia looks off to one side, hugs herself with her arms, and shrugs. "So what? It was just two shots."

"Do you like working here?"

Mia bursts out laughing, but it's a cold, hard laugh. "I don't know, what do you think, Laz? I'm excruciatingly self-conscious at all times and I have to parade around naked in front of a bunch of strangers. I'm a nervous wreck before every shift, and the only thing that evens me out are mouthfuls of vodka every few hours."

"Then why the fuck are you doing this?" I fire at her.

She shrugs. "The same reason as everyone else. I need the money."

"Why? Who's blackmailing you? What debts do you have?"

"It's nothing like that. I have to get the hell out of that house, and soon. I hate it there."

I don't blame her. "I'll take care of you. How much do you need?"

"You don't have any money either."

"Who says I don't?"

"I thought the whole reason you married my mother was for her money."

"No. *My* money. I have an inheritance and stake in the family business that my brothers are keeping from me because apparently I'm too impulsive."

She raises a brow at me as we stare at each other.

"Don't say it," I mutter.

"Your pants are full of cum and your stepdaughter is sitting in your lap."

She said it.

I stare at Mia's beautiful face. What if the mistake I actually made was marrying the wrong Bianchi woman? This girl's far more my speed. She's wild. Sexy. Funny. If I were her husband, I would throw everything I had into making her happy and knocking her up.

"Thanks for the offer, but I'm fine. And I need to keep working because I haven't hit my target for tonight."

I feel my eyes nearly bug out of my head as she stands up from my lap. "You're going back out there?"

Mia looks up at me in surprise.

No.

Tasha looks at me.

She's wearing her cool, professional mask and wearing a cloak of confidence despite the fact that she's stark naked. And wet. I can see how her pussy lips are glistening. What I wouldn't give for one lick.

"Of course I am. I'll see you at home."

She'll see me at *home?* I get to my feet as my temper hits the roof. "You are not working in this place one second longer."

She rolls her eyes. "Oh, please. Don't act fatherly after what we just did. I'm not quitting because you tell me to. This is my life."

I want to shout, or better yet, haul her over my shoulder, but I can feel that bouncer one second away from throwing me out for real this time.

"I told you, I'll look after you."

Mia gives a scornful laugh. "You? Why would I rely on you? I don't trust you. My family hates you more than they hate me, and you could disappear at any moment. I've got my future to think about, and I can only rely on myself."

On the one hand, I'm proud of her for standing up to me. On the other, fuck that for a joke. She's leaving this place and she's not stepping in another strip club as long as she lives. I pull my wallet from the back of my jeans. "How much to hit your target?"

"I thought you were broke?"

"I'm buying-a-business broke, not cash broke. It's hundreds of thousands I'm owed, not pocket money. How much?"

She considers me with her head on one side. "Three thousand."

In this seedy place? I doubt it, but I don't care. I slap eight hundred into her hand. "There. I'll Venmo you the rest. You'll get the same next week, and the week after, and the week after. Now get your shit and let's get out of here, okay?"

Mia holds the bills, glaring up at me. "I'm not letting you become my sugar daddy. If you hate seeing me in this place so much, you don't have to look."

"You're not going to be my sugar baby." I grind my teeth together and then burst out with, "You're going to be my girlfriend."

Mia's mouth falls open. "Are you insane? How's that going to work when you're married to my mother? Don't let one lap dance make you lose your head. You'll be over me by morning, and I'll be worse off than ever. Just take the money back, I don't want it."

She thrusts the bills at me. I pinch my brow and growl. Always with the annoying details when none of that matters right now. I've put my marriage to Giulia Bianchi in one compartment and the life I actually want to live in another. Mia's in the compartment with the things I actually *want*.

Focus on one thing at a time. Get Mia out of this place and safely back home.

I pull my T-shirt off over my head, tug it down over Mia's, and pull her arms through the sleeves. It comes down to her knees like a dress. She's spitting with anger now and trying to get away from me, but I haul her fireman's-lift style over my shoulder and head for the door.

Mia's nails dig into my bare back. "You *asshole*, Laz."

The bouncer blocks the doorway, but I push past him. "Don't bother throwing me out, we're leaving. I'm parked out front, the black Camaro. Can you bring me Mia's things? I have a twenty for you in my car if you do."

The bouncer hesitates, and then heads off to wherever the girls have their lockers. I suppose I'm not the first man who has dragged his girlfriend, wife, or daughter out of this place.

We draw a load of stares from the patrons and passersby in the streets as we head for my car, the shirtless man with a stripper in a T-shirt over his shoulder. I look straight ahead, comfortable in the knowledge that no one can recognize Mia upside down in a wig and an oversized T-shirt. If they recognize me, well, it's not the craziest thing I've ever done in this city.

I open the door of my car and tumble Mia into the back seat. When the bouncer arrives, I take her things from him and pass them to a fuming Mia. "Get dressed. I'm taking you home."

I fish a twenty-dollar bill out of the glove box and pass it to the bouncer. "Thanks, man. She won't be working here again."

The man laughs, shaking his head as he turns away. "Sure, she won't."

I sit in the driver's seat while Mia takes off her wig and makeup and puts her own clothes back on. As soon as she looks herself again, I start the car and we drive in silence toward home.

I pull up two doors down from the house so that Giulia won't see my car if she glances out the window.

Meeting Mia's eyes in the rearview mirror, I say, "The photo of you with your tits out. That wasn't taken at school, was it?"

Her gaze drops away from me and she whispers, "No. Kaleb and his brother came to the club. The bouncer threw them out for taking the photo, but it was too late."

What a couple of pricks. I wish I'd punched them harder. "That's the first and last time you ever lie to me. Out."

She blinks at me in surprise. "What?"

"You're home. Get out." The mood I'm in after what we just did, I dare not risk walking in with Mia and Giulia seeing us together. I can't act natural when all I'm thinking about is dragging Mia upstairs and fucking her hard until she agrees to do everything I say.

Her expression closed and angry, Mia slides out of my car, slams the door, and walks quickly up the sidewalk to our house. I wait to hear the front door slam and then peel away from the curb.

I intended to drive around for another hour and cool off, but there's a tug in my chest. For the first time in a really long time, years probably, I just want to go home.

A few minutes later, I pull into the garage and turn off the engine.

Inside, Giulia's sitting at the kitchen counter while Mia pours herself a glass of juice. My stepdaughter stares at me, and I guess she didn't expect me back so soon.

Neither did I, but I needed to see her here, back to normal.

Giulia wrinkles her nose at me. "Where have you been? You smell like a cheap whore has been rubbing herself all over you."

Over her shoulder, Mia turns pale and her jaw tightens. I can only imagine the hell that would be rained down on her head if Giulia discovers where she's been tonight, and all the other nights she's been dancing at the club. Being dragged down to the basement, tied up, and flogged might not be off the table.

"Me? I ate a lilac-colored ice cream earlier and it wasn't cheap. It was delicious and sweet and just what I wanted."

Giulia throws me a baffled glance and turns back to her phone. Over her shoulder, I give Mia a meaningful look.

"Actually, it was perfect."

You're perfect.

Then I have to get the hell out of there because the inside of my jeans is a mess and I need a shower.

Fifteen minutes later, I'm sitting on the edge of the bed with a towel around my hips, rubbing my hair dry while I search through emails on my phone. I must have Mia's email address somewhere.

I finally find it included in one from Giulia back when she was planning our wedding and she CC'd the whole family. She's even included Mia's phone number in case anyone had questions about our special day.

I grit my teeth, recalling the charade that was our wedding. Giulia was lapping up all the attention she was getting as a bride, acting as if we were in love and this wasn't an arrangement between two people who'd been in the same room on only three separate occasions.

I tried to concentrate on my bride and psych myself up over the idea of sleeping with her. I'm used to looking into the eyes of a woman I'm about to screw and seeing an aching need to feel my cock rammed inside her. Giulia looked right through me.

And then there was Giulia's third bridesmaid and youngest daughter, Mia. She stood behind her older sisters clutching a small pink bouquet, looking as pissed off as I felt. No one paid the slightest bit of attention to her, but I caught her tiny eye rolls and the impatient shifting of her feet. I could also see the outline of her nipples through the thin satin of her bridesmaid gown. The design was simple and clung to her delectable body, and I couldn't stop staring at her all through my vows. I finally got her attention, and she was so disgusted with me. Dislike burned in her eyes, and something else that I suspected she would hate to admit. That it had crossed her mind she'd like to be pushed up against a wall while I tongue-fucked her pussy.

And suddenly, I wanted to screw one of the Bianchi women. I wanted to screw her very much.

Only, it was the wrong goddamn one. If I couldn't screw Mia, then the next best thing was to make her life hell, because that's what

I do when I'm angry.

I act like a cunt.

I send Mia the twenty-two hundred dollars I promised her. A few minutes later I get a notification that the money has been reversed back into my account.

Frowning, I send her a text. *Take the goddamn money. I know you need it.*

I never make 3K in a night. I'll keep the eight hundred for the dance, but I don't want the rest. Thank you for the gesture, I appreciate it. But I can look after myself.

The gesture? It wasn't a gesture, it's a promise to her that I'm not going to sit back and let dozens of skeevy men get their unworthy eyes all over her body.

I type back an angry reply. *Call it whatever you want, but you're never stripping again. I forbid it.*

I smirk down at my phone. Forbid. I sound like a stepdad pulling his stepdaughter into line.

Sure, I just came in my pants while my stepdaughter was grinding in my lap, but I'm laying down the law when it matters.

My phone buzzes a moment later. *I'm not going to stop working. This is the only power I have in the world and you're not going to take it away from me. Tell Mom if you want, cause another huge fight, but she's not going to stop me either.*

Of course I'm not going to tell Giulia, but I'm not going to let other men get their eyes all over the woman I want either.

The woman I want but can't have.

Giulia comes in and sees me sitting on the bed in just a towel.

Her gaze lingers on my body, half annoyed by my presence, half interested. The last thing I need right now is to screw my wife with my head full of Mia.

"Goodnight," I mutter, throwing my towel on the floor and sliding between the sheets.

I pretend to be fast asleep when Giulia gets into bed and puts her hand on my back.

The next day I'm moodily wandering around a secondhand car lot, looking for a muscle car that's been neglected so I can bring it back to life with some love, a fresh coat of paint, and an overpowered engine. If I can't buy a repair shop then I'll distract myself by fixing up one car at home. There's plenty of space in Giulia's quadruple garage, and it will give me something physical to do. I work out every day at the gym and I'm still so goddamn frustrated all day.

Maybe I should have had sex with Giulia last night. If I had, she might have fallen pregnant, and I'd be one step closer to getting what's rightfully mine. But the thought of Mia just down the hall hearing us and being totally disgusted with herself for dancing in my lap and bringing herself to orgasm just hours earlier stopped me. Maybe I can catch Giulia while Mia's out at her sister's or something and screw her quickly.

I stop what I'm doing and tilt my head back with a groan. Jesus fucking Christ. What am I doing, sneaking around my stepdaughter's back with my wife now? This is crazy. How do I get myself into these messes?

I kick a half-deflated tire. I know how I got into this mess. By becoming obsessed with my beautiful, untouchable stepdaughter. She won't have anything to do with me if she hears me screwing her mom. She probably won't let me ever touch her again, period, because she's not as messed up as I am, and I shouldn't be trying to make her that way.

But Mia's lips.

Her *body*.

The way she sasses me and then breaks into smiles.

We're a couple of family fuck-ups together, and I wish I could scoop her up in my arms and carry her away from all this bullshit.

My phone rings and I take it out of my pocket. It's Giulia, and I answer it. "What?"

"Lazzaro."

I lift my head and frown. She doesn't sound normal, and it takes me a moment to realize she's choked up with tears. "What's wrong?"

"Lazzaro, something terrible has happened. Come quickly."

Chapter Six

MIA

"I heard a rumor about you, Miss Mia Bianchi."

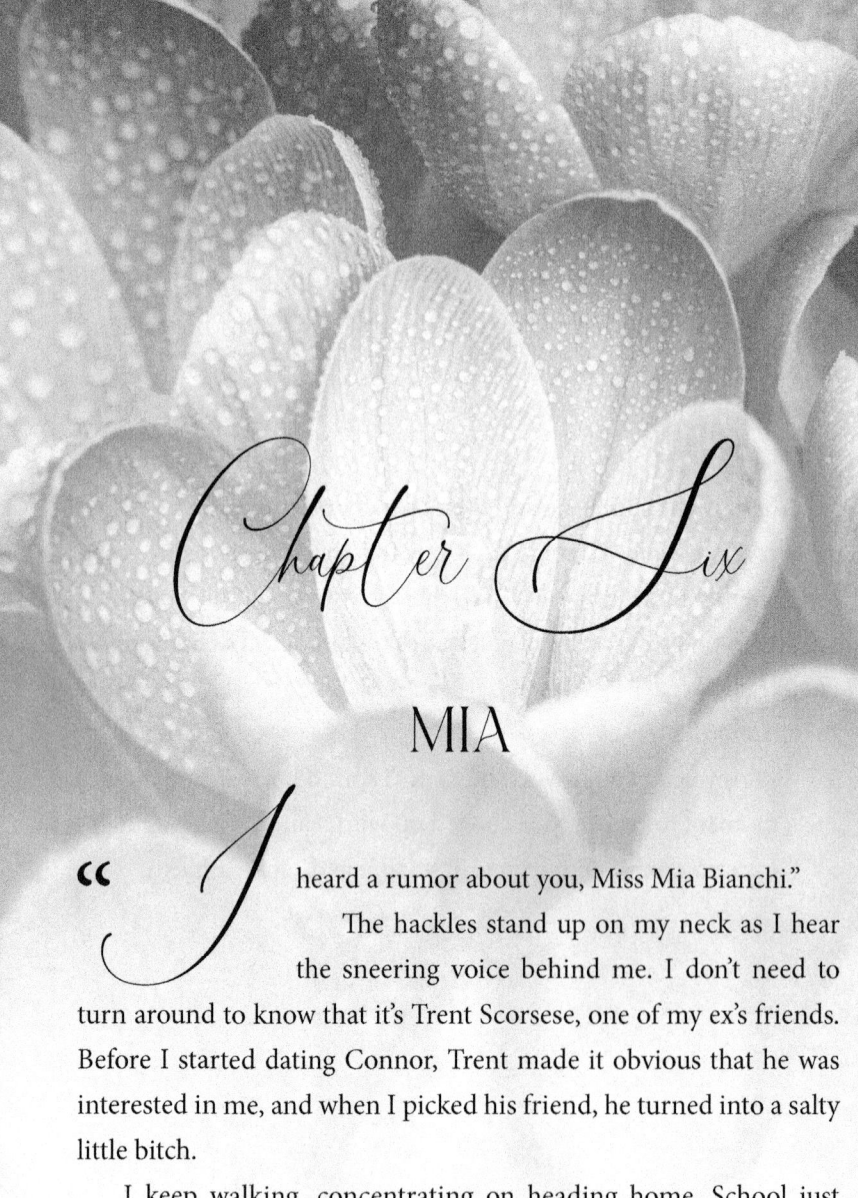

The hackles stand up on my neck as I hear the sneering voice behind me. I don't need to turn around to know that it's Trent Scorsese, one of my ex's friends. Before I started dating Connor, Trent made it obvious that he was interested in me, and when I picked his friend, he turned into a salty little bitch.

I keep walking, concentrating on heading home. School just finished, and I'm in a terrible mood after thinking about one thing and one thing only all day.

My stepfather.

I wish I could cringe over our terrible behavior. That, I could probably live with. Instead, I'm remembering the intense way he looked at me in the private room at the strip club, both hands clenched tight on the seat of his chair like he was holding on for dear life.

Bambi, I want to kiss you so much.

"*I said* I heard a rumor about you, Mia," Trent calls louder.

I waft a lazy hand over my shoulder, not bothering to turn around. "Yeah, yeah. You're obsessed with me. Play another song, Trent."

He jogs ahead of me, turns around and walks backward so I have to look at his face. He raises his eyebrows once, twice. "Something about you in a certain club."

My steps falter on the sidewalk. He knows I'm a stripper? Or he knows about me and Laz? How? I mean, Laz was drawing enough attention to us in the club trying to pull me off stage and then hauling me out over his shoulder, but I didn't think anyone from school was there at the time.

Trent has noticed my expression and his face lights up. "So, it's true. I hear there's even a picture going around, but I can't seem to get a hold of it."

That probably means it's not going around, just the story that there was a photo. If the photo was in circulation, I would have seen it by now.

"I don't know what you're talking about."

Trent grins, having the time of his life at my expense. "You sure? I heard Mia Bianchi knows how to work every pole in town." He makes a fist next to his face and pushes his tongue into his cheek, miming a blow job, like his double meaning wasn't obvious already.

A black car pulls up beside us and coasts along at walking pace. I can't see the driver but a tattooed hand wearing silver rings is clenched on the gear shift.

Trent goes on mocking me. "C'mon, how much for a dance? Twenty? Ten? I hear that pussy is going cheap."

The engine cuts out. A door slams. A huge, angry man dressed in black with blazing green eyes stalks straight over to Trent, grabs him by the throat, and slams him into the nearest brick wall.

In a voice burning with hellfire, Laz seethes, "What the fuck did you just say to her?"

Trent is too shocked to reply to the huge, angry man suddenly towering over him. That, or he can't speak because Laz is gripping his throat so hard.

I grab Laz's other hand before he can drive his fist into Trent's face. "Laz, that's enough. Let go of him."

But Laz doesn't hear me. Or won't.

"Listen up, you sad little dribble of cum. Spread this around that school of yours. If anyone, *anyone*, so much as looks sideways at Mia, let alone spews the filth at her that just came out of your mouth, I will personally take them apart."

Red-faced from the blood that Laz is squeezing into his skull and shaking with fear, Trent nods rapidly.

"Laz, please let go of him. He can't breathe." Laz is a head and shoulders taller than Trent and twice as broad. Maybe Trent deserves to suffer one consequence in his miserable life, but not like this.

He glances at me, then back at Trent. "You're lucky Mia is here, or I would break your teeth. Say *thank you, Mia*."

Trent wheezes something that sounds like, "Thank you, Mia," but it's hard to tell.

Laz doesn't seem satisfied, but he lets go. Trent doubles over, struggling for breath. He's dropped his backpack and Laz punts it down the street with one hard kick.

"Now, fuck off."

As fast as he can, Trent scrambles after his bag and hightails it away.

I turn to Laz with an exasperated shake of my head. "Laz, he's just a bully. He doesn't matter. You didn't need to terrify him like that."

"Is he just a bully? Or is he a man who thinks he doesn't have to treat women with respect?"

I haven't got a reply to that. I don't think I've ever heard one decent thing out of Trent's mouth about a woman. It's one of the reasons I didn't want to date him.

Laz stalks back to his Camaro. "I thought so. Get in the car."

"What are you even doing here?"

Laz grips his open car door, his expression changing from angry to troubled. "Isabel was in an accident. She's in the hospital."

Whatever I thought Laz was going to say, it wasn't that. For a moment, I can't breathe and my whole body locks up. My sister. In the hospital. Those words don't belong together.

"I don't know anything else. Come on, your mom's already there."

We drive in silence. At one point, Laz reaches for my hand, but I'm so sick with worry that I pull away.

I ask at reception where my sister is, and the staff member on duty directs me to the third floor.

I can hear Mom sobbing the moment we step out of the elevator and before we pass through the double doors into the ward. I half walk, half run down the corridor, dreading what I'm going to find when I reach Isabel's room.

An angry voice cuts across the crying before I can reach it. "For heaven's sake, Mom! It's just a broken leg and a broken nose."

Isabel's voice, sounding strong, alive, and exasperated. I sag with relief and Laz loops his arm around my waist to hold me up.

"Thank fuck," he mutters under his breath.

I stroke his chest briefly in thanks and detach from him, conscious even in this situation that I don't want anyone in my family to see us touching each other. His hands leave burning hot marks on my body that only I can see.

"But your beautiful face," Mom sobs.

I round the corner to see Isabel propped up in bed, her right leg in a cast, white tape over her nose and two black eyes. She looks like she was in a fight with a charging bull and lost.

She gives me a weak smile. "Hey, Mia. Hey, Lazzaro. Could one of you get Mom out of here, please? There aren't enough pain meds in the world to deal with her right now."

Laz sighs and heads toward his wife. "Come on, Giulia. Let's go and get you some coffee."

With a little persuading, Mom hiccups herself out of the ward with Laz at her side.

"Thank goodness she's gone. She was ruining my buzz," Isabel laughs to herself. Her eyes have the glazed appearance of someone who's high on pain-relieving drugs.

Of my two sisters, I've always got along better with Rieta. Isabel is so much like Mom that I find it hard to talk to her sometimes, though I still love her.

"Cheer up, I'm not at death's door." She frowns at me, her eyes nearly crossing. "Come to think of it, I haven't seen you smile lately. What's been eating you?"

I give her a tight smile. "I'm fine. What happened to you?"

"A truck ran a red light. I smashed right into him." She mimes a T-bone accident. "I didn't know you could break your nose on an airbag. But seriously, Mia. What's been up with you lately? Or, like, the last five years. The weight of the world is on your shoulders or something."

I swallow, hard. How can she not know? Doesn't she see how Mom treats me? How this entire family acts like I'm invisible most of the time? There's recrimination in her tone, like being unhappy is my fault or I'm wallowing on purpose.

Isabel gives me a knowing look. "High school blues. Boy trouble. I remember it well."

"Isabel, that's not—"

There are footsteps behind me, hurrying closer, and Isabel perks up when whoever it is appears over my shoulder. "Rieta. I guess you're the pretty one now, for a few weeks, anyway."

I stand up and step away from them as Rieta exclaims and Isabel once again describes the accident.

Right behind Rieta is Laz with Mom at his side. She's holding a cup of coffee and though she's deathly white, she's stopped crying.

I lock eyes with Laz. He makes a beeline for me, and we stand silently together with our backs against the wall as Mom and Rieta take the seats on either side of Isabel's bed, discussing insurance policies, lawsuits, and possible plastic surgery for Isabel's broken nose.

No one notices we're here. It's like we're a couple of intruders in another family's room.

"You're the pretty one," he mutters under his breath. A moment later, he shifts on his feet so that his arm is pressed against mine. "You always were."

Five inches of my arm touching his, soaking up his heat and presence. Out in the open for anyone to see. I can't make myself step away.

After fifteen minutes of standing in silence, Laz straightens up and puts his hand on my shoulder, announcing, "I'll take Mia home. Isabel, is there anything I can get for you from your apartment?"

The three of them look around in surprise. They forgot about us.

"Mom will do that. She arranged my wardrobe, and she knows where everything is. But thanks, Lazzaro."

"No problem," he mutters, and we head for the door.

As we're walking through the underground parking garage, I say, "You don't correct the others when they call you Lazzaro."

"I don't give a fuck what those people call me."

When we get home, Laz throws his keys on the counter and pulls his phone from his pocket. "Want to order a pizza?"

I shake my head. "I'm not hungry."

His eyes narrow and his gaze sharpens, and I know something horrible is about to come out of his mouth. "What a performance

Giulia made over a broken leg. I don't think she'd carry on the same way about you, do you?"

"Thanks for pointing that out," I seethe.

"So do something about it."

"Like what? I'm not going to pour red wine on Mom's favorite dress because she loves Isabel more."

He shrugs, but there's a dark glimmer in his eyes. "There are better ways to take revenge."

"I'm not going to suck your dick because my family hates me."

A wicked smile hooks Laz's mouth. My eyes are drawn to his scar as he saunters toward me. "You are going to suck my dick, but because you crave the feel of me bottoming out in your throat."

Desire takes a blazing swan dive through my body. I picture myself on my knees before him, his fist gripping my ponytail while he slowly and firmly fucks my face. Heat slams through me again and again.

Laz lets out a soft groan and pushes his hand through his hair. "That's torture, Bambi. I can see you thinking about it."

I'm more than thinking about it. I can vividly imagine it.

I can feel it.

One thing my ex-boyfriend knows about me is that I really like giving head.

Like, *really* like it.

Some nights I have vivid dreams about some rough, unknown man filling my mouth and throat. I can't see anything. I can't hear anything except for his groans. I don't know who he is, but he has a voice like melted chocolate as he coaxes me to take him deeper. The dream is pure sensation, but I always wake up wet and gasping.

I love the act of giving head. I love that my partner is transfixed the whole time. I love the fact that for once in my life I'm holding all the power.

And I *really* love the fact that I'm good at it.

Not as Tasha.

As me.

"Fuck, I need a cold shower or something." Laz turns away, shaking his head.

The memory of him standing next to me at the hospital with his flesh scorching mine flashes through my mind. I don't want him to go.

I'm not invisible when I'm around him. I'm not a bad memory that keeps intruding. My whole life is bitter, and for once I want something sweet.

I grab two fistfuls of Laz's T-shirt and pull him back to me. His eyes widen as my back hits the wall, and he captures my waist with his hands.

"Just shut up," I whisper.

His lips are so close that I feel every word against my mouth. "I didn't say anything."

I release his T-shirt and slide slowly down the wall until I'm kneeling at his feet. Big feet in scuffed black boots, as attractively worn-in as his ripped jeans. Everything about Laz says that he knows how to have a good time. All you have to do is ask him how.

My sweaty palms are pressed against his stomach. I can feel him breathing. Waiting.

If I were a good girl, I wouldn't be doing this.

If he were a good man, he'd step away and tell me to get up.

I guess we're bad people because my fingers hook into his waistband, next to the button, and Laz doesn't stop me. He probably thinks I'm hesitating. That a war is going on inside me. Should I? Shouldn't I?

But I've already decided that I'm going to do this. I'm making a meal of it because the tension must be killing him. He *really* wants this. I knew it when he left that heart painted in cum on my sheets. I can see how much he craves it right now as the swelling in the front of his jeans gets bigger and bigger. The thick ridge at the head of his cock is visible through the denim.

Slowly, I lean forward and plant a kiss right there.

Laz groans.

I flick open the top button on his jeans.

He groans louder.

That's right, you gorgeous asshole. Give me a groan for every little thing I do to you. His zipper needs only the slightest encouragement for the teeth to burst apart. His cock is angled to one side, thick and swollen, and a pang goes through my pussy as I imagine him buried deep in my mouth.

But not yet. I'm driving myself crazy with teasing him. I pull his briefs down, and the heavy weight of his dick swings forward.

Laz has one of the most gorgeous cocks I've ever seen. He's buzzed off all his hair, making him look huge. The skin is soft and flushed pink, with a thick vein standing out along his length. I run my tongue up the underside of him, and slowly look up and meet his gaze. I can't help my self-satisfied smile when I see the expression of utter focus and desire on his face.

I swallow the head of his cock, and he groans, curling his fist into the hair at the nape of my neck.

"Mia," he says roughly in a voice I've never heard from him before, deep with need and desire. A curse and a surrender. "Mia. Fuck, yes, Mia."

I suck him slowly up and down. He can't stop saying my name and every time he does, my heart swells more and more until it feels like it's going to burst.

With clumsy hands, he unbuttons my top and reveals the camisole underneath. He shoves it from my shoulders and exposes me, moaning as he runs his fingers up my breast.

A thrust of his hips, and the back of my head hits the wall and his cock slides deeper. It's my dream. My favorite dream. The angle is just right. Laz is filling my throat so perfectly that I don't gag, and I barely need to breathe. I hold on to his hips so I can feel their motion with my fingers as well. I wonder if you can come just from giving head. If I'd bothered to remove my jeans before I got onto my knees I could be touching myself, and I roll my hips in needy frustration.

"Horny, Bambi? I'll take care of you in just a moment. Right now, you're not going anywhere."

The growl in his voice makes me moan around him.

"Your perfect lips are going to send me over the edge. I would fuck you like this all day if I could."

I can tell from his voice that he's hovering just on the edge of coming, and he's slowed down his thrusts. Trying to draw it out as long as possible. But he can't. His body is growing rigid beneath my touch as he tries to cling on, but then he climaxes with a shudder. He floods my mouth with his cum, his hips thrusting haphazardly.

Laz barely gets his breath back before he's gripping my shoulders and gasping, "Don't fucking swallow. Don't spit either. Just hold it."

He takes a deep breath and grabs my chin, drawing my face up to his.

"Let me see it, Bambi."

I open my mouth and let his cum roll over my tongue. Laz sinks his teeth into his lower lip and smiles, his hair hanging into his eyes. "You're the hottest thing I've ever seen." His voice is husky with desire. "Now, swallow like a good girl."

I do as I'm told, looking him in the eye the entire time. Laz hooks his hands under my arms and hauls me up. My back hits the wall and his mouth descends on mine. His kiss is ravenous as he tastes himself in my mouth. His tongue delves into me and slides against my own.

I need to fuck you, the thrusts of his tongue say.

He breaks away from my lips and plants breathless, hungry kisses on my throat, my breasts. His cock is between us, semi-hard and glistening.

"I'm going to bang you with my fingers until my dick gets hard again. Should only take about thirty seconds because I'm insane for you, Bambi."

There's a grating of metal, a jangle of keys, and street sounds from outside, and then the front door slams. Two female voices reach us from the hall. Mom and Rieta.

Shit. Shit. *Shit.*

I pull my camisole up and frantically button my cardigan. Laz looks more annoyed than anything else as he slowly steps back and shoves himself back into his jeans.

Reality is flooding back as I hear my mom and sister coming closer and closer. I just gave my stepdad head while my other sister is lying injured in a hospital bed. He face-fucked me into the wall. There's acting crazy, and then there's being plain stupid.

"This isn't over."

"Yes, it is," I whisper feverishly. He's cheating on his wife in her own house. Mom is suspicious and critical of everything I do. She's going to find out if we carry on like this.

But Laz either doesn't hear me or pretends that he doesn't.

"Your lips are BJ messy," he says as he buttons his jeans. With a wink, he turns and disappears into the hallway to greet his wife.

Chapter Seven

LAZ

Over the next few days, Mia's face burns whenever she lays eyes on me or when her mom walks into the room. I make it my mission to get close to her as much as possible because the sadistic pleasure I feel seeing her squirm is off the charts.

Before school one morning, I come into the kitchen just as she's lifting a mug to her lips and murmur, "Swallow like a good girl."

She chokes and nearly spits out her coffee. Wiping her chin, she checks that no one else is around and hisses, "Have you no shame?"

Please. Where's the fun in feeling shame when there's heart-pounding, honey-sticky pleasure to be had from a girl who sucks dick like she's trying to swallow my soul?

I'm not the only one who thinks so, either. I catch Mia sneaking looks at me as often as I find myself hungrily devouring her peachy ass and the curve of her breasts. All I have to do is raise my arms above my head and stretch and she zeros in on the hard line of muscle at my hip that disappears inside my jeans, the adorable little slut. And I mean that as a compliment. There's nothing hotter than when a girl abandons all her inhibitions for you. I want to whisper in her ear what a delicious little slut she is for me while I'm buried deep inside her and feel her clench around me in sheer delight.

Just for me.

One afternoon she's eating strawberries, slowly, one by one, sucking on the tips before biting into them and letting the juice run over her tongue. I'm ready to burst in my jeans as she stares at me across the kitchen counter.

Giulia is calling out for Mia from another part of the house, growing more and more irate with every passing moment.

"Your mom wants you," I mutter, my gaze trained on her juicy lips. What I wouldn't give to shove my thumb into her mouth along with all that sweet fruit and feel her tongue moving against me.

"*Mia.*" High heels click angrily on the tiles. Giulia bursts into the kitchen, her face pale and angry.

Mia looks up from her strawberries and turns to her mom, blinking like she's just woken up from a dream. "What?"

"For heaven's sake, Mia. What's going on in that head?"

My dick, I mouth, hiding my lips behind the glass of water I'm drinking. Mia can't get me out of her head, and I'm hungry to know all the ways she's picturing me screwing her. I want to make every single one a reality as soon as possible.

"I've been calling you for ten minutes. I need you to take all the decorations in the living room around to Isabel's apartment and put them up."

"I'll drive her," I say automatically, and Mia shoots me a suspicious glare.

"I'll go by myself, thank you."

"No, take Lazzaro with you," Giulia says, reaching for her handbag. "I need you to finish quickly so you can come back here and make the punch for the party. The recipe is on the fridge. I'm going to pick up the food. Remember, everything needs to be ready by seven."

Isabel is being discharged this evening, and Giulia is throwing her a welcome-home party. Mia takes the keys to her sister's apartment from the hook, grabs the box of decorations, and follows me out to my car, dragging her feet.

As we drive, she gazes into the box of decorations. Cheerful, bright colors. Giulia made them herself. Her baby getting injured seems to have thrown her into a homespun, motherly mood.

"It was my birthday last month. Mom threw me a dinner party at home."

My brows lift in surprise. "A party? Uncharacteristically thoughtful."

Mia stares out the window with her arms around the decorations. "You would think so. No one wished me happy birthday. Uncle Roberto cut the cake in the kitchen and handed it out, not realizing there were candles or that it was my birthday cake. Mom was talking nonstop about her wedding to you, and she just accepted a piece and started eating it."

It starts raining, fat drops of water hitting the windshield.

I picture Mia sitting at the end of the table, watching everyone eat her birthday cake like she's not even there.

No one can hurt you like family can.

Just because you tell yourself it doesn't matter it doesn't mean you stop caring about that sort of pain.

"Listen to me. I'm eighteen years old and I sound like such a baby." She shakes her head as she stares out at the rainy street. "I have to get out, Laz. I know you're going to turn up at Peppers tomorrow night and try and keep me from dancing, but if you ruin my dreams then you really will break my heart."

I grit my teeth and shove my hand through my hair. I knew she was going to say that. Saturday night has been looming closer and closer all week, and I've hated every minute that's drawing her closer to getting back on that pole.

She shrugs. "But then, hurting me has been your goal all along, so now you know exactly how to do it."

Tormenting her has been my cardio lately, sure, but for sport. This miserable, downcast Mia is never what I wanted. She feels like she's circling the drain and I don't know how to pull her back.

"You shouldn't have to resort to something you hate in order to escape," I say, my hands clenched on the steering wheel.

"Who says I hate it? I like being Tasha. Tasha is free." Mia holds my gaze, but her top lip wobbles and her eyes grow watery. She looks away, blinking angrily.

At Isabel's apartment, she puts the box of decorations on the coffee table, and we stare around at the neat and designer living room that's decorated very much like Giulia's house. Minimal. White surfaces. No soul.

"Why did you even want to help me with this?" Mia asks, rummaging around in the box.

I meet her eyes with a meaningful expression on my face. For no virtuous reasons, that's for sure.

Mia flushes red. "Do you have no shame? No guilt over what we did?"

Sneaking around behind my partner's back isn't something I've done before or ever imagined doing. I wish I could say I hated this, but the only time I can breathe is when I'm around Mia. I'm struggling to care about what's right and wrong.

"Shame isn't in my vocabulary, Bambi."

Mia lowers her eyes, and I can tell from her pained expression that it's in hers. Her movements as she drags out some bunting are forced and angry and pain flashes over her face.

"You need to keep your hands to yourself from now on."

She's right, I do need to do that.

But needing and doing?

Different things entirely.

There is a row of photographs on the mantelpiece, and I go over and study them. Then I frown. Picture after picture of Giulia and her daughters. "Bambi?"

"Yeah, I know."

"You're not in these photos. It's just your mom, Isabel, and Rieta."

"I said I know. Isabel likes just photos of her family."

"But you are her family!" Mia's not in any photo in the apartment. Now that I think about it, Mia's in barely any of the photographs that Giulia has put up around her own house either. The ones that do feature her are family shots where Mia is in the background. There are none of just Mia, or even Mia with her sisters.

Mia strides over, rips the frame out of my hand, and slams it down on the shelf so hard that I think the glass is going to shatter. "Can you please focus so we can finish and get out of here?"

"Mia—" I reach for her, but she throws me off angrily.

"I don't need you trying to screw me right now, Laz." Her eyes are wilder than I've ever seen them before.

"I'm trying to comfort you."

She thrusts an armload of white and yellow decorations at me. "I don't need your pity. I need you to hang this bunting."

There's a nauseating taste in my mouth as I hang the cheerful decorations around Isabel's apartment. At least my brothers acknowledge my existence as they tell me I'm a fuck-up. The way Mia is being excluded is twisted. She didn't even do anything wrong.

I get angrier and angrier watching Mia fiddle with the decorations and make them perfect for a sister who treats her like dirt, until I rip the box out of her hands.

"It's done. We're leaving. And you're not coming to this party."

"What?"

"I'll tell Giulia you're sick. You have a headache."

As I hustle her out to my car, she tells me, "Laz, I've been dealing with this all my life. I don't need your pity or your interference. I need you to let me do my job at Peppers so I can get the hell out of here as soon as possible."

"Over my dead body," I growl.

"That can be arranged. If you get in my way, I'll tell Mom exactly how you know I work at Peppers and all the gory details about the dance you paid for. If she doesn't believe me, I'll ask the bouncer to back me up. Jimmy is on the girls' side, whatever they ask for."

"You'll be screwed."

"And so will you, and whatever plans you have for your money. Mutually assured destruction." She tosses her hair over her shoulder and gazes at me over the top of my Camaro. "Your move, Laz."

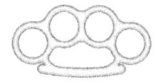

Mia goes to the party. I go to the fucking party, and I watch as Mia pours drinks and hands around cheese plates like she's staff, not family. All the while, I'm stewing on her threat to tell her mom everything. Tomorrow night, dozens of men are going to be drooling all over Mia, and she's going to be rubbing her bare snatch in their laps while she coos at them that she loves their tattoos. My blood pressure shoots through the roof.

When I've finished my glass of red wine, I pull out my phone and approach Isabel, who's seated on the sofa like a queen. Her leg is in a cast and the bruises are slowly fading from her face.

"Let's get a photo of you and your sister."

Isabel looks around for Rieta and notices she's on the other side of the room talking to some cousin.

"No, your other sister. You do know you have another sister, right?" I snap my fingers at Mia who's walking toward the kitchen with a trayful of dirty glasses. "Waitress. Time for a photo with your dear, darling Isabel."

Mia shoots me a dirty look and disappears into the kitchen.

"You're funny," Isabel deadpans at me.

"Yeah. It's why you're all laughing so much," I mutter, shoving my phone back into my pocket and following Mia.

She's ramming plates into the dishwasher and won't look at me.

I fold my arms and lean against the kitchen counter, searching for the cruelest thing I can say to her. "It's like you enjoy them walking all over you."

Mia snatches a butter knife from the counter and brandishes it at my throat. "I will nuke your life if you don't stay the hell away from me."

Excitement blazes through my chest as I see the fire in her eyes.

She's what I crave.

She's what I *need*.

I lean dangerously close, the tip of my nose is nearly touching hers, and the knife she's holding presses into my throat. "Challenge fucking accepted."

There's a special trick with Mia's bedroom door. It sticks if you turn the handle and push, and the noise it makes is loud in the dead of night. Instead, if you lift it before you push, it opens as smooth as butter and as silent as the grave.

Mia's breathing is soft and even as I approach the bed, devouring the sight of her laying on the mattress with the sheets tangled around her legs. She's wearing that adorable little PJ set. Tiny white shorts. A camisole with ruffled straps. It reminds me of her delicate little stripper G-string, and I feel myself getting hard in my sweats.

Carefully, I get up on the bed with her and straddle her body, and then pin her down with a hand over her mouth. She rouses quickly as she tries to turn her head and realizes she can't, and her eyes fly open.

I put my finger to my lips. "*Shh.*"

Her eyes blaze with fury, and I take my hand away from her mouth.

"I told you to stay away from me. What are you doing here?" she hisses.

I walk my knees down her body and press one between her thighs. "No talking. Just lay back and try not to be loud."

Even in the semi-darkness, I see the blush erupt over her cheeks as I curl my fingers around the waistband of her shorts. I need to get my mouth on her. I've been obsessed with the idea for weeks, and I can't go a moment longer without tasting her.

"But Mom—"

"She's fast asleep."

I plant a kiss slowly on her belly and feel her shiver beneath me. Mia's still furious with me, but she wants this. She needs this as much as I do.

Mia casts a desperate look at the door. "What if she wakes up?"

Screw what-ifs. Mia is the only thing I care about right now. "I said no fucking talking."

She clutches my wrist. "I'm not ready for that."

Heat slams through me. Implying that there will be a time when she will be ready—*panting*—for me to fuck her?

"We're not having sex. I'm going down on you."

Mia's brows draw up and together. "Really? Why?"

I'm not answering any more stupid questions. I slide my hands under her ass, take hold of her shorts, and pull. Mia lifts her hips up to help me and, judging from her expression, she's shocked by her own movements.

I lift each of her slender legs in the air and pull the tiny garment off her, and stare down at her perfect, delicious body. With her ankles in my grip, I push her heels against her thighs and spread them open.

"That's it, Bambi. Let me manhandle your body just how I want."

Her ass is against my sweats, and I press my hips into her slowly, aching to pull my cock free and plunge into her.

"So fucking beautiful." I run my finger down her slit and the ruffles of her inner lips.

My mouth waters. I have to taste her. I slide down the bed and I'm about to taste her, when I look up at Mia's face. She looks terrified.

I stop what I'm doing and frown. "I'm not going to bite you."

Mia nods, but her lips are pressed tightly together.

"I can stop if you don't want it." I start to sit up, but she shakes her head frantically.

"No, don't. It's just . . ." Mia's eyes dart around the room, and she's squirming like a girl who's never been kissed.

"You're acting like a man's never gone down on you before."

Mia opens her mouth and then closes it again.

My head rears up with indignation, and I nearly shout before remembering we have to be quiet. "What the fuck? No one's ever gone down on you before? But that's not possible. You give killer blow jobs."

She seems genuinely puzzled. "What's that got to do with it?"

Jesus fucking Christ. I guess I shouldn't be surprised that she lets her boyfriends treat her as badly as her family does. "For starters, it's only good manners to give as good as you get. What's wrong with high school boys these days? By the time I graduated, I had five different women come all over my face. That's what you call an education."

Mia glances from my face to her pussy and back again. "You like . . . doing this?"

"Are you kidding? I love it."

"I thought . . ." she swallows and trails off.

"You thought this was something only men who were weak or pussy-whipped do, and they don't really enjoy it? I don't know who fed you that bullshit, but I love doing this."

I plant a kiss on her clit. Mia tenses up, and then slowly relaxes. I brush her with my tongue, just gentle laps.

"That feels weird," she whispers.

"Weird how?"

"Weird . . . and amazing."

I smile and grow bolder, spreading her open with my fingers and licking her firmly. She yelps as my tongue slides over her clit.

"Quiet, Bambi."

Mia grabs hold of my wrists and sinks her teeth into her lip, nodding quickly.

I angle my head the other way, a smirk spreading over my face. "Good girl. You can go back to being mad at me tomorrow."

"I'm mad at you now," she whispers, her head arching back on the pillow and her fingers tightening around my wrists.

Sure she is.

It's been too long since I've gone down on a woman, and I'm like a starving man as I spread her open even more. She tastes even better than I thought she would. I've been vividly imagining her taste ever since she was bent over in front of me and running her nails through her pussy lips.

"We shouldn't be doing this," she moans, anxious and horny at the same time.

I don't give a damn what I should or shouldn't be doing with this girl. All I know is she feels better than anyone I've ever laid hands on and making her smile and come is my number one priority.

"You're really enjoying doing that?" she asks hesitantly.

If she's not going to believe me, I'll have to show her.

I sit up, take her hand, and press it to my cock, which is rock hard and straining against the fabric of my sweats. I would take off my clothes, but the sight of her pressed against my naked body would tip me over the edge, and I'd start coaxing her to give it up now.

Just the tip, Bambi. Just to see how pretty you'd look if we went all the way.

Then I'd lose it, and one thrust later, I'd be balls deep in her, one hand over her mouth while I fucked her hard. Desperate not to be heard while my wife is just down the hall, and aching to blow inside of Mia.

She explores my cock slowly with her fingers and I nearly throw caution out the window as I stare at her glistening wet pussy. My pretty baby is aching for me, so why am I holding back?

My chest lifts with a ragged breath. It's not about me tonight. I'm going to show her how much I love giving head, because I'm determined to do this as much as possible from now on.

I drop back down and go to town on her pussy, licking her with determined swipes of my tongue.

"How does that feel?" With her moaning under her breath and gasping, I don't need to ask, but I want to hear her horny voice.

"So good, Laz," she whimpers, clenching and unclenching the sheets on either side of her. "Laz. *Laz.*"

She wraps her legs around my head and shoulders, and I'm in heaven. The world feels right between Mia's thighs, and I give her what she's been missing. Her head lifts up from the bed as she comes, and I keep on working her clit with my tongue until she collapses back, her nails digging into my shoulders.

Mia breathes hard in the darkness. "I thought nothing was going to top the orgasm I had on your fingers."

She fucking thought. I move up the bed toward her and she wraps her arms around me. I slide my hand against her ass and scoop her closer, my fingers just delving in her wetness.

Mia nuzzles into my chest. Is there anything sweeter than a girl who clings to you after you've made her come?

My pulse throbs in my cock, aching to slam inside of her. I can picture myself buried inside her tight, wet heat. I can *feel* it.

Mia wraps both of her naked legs around my thigh and squeezes, moaning as she rubs her pussy against me. The sound and feel of her short-circuits my brain.

"Stop that," I growl, barely clinging to reason.

"Stop what?"

I can only hold back for so long. I sit up and rest on my knuckles, braced over her half-naked body. She stares up at me, breathless and beautiful.

"Make your choice, Bambi. Either I leave, or I'm going to fuck you right here and now."

Chapter Eight

MIA

My sneakered feet pound along the rain-slicked sidewalk. Far down the street, the neon lights of Peppers are blinking on and off. My work clothes are in a backpack that's slung over my shoulder.

I'm on my way to dance naked in front of strangers who'll do their best to cop feels of my ass and tits while spending as little of their money as possible. Meanwhile, I'm still back with Laz and the feral, demonic gleam in his eyes as he said, *Either I leave, or I'm going to fuck you right here and now.*

His touch makes me crazy. His tongue makes me lose my mind.

I crave to wrap my legs around my stepdad while he buries his cock deep inside me. Deliver my virginity, my total surrender, to the absolute worst man possible.

I wish I'd done just that instead of sending Laz away.

Or do I?

I don't know anymore.

When I'm thirty feet from the alleyway that leads behind the bar to the entrance the dancers use, the man who consumes my thoughts steps out from behind a parked car and blocks my way, a bleak expression on his handsome face.

"Get out of the way, Laz," I say quietly.

"Mia, please—"

"It's Tasha tonight."

He gazes at me for a long time, his green eyes searching mine. "Is there alcohol in your bag? Can you even do this sober?"

I swallow around the lump in my throat. There's a handful of single-serve vodka bottles in my bag that I swiped from the bar at home.

"Let me take care of Tasha. I'm begging you." Laz actually sinks down to his knees in front of me, right onto the wet sidewalk.

I glance up and down the street. At this rate, we're going to be recognized, and I'm not wearing my wig yet. "Laz, stop it. Get up."

"I won't. Not until you promise to come home with me and let me take care of you."

Something snaps inside of me. My breaths are coming too fast, anger and frustration making my adrenaline spike. "I'm supposed to rely on you now? Mom could find out about us at any moment, and you could be gone just like *that*. You could die because my uncles will kill you for betraying her. What then? How am I supposed to trust anything you say or do?"

He gets to his feet and pulls me against his chest. "Breathe, Bambi. We'll figure it out."

Laz has made my life a thousand times more complicated. I struggle in his arms, trying to pull away, but he's too strong for me. I slump in his hold, too tired to fight anymore. "This was my secret. My way out. You've made everything so much harder."

"Yeah. I'm told I do that," he mutters.

I groan and push my face against his chest. Clinging to him, my fellow fuck-up.

"You're wonderful as Tasha," Laz whispers. "Beautiful and fearless. The moment I saw you, I couldn't take my eyes off you. But you know who's twice as entrancing? Mia, when she's curled up in an armchair reading a book, so absorbed in what she's doing that she doesn't notice she's wrapping and unwrapping a strand of hair around her finger. I can't stop staring at that girl. She's real. She doesn't have to be anyone else."

That's the sweetest thing anyone's ever said to me, but I need Tasha. She's the one who's going to pay for my freedom.

"I'll come home with you tonight," I tell Laz. "I'll skip this week. But I won't make any promises about next week."

Laz groans in relief and squeezes me tight. "You won't miss out on a paycheck. I'll give you what you would have made."

That's not what I want from him, but he can't give me what I truly want, which is to unfuck this mess we're in together.

"You don't want me to be a stripper, but you're happy to turn me into a whore." I look around and spy his car and, extricating myself from his arms, I head over to it.

"That's not what I'm trying to do," he says after he gets in and starts the engine. He's tense as he drives, the muscles taut as ropes in his tattooed forearms.

The inside of Laz's car is fogging up because of the cold night air, and I can barely see out my window. All the streetlights and traffic lights are colored blurs. Maybe he's not trying to force me into having sex with him in exchange for money, but that's what it will feel like, no matter how much I want him. I'll be Lazzaro Rosetti's whore. His dirty little secret.

"What will you do once you're free?" he asks me.

I stroke my fingers through the condensation, making patterns on the glass. "Just be. There's nothing else that I want."

"How about you just be mine," he says in a low voice.

I reach over and touch the wedding ring on his finger. "You're spoken for, remember?"

He gazes bitterly at the ring. "I'm going to do something about that one of these days."

"And then we'll be two broke fuck-ups instead of one. Don't kiss your dreams goodbye for me, Laz. I'm already drowning under the weight of my own mistakes. I don't need yours on my conscience, too."

Laz drops me at home and drives off into the night. It's raining once more as I head inside, wondering if I should just go back to Peppers and start my shift anyway. As I think about plastering a smile on my lips and swinging around that pole while people offer me wrinkled dollar bills, my heart shrivels up.

Mom looks up from the sofa with a frown. She's wearing a white cashmere lounge suit and gold jewelry. "You're home early. What happened to your shift?"

"They didn't need me. I'm tired, so I'll just go to bed."

I head for the stairs, but Mom stands up and beckons me to the shelving at the back of the room. "While you're here, I have something to show you."

She picks up a framed photograph and hands it to me, and I recognize the picture. I recognize when it was taken, anyway. Six months ago, at a professional studio. Mom, Isabel, Rieta, and I all had our pictures taken, some as a group and some individually. Shots of the three of them appeared on the walls in this house and my sisters' places, but I never saw any photographs of me.

I stare at myself in the picture. I'm smiling, but my eyes are empty, like I suspected that no one would ever look at this picture, so I'd mentally checked out. "Why are you only getting this framed now?"

Mom hesitates. "Well, if you must know, it was something Lazzaro said the other night. He pointed out that Isabel didn't have any photographs of the four of us, and I forgot that I had these taken." She smiles at me. "You look beautiful, don't you? I love that color on you."

She gives me a squeeze and turns around to place the photograph on the mantelpiece and smiles fondly at it. I cut my eyes away, unable to look at it.

"Mia? What's wrong?"

I'm messing around with your husband behind your back.
Laz crawls into my bed in the middle of the night and we all but fuck.

My stepdad is the most dangerous and beautiful man I've ever laid eyes on, and I can't stop myself from thinking about touching him, kissing him, coming hard in his arms.

I imagine the way her face would fall if she heard me admit to any of that. Maybe I've been turning Mom into a villain so that I don't have to feel guilty about craving Laz, kissing Laz, rubbing my pussy all over Laz.

A wave of shame and horror washes over me. How did things get so far out of hand?

I really cried to Laz because Uncle Roberto cut my birthday cake without singing happy birthday. I felt sorry for myself over a *birthday cake* and used it as a reason to nearly screw my mom's husband. Sure, my family has a tendency to treat me like an afterthought, but I'm a teenager. Don't all teenagers think their life sucks and their family sucks even harder?

A sour taste fills my mouth. I think I'm going to be sick.

"I'm planning a party for next month," Mom continues brightly. "My two-month anniversary with Lazzaro. Something to bring our two families closer together."

He'll hate that, but this is what Mom enjoys, throwing parties for people like her. Laz's brothers will probably have a great time. They have the same polished attitude as Mom and my uncles.

"Sounds great," I manage in a hoarse voice. "Sorry, I have to . . ."

I gesture over my shoulder and hurry out of the room, worried that if I stand still I'll start retching. In my room, I curl up into a ball on my bed, hugging my knees. I feel so dirty. I let a man who's too old for me use me to take revenge on the woman he didn't want to marry. When he finally gets his money, he'll disappear and leave me behind, and I'll have nothing but regrets to show for our sordid time together.

The night passes painfully slow, and I barely sleep at all.

When I come downstairs in the morning, Mom is cooking Sunday brunch. Waffles and bacon, and she seems happier than she has in weeks. She even drops a kiss onto my head when I make myself coffee and perch on a stool.

My guilty conscious tells me it's because she knows about me and Laz, and she's showing me she wants me to confess and that she won't be angry with me.

Laz comes in from the garage a few minutes later and washes the engine grease from his hands in the sink. The T-shirt he's wearing hugs his muscles, and I look away quickly before I can start fantasizing about him.

"Just in time, darling. Sit down and have breakfast with us," Mom coos at him.

Laz stares at Mom like he doesn't know who she is as he shakes off his wet hands. After seeming to decide that the place settings, the bowl of strawberry pieces, and basket of waffles hold no threat to him, he shrugs and sits down at the counter with us.

Steaming waffles and bacon are set before us. I haven't got an appetite, but I force down a tiny bit of food so Mom doesn't figure out that anything's wrong.

Mom turns to her husband with a bright smile on her face. "Lazzaro, you came in so late last night that I didn't get to tell you the good news. I'm throwing us a party to celebrate our two-month anniversary."

Laz gives a mirthless laugh and shakes his head as he reaches for the strawberries. "Oh, yeah. Something to celebrate."

"It will bring our two families together, and everyone will get to see how well Isabel is doing since her accident. It's the perfect occasion."

"What day? Maybe I'm busy," he mutters. "Or dead."

Mom shoots him a disapproving glance and smacks the back of his hand like he's a naughty boy. "Oh, hush. The twelfth."

I look up in shock, a piece of bacon halfway to my lips. "The twelfth? But that's the anniversary of Dad's death."

Laz looks up and frowns.

"Is it?" Mom answers vaguely, spooning sliced strawberries onto her plate. "I'd forgotten. Anyway, the party starts at two in the afternoon for drinks, canapés, and then a sit-down meal at five."

"I can't. You know I go to the cemetery that day."

Mom shrugs, her smile growing brittle. "You can go the day after this year. It's not as if Ennio will notice if you're there or not."

That's hardly the point. Of course Dad won't notice if I'm there, but it's something I've always done and she knows that. Every year she makes some flippant comment about it, but she's never actually stood in my way before.

"He'll notice Mia's absence from the cemetery more than you'll notice her presence at the party."

I shoot Laz a grateful look, and he gives me a tiny smile in return.

I turn to Mom. "You can have the party without me. Laz's right. No one will miss me." No one except him. It might have been fun to sneak away and do shots together.

Mom puts down the syrup bottle, every trace of a smile disappearing from her face. "Mia. Life is for the living. I don't know what makes you think you can pretend you're not part of this family."

Laz puts down his fork and sticks his hand in the air. "I'll take a wild stab at that."

"No one asked you," she shoots at him, her voice filled with venom. "I don't want to hear any more excuses, Mia. You're coming to this party."

"Can't you move the party a day earlier or later? Isn't your anniversary on the tenth anyway?"

"The tenth wasn't available. I booked the room for the twelfth, and I can't change it with the Regency. It's the most popular venue in the city, and they're booked out solid for months. I could only secure the ballroom because there was a cancellation."

"Then I'll go to the cemetery in the morning," I tell her.

"I need you to help me set everything up in the morning. Your family needs you, Mia. Why are you being so selfish?"

"How can you say I'm being selfish? You know what that day means to me."

Mom's nostrils grow pinched and white with anger. "I made you this lovely breakfast, Mia. I put that photograph in a beautiful frame. I thought you could be as thoughtful to me as I'm being toward you."

Laz reaches for the syrup and pours it all over his waffles. "You should have married Faber. He loves emotional blackmail, too."

I spent the whole night feeling guilty because Mom was being so nice all of a sudden. I should have realized she had an ulterior motive.

"Tell me," I say, my voice shaking with anger. "Did you get that photo framed because you scheduled your party on the anniversary of Dad's death by accident, or on purpose?"

Mom flushes red. "You unreasonable, ungrateful child. After all I suffered to bring you into this world, and this is the thanks I get? If you don't want to be part of this family, then you can pack your things and get out. You're eighteen years old, and it's time you started taking some responsibility."

Laz gives her a dirty look. "It's a party, Giulia. Why are you being such a bitch about this?"

I wipe my hands on my napkin and stand up. "Thank you for breakfast. If you need me, I'll be upstairs choosing my dress for your stinking party."

As I walk out of the room I hear Laz growl, "You'd kick your own daughter out over a party? Classy move."

When I'm alone in my room, I throw myself on my bed and pull out my phone to check my banking app. If Mom does kick me out, how much money have I got to work with?

Thirteen hundred dollars. After paying rent and deposit on some shitty apartment, I'd have nothing left. I've only worked a handful of Saturday nights, and the first two times I barely broke even after tip out and house fees. When my confidence grew, so did my earnings, but not fast enough.

I sigh and drop my phone.

A moment later it buzzes. It's a text message from Laz.

I'm sorry. I should have let you go to work. I'm sorry. I'm sorry. I'm sorry.

I can feel his outrage over what Mom's done and it warms me a little. I stare at the message, wishing I could feel Laz's arms around me.

A moment later, my phone buzzes again. *Will you still be my Mia even if I have to share Tasha with other men?*

He was so jealous and torn up about me in that strip club, but he's willing to swallow it down for me? *You would be okay with that?*

Fuck, no. It's killing me, Bambi.

I sigh and shake my head.

I'll buy every lap dance so no one else gets their hands on you. I'll do your pole dances for you. I can shake my ass real good.

I grin as I picture Laz on the pole at the club.

Since when am I your Mia?

Since you became the only thing I care about.

I feel a jolt as I realize I'm smiling, and it's because of Laz. I can't remember the last time anyone else made me forget about my worries for a while.

Everything's getting so complicated, I type back.

No shit. But one thing's very simple.

What's that?

I care about you, Bambi.

I hug my phone to my chest. I care about him, too. Maybe I'm going to hell, but all I want is some peace and quiet, and Laz.

Just me and Laz, always. Am I crazy, or would that be perfect?

"Knock, knock."

I look up from my homework to see Laz filling my doorway,

wearing a pair of jeans so tight that they would make an angel blush. I wonder if it hurts to get a hard-on in those, or if it aches in a good way. Sometimes when I get turned on in tight jeans I purposefully squeeze my thighs together and it feels amazing.

"Your Mom's gone out," he tells me with a wicked smile.

I roll my pen absent-mindedly along my lips. Is this when it happens? Are we going to have sex in my bed while Mom is out? I don't think I'll be able to relax if I'm listening for her car the whole time. Then again, Laz has a habit of blocking out my awareness of everything but him when we're together.

But instead of pulling off his T-shirt, he digs his phone out of his back pocket as he strolls toward me. "It's time for some revenge, Bambi."

I stare at his chest, kind of wishing he'd take off his shirt. "Hm? Sorry, what?"

Get your mind off his dick.

"Revenge," Laz says again. He cups my cheek and plays his thumb over my lips. "Ruin her party."

I suck in an alarmed breath. "I can't do that."

"Yes, you can. She scheduled it on the anniversary of your dad's death knowing it would upset you. If you don't wreck it, I will. But it's easier if you help me."

"Why?"

"Because my Giulia Bianchi impression isn't up to much."

He taps his phone a few times and I suddenly realize what he intends for us to do. We couldn't.

We *shouldn't*.

That's just plain wicked.

A thrill goes through me.

"Let's do it together. I'll hit dial. You speak."

He presses Call and puts it on speaker phone. It rings a handful of times and then someone picks up.

"Hello, you've reached the Regency Hotel. How may I help you?"

Laz speaks in a cheerful voice. "I'd like to speak to the events coordinator, please."

"One moment."

Another dial tone sounds, and then a woman picks up and announces herself as Kelly, the events coordinator.

Dead air. Laz stares at me.

"Hello?" Kelly says again.

My jaw works.

Am I really going to do this?

I reach out and hit the red button, hanging up the call.

Laz rubs the back of his neck, his face falling. "Ah, Bambi. Why'd you do that?"

Because this isn't just about the party.

"I can't. We can't. You're *married*. I know she's unreasonable and selfish sometimes, but she's my mother."

"You're too fucking noble," he growls.

"And you're going to get yourself killed."

He gives me a hard, sarcastic smile. "No shit. I'm a Rosetti, after all."

"What?"

Laz breezes past that statement. "There are only two things I want, my money so I can buy my garage, and you. I can't have my money yet, so I'm going to have you."

He tries to kiss me, but I put my hand over his mouth, stopping him. "I'm not your consolation prize."

He takes my hand away. "Bambi, you're my grand prize."

Our lips are so close together. I could kiss him right now. A lover's kiss, more about feelings than sex. Wanting my stepdad is one thing.

Falling in love with him?

Insane.

I pull myself out of his grip and back away.

"I can't be your anything. I really like you, I care about you, I'm always thinking about you, but this isn't right."

The expression in his eyes flickers between anger and pain. "If you wanted to say the words that would make me back off, those aren't it." He moves toward me like a hunter stalking prey. "You like me? You care about me? That's oxygen to me."

I was trying to remind him that he has good qualities and not to throw his dreams away on an affair that might get him killed.

I'm reminding myself, too. He's the man who goes up to bat for me when no one else will. His protection feels like warmth pouring through my body. We can't destroy all that goodness by acting like idiots.

Laz takes me in his arms and his mouth descends toward mine in a hungry kiss.

I have only a split second of sanity, but it's enough. I rip myself away from him and run downstairs. I need a cold drink. Maybe a swim. Something to clear my mind.

There are male voices in the lounge, and I realize that my uncles have come over. In order to get to the kitchen or the pool, I'll have to pass by them, and I'm terrified that one look at me, and they'll see shame painted thickly over my body.

"... being so difficult over the party. I don't know what I'm going to do with her."

That's Mom's voice. I freeze halfway.

"Difficult?" scoffs Marzio. "That girl was born a problem."

I cross my arms and hug myself, wishing I knew what to do to make my uncles forgive me for being born. I've always been nice to them. Polite to them. Tried to stay out of their ways and not draw attention to myself. It's never enough.

"Have her married off as soon as possible. Get her out of this house."

"Maybe," Mom replies, but she sounds uncertain. I feel a flood of gratitude that she's not talking about me like I'm the problem child. "But who would take her?"

My heart plummets.

"We told you nineteen years ago what to do about that child, but you wouldn't listen to us," grumbles Uncle Tomaso, and someone else mutters his agreement.

"I thought she would fit into the family eventually," Mom replies. I can't see her, but she sounds tired and frustrated.

"All she does is cause trouble and bring shame down on our heads."

"You must regret not following our advice, Giulia."

What advice? What are they talking about? What happened nineteen years ago that—

Oh.

Oh.

My insides freeze in horror.

Don't say it, Mom.

Don't say it.

Please, I'm begging you.

"It's too late for an abortion now." Mom laughs lightly. "I'll handle Mia. She has her little moments of rebellion, but she'll do as she's told. She always does."

Feeling like you're not wanted is one thing. It plays on your mind in the dark, but you can shake off the misery when the sun rises.

Knowing you're not wanted?

Self-hatred and shame deluge my body and soul so fast that I gasp and run for the stairs. I made myself so small for my family, so quiet, so they could pretend I didn't exist. It was never going to be enough because they didn't want me to exist in the first place.

I blindly try to find my bedroom, and run up against a tall, broad figure in black.

Laz clutches my arms. "Bambi? What's wrong? What's happened?"

I can't speak I'm crying so hard. I open my mouth, but a sick feeling crawls up my throat so fast and I know I don't have time to explain. I push past Laz and dive for the bathroom door, shoving it open and scrambling to reach the toilet.

Uncontrollable retching racks my body. My stomach feels like it's trying to turn itself inside out as I throw up.

"Ah, my little Mia," he murmurs, gathering my hair in his hands and then gently rubbing my back. "Are you sick?"

I wish he'd leave. It's disgusting for him to see me like this.

Finally, my guts stop heaving. I wipe my mouth with some toilet paper and flush the whole mess down. I can't meet Laz's eyes, so I rinse my mouth out and splash cold water on my face.

"Should I go to the drugstore for you? Have you got food poisoning?"

Blotting my face with a towel, I shake my head. "It's nothing. Just something I overheard Mom and my uncles saying."

"What did they say?" he asks coldly.

"It doesn't matter," I reply, applying toothpaste to my toothbrush and shoving it into my mouth. I scrub every tooth and my tongue to the back of my mouth as hard as I can.

Laz watches me, his arms folded tightly across his chest and murder flickering in his eyes.

I spit and rinse my mouth, and my gaze drops to Laz's jeans where I can see the outline of something rectangular. I move past him and shut the bathroom door. "Get your phone out. Make that call."

His arms loosen in surprise. "Really? You mean that?"

I nod. Now that the sickness is passing, all I'm left with is anger.

I watch Laz make the call and get through to the right person, and he holds the phone out to me. There's a smile on his beautiful, scarred lips.

I take a deep breath and assume my mother's clipped, imperious tone. "Kelly. It's Giulia Bianchi here."

"Oh, hello, Ms. Bianchi. What can I do for you today?"

"I . . . need to cancel my party." I fumble my way through the conversation, telling a clearly peeved Kelly that I understand I won't get my money back.

"Can I ask the reason for this cancellation?" Kelly asks, and with her attitude you'd think I was rejecting an audience with the Queen of England.

"I changed my mind."

"There's a waiting list for this venue. I won't be able to rebook the space for you for months if you change your mind again."

"I won't." I reach out and hit the red button on Laz's phone and hang up.

I cover my mouth with both hands, shocked and delighted at the same time. Laz is staring at me like he can't believe I actually went through with it. I can't believe I went through with it either.

I move my hands aside and whisper, "I've never done anything like that before."

"How did it feel?"

"Amazing," I breathe.

"You bad fucking girl." Laz pulls me closer, takes my face in his hands, and kisses me hard, his tongue parting my lips. My heart is beating wildly as Laz perches me on the vanity and moves between my thighs, pulling them around his hips. He overwhelms me.

Invades me.

Conquers me.

It's the most intense kiss of my life.

I take his lower lip between my teeth, biting down gently. He groans, and I revel in my newfound power. I'm done being a good girl for the Bianchis.

From now on, I'm going to be a bad girl for Laz Rosetti.

Chapter Nine

LAZ

A furious scream emanates from downstairs and rocks the house to its foundation.

I turn over in bed, smiling to myself, because I know why my wife is doing a banshee impression this early in the morning.

Footsteps race up the stairs and the bedroom door flies open.

"The party is canceled."

"Mmph," I mumble sleepily.

She grabs my shoulder through the blankets and shakes me. "Did you hear me? I said the party's canceled."

"Why did you do that?"

"I didn't!" she shrieks, the sound shredding my eardrums. "I just got a call from the caterers saying the venue refused to allow them to deliver the food and drinks, so I called the Regency Hotel. They said I canceled it myself weeks ago, but I did no such thing. What am I going to do without a venue?"

"What a shame. Close the door, will you? I'm still sleeping." I pull the blanket over my head and close my eyes, a grin on my lips.

Giulia screams again and slams out of the room.

I keep out of the way for most of the day while my wife makes angry phone calls to everyone on the guest list, ranting about the terrible customer service at the Regency.

Around three, I walk into the kitchen, tossing my keys up and down in my hand. Mia's risked coming downstairs for a muesli bar and a glass of juice. "Let's go, Bambi."

She crams the rest of the bar into her mouth just as Giulia stalks in and glares at us with puffy eyes.

"Where are you two going?"

I don't bother to look at her as I head into the garage. "The cemetery."

"You shouldn't call me Bambi in front of Mom," Mia tells me when we're driving along the street.

"I shouldn't do a lot of things." After I change gears, I reach over and touch her cheek. "Like this. You look beautiful, baby. How are you feeling?"

Mia reaches up and takes my hand, squeezing my fingers. "Happy I'm not at the party. Guilty about the party. It's complicated."

It sure is, but my girl is doing what matters to her today, and that's all that matters to me.

The cemetery is in the northeast of the city, a somber place with black wrought-iron gates, sweeping lawns, and hundreds of nodding roses in orderly rows.

We walk in silence up the long avenue, lined with gravestones and shaded by trees with thick green leaves.

Mia leads us right to her father's plot. She kneels down and tenderly brushes grass clippings and dirt from the base of the gravestone. I hang back a little, my hands in my pockets, aware that I'm probably the sort of man Mia's father would be warning her away from if he were still around. I peer at the name carved into the marble. Ennio Russo.

She grew up beautiful, Mr. Russo. You'd be proud of your daughter if you were alive. And, my God, you'd hate me.

Mia has a bouquet of flowers with her, and she takes her time arranging the blossoms in the holder at the base of the gravestone.

Finally, she touches the marble where his name is carved and stands up. "I've spent far more of my life without him in it by now. But I still miss him."

"What do you remember about him?"

Her eyes are unfocused while she plays with the chain around her neck. "He used to come and pick me up every Saturday afternoon and we'd go to the park or to get an ice cream. It was always fun while I was with him, but Mom had a habit of spoiling my enjoyment by picking fights with him or telling me that Dad was uneducated and unconnected, and I was lucky she had custody of me. I don't know why she had to do that."

"I think I do," I mutter.

"Yeah?"

"She's a bitch."

"She was jealous, I think. Weirdly possessive. She ignored me most of the time and then lavished me with all kinds of attention when Dad was due to come around. It was so confusing."

I don't have the expertise or energy to unpack a woman like Giulia Bianchi, but if I had to guess, I'd say she was a raving narcissist.

As we turn to go, some names on a group of gravestones catch my eye, and I feel the sad, bitter twist of my heart.

Rosetti.

Rosetti.

Rosetti.

Mia starts to turn around. "What are you looking at?"

Ennio is a lucky bastard in some ways. I wonder if a beautiful woman will lay flowers on my grave when I'm gone.

I put my hand on her shoulder and steer her toward the exit. "Nothing. Fancy a beer? I know a place."

The place I know is on the other side of town, up a long and windy road. It's one of my favorite drives in this city, up into the hills where it's peaceful and you can leave everyone and everything behind.

We haven't seen another car for twenty minutes when I park at a deserted lookout. The city is spread below us, and Mia's face is lit with delight.

"I've never been up here before. I didn't even know you could get such a good view from these hills."

We sit on the hood of my car, watching the sun go down and swigging from bottles of beer we picked up along the way.

I peel the label from my beer bottle, roll it in my fingers and throw it out into the void. "I think I'll be dead soon, Bambi."

She stops with the bottle halfway to her lips. "What? Don't say that."

"That's just how it is with Rosetti men." I clench my jaw, glaring at the setting sun. "We passed all their graves today."

It felt like they were lined up and waiting for me.

"I keep messing up. That's never mattered to me before, but this time I might actually have something good on my hands. Something that makes me not want to go."

I look at Mia, her face burnished with golden sunlight. She's the only thing that makes me want to be a better man, and the harder I pursue her, the more likely I am to wind up six feet under.

"I shouldn't be here with you. I should be trying my best to make things work with your mom. It's the fastest route to the things I thought I wanted."

"But . . .?" she asks.

"But I can't stop thinking about you." What a terrible seduction technique. Honesty isn't sexy.

Or maybe it is, because Mia leans over, tilts her face up to mine, and kisses me. A slow kiss, filled with the passion of unspoken words.

I think I need you.

What if you're my person?

I'm half in love with you already.

The beer bottle slips from my fingers and clatters onto the gravel. Still kissing her, I stand up and swing around to face her, both of my hands cupping her jaw.

I kiss her like I'm about to be ripped away from her forever.

There's no one around. It's just me and her up here, and I pull her top up over her head. She's not wearing a bra and her nipples tighten in the cool air. With an arm around her waist, I lower my mouth and suck one of her nipples into my mouth. She cries out and threads her fingers through my hair, holding on to me.

I need her. I need her so much.

Mia helps me get her pants off her. Her body is delicious in the light of the setting sun, and I drink my fill of the sight of her. Her warm skin painted golden. The way her long, curly hair is rippling in the breeze. The whole city is spread below us. They can't see us, but it feels good not to hide away for once.

I pull my T-shirt off and she rests her palms against my chest while I undo my jeans and push them down. I get my mouth on her. I get my tongue inside her.

Bambi on the hood of my car, gazing up at me with her legs spread and giving me those fuck-me eyes.

"I want you so much. Can I have you, Bambi?"

Mia nods. "Please. Laz—"

My name sounds so good in her mouth. I want her saying it as she comes. I'm so needy to be inside her and she's just so wet spread open before me. The sweetest invitation I ever saw. I take my cock in my hand and guide it down to her entrance, coating myself with her slippery wetness.

"Laz, remember I told you—"

She speaks at the same time as I thrust into her. Fucking *finally*.

My cock is buried inside her cute little snatch, and I get to pound the living daylights out of her, like I've imagined hundreds of times by now.

It takes me a moment to realize that Mia yelped in pain and her face is screwed up.

Oh, shit. That was too much all at once. I'm being rough with her.

"I'm so sorry, Bambi. I got carried away. I'll warm you up with my fingers, I just—" As I draw out of her, I freeze. "What the hell?"

There's blood on my cock.

Maybe she's on her period and she didn't realize?

An ominous feeling growing stronger and stronger inside me tells me she's not on her period.

"I'm a virgin."

"You're a *what*?" Horror plunges over me. But she can't be a virgin when she sucked me like that and danced in my lap. "Mia, what the *fuck*. Why didn't you tell me?"

She gapes at me. "I did tell you. The day you beat up Kaleb and his brother."

I mentally riffle through the conversations we've had that even allude to sex, and I come up blank. The day I beat up those idiots I propositioned her in the bathroom, and she turned me down flat. She never said, *I'm a virgin, Laz.*

She slides off the hood of my car and drags her underwear up her legs. "I can't believe you don't remember."

I pull my jeans up and button them. "The word virgin never passed your lips. What did you even say to me?"

Mia collects her clothes, humiliation and anger etched on her face. Or is it pain? Jesus fucking Christ, I just impaled a virgin like she was an experienced sex kitten. I barely warmed her up first.

"You wanted to screw in the bathroom, and I replied, *What an enticing first time.*"

First time.

First time *ever*.

I shove my hands through my hair, groaning and wishing I could rewind the last five minutes. "Fuck. I thought you meant first time with me."

Nothing about Mia has ever screamed virgin to me. I've never been with one, but aren't virgins supposed to be trembling violets? Every time she's kissed me, I've felt her desire. She danced in my lap like a woman who knows her way around a man. Her blow jobs are supreme.

Or was this my own assumption because pinning her down and messing with her was too much fun? Being an asshole to her was delicious revenge against the wife I didn't want.

She pulls her clothes on, and when I try to touch her, she shoves me away angrily. "Even if you didn't realize, I tried to tell you just now, but you wouldn't listen to me."

Her voice sounded like she was turned on, not begging me to stop. Or was that what I wanted to hear?

"I'm so sorry, Bambi," I say in a hollow voice. "If I'd realized you were a virgin then I never would have done it like that."

She slumps on the hood of my car, and her misery is so painful to witness that I wish she'd stay angry with me. The light has faded from the sky, and we're left in chilly darkness.

"Maybe this was so terrible because it's a sign that we shouldn't do this," she whispers. "Us. It's wrong. It's twisted."

I want to reach for her, desperate to touch her but unable to bear it if she slaps me away. "No. It's a sign that I need to do better. I've messed up. I'm always messing up, but this time I care. I'm really sorry, Bambi. Please let me make it up to you."

She puts her hands over her face and my stomach seems to vanish from my abdomen. Oh, God. Is she crying? Please don't let her be crying. If she is, I'll fling myself from this lookout and smash myself to pieces on the rocks below.

I took her virginity and she's *crying*.

She raises her head, and there are no tears on her face, but her expression is hollow. She gets into the passenger seat without looking at me. "I'm fine. Let's just go home."

With a sick feeling in my guts, I slide into the driver's seat.

I don't know what to say the whole way down through the hills and back through the city.

Why do I always ruin everything?

I'm so fucking *cursed*.

Before I can pull into our street, I stop the car. Mia reaches for the doorhandle, thinking I'm dropping her off out of sight of the house, but I reach out and grab her wrist.

"No, wait. Please."

"Laz, I want to go home."

There's so much pain on her face, and I hate it. This day isn't going to turn into a double shitburger for her on the anniversary of her dad's death, losing her virginity in one of the worst ways possible.

"No. Not happening." I turn the car around so fast and speed back down the street.

"Laz! What are you doing?" she asks, her brow wrinkled with confusion.

I don't reply because I have no words. I have to show her what I mean.

Ten minutes later, we pull up outside one of the swankiest hotels in the city. Not the Regency. This one is better, in my opinion. More modern. Less stuffy.

"I'm not very good at saying sorry. I haven't had much practice, though with all the things I've done, I should be an expert." I nod at the hotel. "This is how I would have done it if I'd opened my ears and listened to the things you were trying to tell me. Brought you to this hotel. Booked the best room for the night. Made you come. A lot. Fucked you slow and hard on the sheets of an enormous bed until I broke you into the shape of my cock, and only my cock."

A pink flush creeps into her pale cheeks.

"Will you let me make it up to you? Not sex," I say quickly. "Not if you don't want to. I'll wash your hair. Feed you strawberries. Paint your toenails. Whatever you want. The night is yours and I'm your footman. Your servant. Whatever you want me to be."

Mia chews her lip, looking from me to the hotel and back again. "You want to make it up to me?"

"You have no idea how much. I'll just book you the room and leave if that's what you prefer, and I'll go sit in the cold and think about what I did, praying that you'll forgive me."

Mia stares at me with a wrinkled brow. She seems confused.

Doesn't she want me to try and—

But then I realize. I don't think anyone has ever apologized to Mia for treating her badly or cared enough to do anything to win back her favor.

"I mean it, Bambi," I say softly. "It matters to me that I hurt you. If you don't want to go inside, we can go somewhere else. Wherever you like. It's your call."

"No one's tried this hard to make me happy before. It's weird."

I take her face between my hands. "Please let me try."

Her eyes grow even bigger and more liquid than usual. "Are you sure you want a virgin who can't even tell you properly that she's a virgin?"

Please. Like any of this is her fault.

"You think I'll let this be over before I've given you the first time you deserve?"

A hopeful smile touches her lips. "Can we pretend something when we go in? The staff are going to wonder why we turned up without any bags. Can we tell them . . ."

I hold my breath.

Her courage fails her, and she shakes her head. "Never mind."

"Tell me. Anything."

She peeps at me through her lashes. "Can we tell them we just got married? It was spur of the moment. We got carried away and now we're celebrating."

A smile spreads over my face. There's a ring on her right hand. I pull it off and slide it down the ring finger of her left hand, and then admire it in the streetlight that's falling through the window.

Well, fuck. That looks so perfect that if I wasn't married already, I'd wife this girl immediately.

"Come on, Mrs. Rosetti. Let's go get you that bridal suite."

We're holding hands and grinning like idiots in love when we walk into the hotel. I don't know which room we get in the end. I can barely listen to the staff because Mia has her arms clasped tight around my waist.

We don't look like newlyweds in our street clothes, but Mia feels like my bride. The room is huge with acres of bed and a separate lounge, and a view of the city that's almost as good as the lookout.

"Can I run you a bath, or—"

Mia grabs my face, comes up on her toes and kisses me. Our tongues are soft, and they melt together.

"I'm so sorry," I murmur urgently between kisses.

She puts a finger over my lips. "Let's start over. You're my husband. This is our wedding night. How do you want to spend our wedding night?"

I want to spend it with my tongue on her clit, making her come until her legs are shaking.

I pick Mia up and carry her through the suite to the bedroom. There's no champagne, there are no rose petals strewn around. It's disappointing because I want those corny things for us.

That's when the realization hits me.

I'm going to marry this girl one day. For real. I'm going to see her in the white dress clutching a bouquet of flowers. I want us to eat cake off each other's fingers. Then I want to take her to a room like this and fuck my wife senseless on a pile of rose petals, and place champagne kisses on her mouth and pussy.

"Laz? What are you thinking about?"

I realize I've been staring at her, and I smile. "You."

I rip the bedclothes back and lay Mia down on the sheets.

"We can just kiss," I remind her. "We can sleep together without having sex."

She blinks her beautiful lashes up at me. "Why wouldn't I want to have sex with my husband?"

And just like that, I'm instantly hard. I try to ignore what's going on with my dick, though, as that's what got me into trouble up at the lookout.

Don't fuck this up, Laz.

You've got one chance left with this girl.

Don't fuck it up.

Mia's touches are tentative, exploring my body slowly between kisses. Her slender fingers slide beneath my T-shirt sleeves and along my throat.

"I never really get to touch you. Can I touch you?" she whispers.

"Bambi, you can do whatever you want with me."

She strokes her fingertips over my chest and down my stomach. Carefully, slowly, she pushes my T-shirt up to my ribs. "I spend every minute I'm near you looking at you as much as I dare. Secretly drinking you in. Praying that no one realizes I'm hungering for you."

"Me?" I ask, stupidly. I had no idea.

"Of course you, Laz. Even when I hated you. On your wedding day, I couldn't stop staring at you in that gray suit. I told myself that it was because I hated you so much and I kept reciting, *What a dumb shirt he's wearing. What a stupid pair of pants that hugs his ass. I hate the way the flowers in his boutonniere bring out his eyes."*

I noticed Mia looking at me, but I thought it was only because I was staring at her.

She pushes her hands all the way beneath my T-shirt, and I sit up a little so she can pull it off over my head. Then she sits astride me, brushing back my hair and circling my nipples with her fingertips.

I feel like her plaything. I love being her plaything.

"I was so scared to touch you at first," she confesses. "I worried that once I had a taste for you, I wouldn't be able to stop wanting you."

"And?"

She lifts her beautiful brown eyes to mine. "Now I'm obsessed with you."

I groan and pull her mouth down to mine.

Mia undoes her shorts and wriggles out of them, but I stop her when she reaches for her tee.

"Can we leave your T-shirt on?" I pull it up to expose her tits like I did just a few short weeks ago in my car. Not only is it cute, but it's also really fucking hot. "Now come up here and sit on my face."

I capture her thighs with my hands as she walks them up my body, a little bit shy but willing to go with it because she's turned on. I lick her eagerly, and she gasps and settles over my face.

"What a good girl," I murmur between licks, loving how she's responding.

Mia clings to the headboard, half moaning, half laughing. "I feel like a princess."

"You taste like one, too." Soft, sweet, and delicious. I can't get enough of licking her, and I love the little noises she makes as my tongue brushes over her clit. She makes them again and again, until I realize she's moaning and writhing so hard that she's going to come.

And then she does, squeezing my head with her thighs as she rocks back and forth on my face.

I sit up, taking her with me and dropping her gently onto her back. "We can stop here. I don't care."

"No, please," she cries, gripping my shoulders and digging her nails in. "I need you."

Mia reaches for my jeans and undoes them, pushing them down and off me, and we see something that surprises us both.

Her blood, smeared on my cock.

She runs her fingers down my shaft, as transfixed by the sight as I am. The evidence that I'm the only man who's ever been inside her.

"Shit, Mia, that must have hurt. I'm sorry."

She shakes her head, still gazing at me. "I don't care anymore."

I sink my teeth into my lip for a moment. "Maybe it's messed up, but your blood on my dick is so sexy."

I wish I could keep this little smear of red that proclaims she is mine, now and forever, but if I have to lose it, the best place is in her pussy.

"Please, Laz," she breathes.

Oh, Jesus Christ. I will go crazy just from the sound of her needy little voice. She wraps her hand around my shaft and so do I, and together we guide it into her tight, slippery channel. She moans as the head of me slips into her, and then inch after inch of my length. I move as slowly and as carefully as possible, holding back like I haven't done in years.

"Am I hurting you?" I ask through gritted teeth.

Mia sits up on her elbows and stares at herself. Stares at me driving into her with careful thrusts, edging my way deeper. Her pretty pussy is getting my shaft so wet.

She looks up at me with flushed cheeks and dilated eyes. "I think you were made for me, Laz."

I relax a little and thrust deeper, and she moans in pleasure. I'm lost in those big eyes, my cock buried inside of her.

I think she's fucking right.

Chapter Ten

MIA

I've heard a lot about sex, how it can be good, how it can be bad, how it's messy, and how it's wonderful. I wasn't prepared for how beautiful a man would look with his cock buried inside me, or how strangely delicious it was to feel the stretch and burn of his thrusts.

I really wasn't prepared for how vulnerable Laz looks as he thrusts carefully, covering my mouth with desperate kisses, and fisting his hands in the sheets.

"Bambi. Baby," he moans, staring between us at the place where we're joined. The thickness of him is almost shocking.

He pulls out suddenly and shimmies down between my thighs. "I need to make you come again," he says, licking me urgently.

Pleasure shoots through me. My sensitized flesh is craving his touch, and he gives me what I need without mercy. My legs shake as my orgasm approaches, and he grips my thighs hard and doubles down. I remind myself to be careful, not to be loud, but then remember where we are and that I can do whatever I want.

I throw my head back with a loud cry and give in to my climax completely.

Laz moves up my body, and the moment I open my eyes, he plunges into me again. I gasp and wrap my legs around him.

"Can I cum in you?" he asks with a groan, and I nod and capture his face in my hands. I want to see what he looks like in the final moment. I bet he's beautiful.

Laz groans harder and ups the speed of his thrusts, pulling all the way out and then plunging in again. That must feel insanely good for him because his cheeks flush and his breathing grows harsher. Then he thrusts deep and quickly, his tempo rising until he suddenly cries out.

"*Fuck*, Bambi."

I feel his whole body go rigid and his cock spasm. Then he slumps slowly down on his elbows and kisses me woozily.

I twine my fingers through his, my left hand and his left hand, and our rings clink softly together. There's a fierce longing in my chest. I want this man all to myself. I don't want to share him with anyone.

"Was it a good first time?" he asks, pulling me tighter against him.

"The best," I whisper, stretching luxuriously and fanning all of my toes.

"I'm glad, my beautiful wife."

We order room service and eat burgers and fries with ketchup in bathrobes while looking out over the city. Only crawling into bed and settling down to sleep in each other's arms when our eyes are heavy.

I'm so glad I ruined Mom's party is the last thing I think before I fall asleep.

In the morning, I wake in Laz's arms and nuzzle closer to him. He murmurs sleepily, wraps his arms tighter around me, and kisses the top of my head. "Good morning, wifey."

I laugh against his chest, giddy that the fantasy isn't over just yet. Laz pulls me tight against his hips and I feel how hard he is.

"Let me wash your hair," he says, stroking his fingers through it.

I wriggle against his erection, still feeling too sleepy to get up. "Are you sure you don't want to stay in bed?"

"I can fuck you in the shower," he points out.

And just like that, my pussy is one awake bitch.

The bathroom is huge and luxurious with a walk-in shower that has multiple jets. While he lathers up my hair, he asks me silly questions, like what my favorite odd food combinations are.

"Peanut butter and pickles," I reply.

"You weirdo."

"Oh, yeah? What's your odd combo?"

"I like dipping Oreos in juice, but that's not weird. That's practically gourmet."

"Ewww."

He tickles me, and I screech like a pterodactyl I'm laughing so hard.

It's not until he's rinsing the conditioner from my hair that his cock bumps against my ass and I remember his promise of shower sex. I wriggle against him until he's nestled into my ass.

Laz groans and kisses my neck. I'm so turned on and wet that when the plush head of his cock slips between my lips, he slides right in.

My palms land flat against the tiles, and I walk my feet apart. One of his large, tattooed hands lands next to mine, and I stare at how perfect we look together as he carefully thrusts into me, his lips against my ear.

"Are you sore, Bambi?"

I shake my head, the water flowing down my skin and around the place where he's thrusting deep inside me.

Laz groans and starts to fuck me in earnest, his powerful body making smacking sounds with every thrust. I arch back into his grip on my waist.

My clit is right there, and I play with myself, rubbing hard in time with his thrusts. My eyes are closed, and I feel surrounded by Laz. Cocooned by him. There's only him and me, the sound of rushing water, and the ecstasy that's building inside me.

I come in a joyful rush, the water cool against my hot skin, and then revel in the sensations of Laz pounding me with pure abandon and coming with a groan in my ear, wringing every last drop of pleasure out of this moment.

Because it's over too soon. The water is turned off. We dry off and get dressed. There's no packing to be done as we didn't bring anything with us, so we share a final kiss behind the closed door, and then leave it all behind.

We hold hands as we ride the elevator down and check out. When we pass through the front doors out into the fresh air, we let go of each other.

Laz casts me a look that's as wistful as I feel as he digs the valet ticket out of his wallet and his Camaro is brought around.

Back home.

Back to Laz being my stepfather.

Back to shitty reality.

"Where the hell have you two been?"

The moment we enter the house Mom confronts us with tired, angry lines around her eyes. She probably had too much wine, barely any sleep, and she's still in a rage from yesterday.

Her gaze darts from me to Laz and back again, preternaturally sharp, like she's watching a replay of last night's events just by looking at us.

Behind my back, I pull the ring off my left hand and stick it back on my right. I don't know what to say. I don't know how to act. I totally freeze.

Laz shrugs casually. "Mia was upset after the cemetery. She didn't want to come home, so I took her to a hotel."

My eyes nearly bug out of my head. So, we're not bothering to lie? I thought Laz would spin a tale about his car breaking down in the woods and us shivering under our jackets all night or something.

"Why on earth would Mia be so upset about something that happened years ago?"

"Maybe you should ask yourself that question, Giulia. You're the one who nearly took yesterday away from her."

Mom glares at him and turns to me. "You're only eighteen. You're still in school and you stayed out all night. I was worried sick."

I pull my phone from my bag, but I haven't missed any calls or messages. "I didn't know you were worried. You didn't call."

"I'm your mother, Mia. Of course I'm worried." She turns to Laz. "A man with a reputation like yours shouldn't be spending the night alone with inexperienced young women."

"Whatever, Giulia. I took my stepdaughter to the cemetery, and then to a hotel and screwed her." His voice is dripping with scorn even though that's exactly what he did do. With a shake of his head, he turns toward the kitchen. "Who wants coffee? My head is going to explode."

He saunters off without waiting for a reply, leaving Mom and me staring at each other.

"I have my eyes on you, young lady."

My stomach lurches. Can she smell it on me, the sex I had with her husband?

"If I find out that you had anything to do with my party being ruined, I will throw you out of this house so fast your head will spin."

I almost sigh with relief. Oh, yeah. That. Her bringing up the party reminds me of what I overheard between her and my uncles. "It's too late to get rid of me now. Nineteen years too late."

Mom's eyes widen. "Have you been eavesdropping on my private conversations?"

"It's not really eavesdropping if I'm standing in the hall and overhear you against my will. You and my uncles were talking about me at the tops of your voices."

Her mouth works like she's trying to spit out something bitter. "I can't keep you in line any longer. My brothers have been saying for weeks that you need a husband to control you, but I thought it would be better if you finished high school first. As usual, they were right."

"Like they were right that you should have got rid of me? Maybe you let me be born, but you banished me from your heart a long time ago." I throw back at her, and she's astonished that I'm talking back to her.

Then she's livid, and seethes, "You ungrateful child."

Laz has heard us arguing and he's standing in the doorway. "Giulia, she's eighteen. She's too young to get married."

She shoots him a haughty look. "I was engaged at seventeen. I ate my leftover birthday cake the night before I was married."

"And look how well that marriage turned out for you," he shoots back.

"How dare you! Who are you to lecture me about marriage?"

While they argue, I try to slip away.

"Where do you think you're going, young lady? I have things to discuss with you. Are you going to drop out of school, or would you prefer the wedding to take place after you've graduated? Personally, I don't know why you're still attending classes."

I stare at Mom. I'm still attending classes because I have no idea what I want to do with my life. Maybe I'll attend a community college once I'm out of here. I don't have the grades for the Ivy League or any of the decent schools, but I still want my high school diploma. "Don't tell me you're serious about me getting married?"

Mom gives me a tight, unfriendly smile. "I'm deadly serious. I've had enough of you coming and going as you please and defying me at every turn. We can figure out the details later. Meanwhile, I'll start making calls."

And with that, she turns on her heel and walks smartly upstairs, an expression on her face bordering on spiteful.

She knows I ruined her party.

She can't prove it, but she knows, and this is how I'm being punished.

"Laz," I whisper, my voice shaking with emotion. "I don't want a husband, especially not one that Mom chooses."

He comes toward me and palms the nape of my neck with his large hand, staring deep into my eyes. "Over my dead body are you getting married. It's not happening."

"What are we going to do?" I'm amazed how natural it suddenly feels to say *we*. How good it feels, too.

Me and Laz.

Against Mom.

Against the world.

"I'll think of something. Meanwhile, try not to worry too much. Just focus on school." Laz darts a quick look around before taking my face between his hands. "And on me."

He covers my mouth with his in a searing kiss that I feel right down to my toes.

"Come on. I'll make us that coffee."

Over the next few days, I live in fear of men arriving unannounced at the house bearing engagement rings. I overhear Mom on the phone asking people about their unmarried sons and brothers. She's got a list on her tablet, and she makes notes as she talks. How much this man earns. How long this one has been divorced.

If I don't sign the marriage certificate, I can't get married. I remind myself of this over and over. It's not like Mom has any leverage over me apart from throwing me out of this house, and I've been half expecting that would happen anyway.

Everywhere I go in this house, I see Laz or am reminded of the night I spent with him. His voice rumbles from downstairs when I'm in my room. His scent lingers in the air when he's not there. I often hear him whistling to himself or playing rock songs on the radio when he's working on his car. There's only one man on earth that I'd even consider marrying, and he's married to someone else.

Miserably, I imagine a future in which I'm married as well, and Laz and I both sneak around behind our partners' backs. I hate it. I'm already racked with guilt half the time, and I take no pleasure in knowing I'm stealing someone else's man. Yet I can't help wondering when I'll next feel Laz's powerful arms around me and his tongue in my mouth.

I'm in the middle of some history homework when my bedroom door opens and Laz enters. He's wearing a loose dark gray shirt with his black jeans, and the soft fabric looks so good against his muscles and accentuates his strong throat.

I wonder if he's about to tell me Mom's set my wedding date when a heated smile slips over his lips. He's here for something else.

Me.

Laz takes my hand, pulls me to my feet, and kisses me.

"What—"

"Your mom's out," he murmurs between hungry kisses.

Shit, shit, shit. This is so sordid. This is so messed up. But I can feel myself getting hot and wet as his hands rove over my body.

"You let me raw you, baby. You're a risky bitch and that was so hot it's all I can think about. I need to see you brimming with my cum again."

"I'm not risky. I'm on the pill."

He pulls back. "You're on the what?"

"You heard me."

"But you were a virgin."

I shrug. "Plenty of women take the pill to regulate their periods. Plus, it stops my skin from breaking out."

Laz frowns at me. "Stop taking it."

I laugh, wondering if I heard him right. "What?"

"You heard me. I want to raw you properly."

I glare up at him and hold up fingers as I speak. "One, are you crazy? Scratch that. You're definitely crazy. Two, I could get pregnant. Three, are you freaking crazy?!"

He grins and hooks a finger into the neck of my T-shirt, dragging me closer. "That's so sexy. Say *I could get pregnant* again."

I swat his hand away. "You're not listening to me."

"I hear you loud and clear, Bambi." Laz lets go of me and starts going through the drawers in my bedside table. Then he moves on to my chest of drawers, pawing through my underwear and socks and feeling right to the back.

"What are you doing?"

"Looking for your prescription so I can throw it out."

I don't keep my pills there, so I just fold my arms and watch him scattering panties about. As the minutes pass he grows increasingly annoyed.

Finally, he rounds on me. "Where are they?"

"You are unbelievable, Lazzaro Rosetti. I'm not telling you where my pills are, and I'm not going to stop taking them."

His smile grows wicked. "C'mon. You love being bad with me."

"That's not bad, that's insane! I could get pregnant."

He groans and slants his mouth over mine. "That's so hot. I want you pregnant. Have my baby and let's run away together."

I try to tell him off, but he grasps the nape of my neck and parts my lips with his tongue, invading my mouth with the determination of a man who's going to get what he wants.

When he fists the waistband of my shorts and pulls them tight against my clit, I moan into his mouth. "You're too much."

"I'll ease it in. I'll be gentle."

He starts to pull my shorts and underwear down. "I'm not talking about your dick. I mean your *everything*. Your attitude. Your ego. Your crazy ideas."

Laz gets me out of my clothes and cups my ass in his large hands, pressing me against his hard cock. We're going to get caught. We're so going to get caught, and we're going straight to hell, or to the bottom of the lake with concrete boots or wherever terrible people go when they do things that are really bad.

And wrong.

And *twisted*.

Laz presses kisses to my throat, and putting his lips against my ear, he says in a hot, breathy murmur, "Let me fuck you in your bed while your mom is out. I want to blow my load in this pretty snatch of yours."

Mom could come home any minute. I picture myself bent over the mattress with both hands over my mouth while Laz screws me firmly and thoroughly from behind, his large hands gripping my waist. The fact that we could get caught, the idea of doing something so reckless, has short-circuited my brain.

He walks me back toward the bed, and I know that as soon as he unzips his jeans he's going to be inside me. My core turns molten at the thought as we fall back together on the mattress.

My phone buzzes next to my head and I glance at the screen out of the corner of my eye. There's a message from Mom. Well, shit. This can't be good.

"Wait a sec," I tell Laz breathlessly, and pick my phone up and hold it up before my face.

Please wear your red slip dress at dinner on Wednesday night. Put some makeup on and do something nice with your hair.

Why? I send back, though I think I already know the answer.

Fabrizio Rosetti is coming to dinner with one of his bachelor friends. Drago Lastra.

I must look horrified because Laz grabs my phone from me and reads the screen.

"Drago Lastra?" he exclaims, his voice ringing in the silence of my bedroom. "That fucking predator?"

"Who's Drago Lastra?"

His lip curls. "Only one of coldest, most vicious bastards I've ever met. Jesus Christ, your mom must know his reputation. It's like she wants you to get eaten alive, the cruel bitch."

I swallow hard. "Maybe she does. I think she hates me because she knows I ruined her party."

"That stupid party." He takes my phone from my hand and tosses it onto the nightstand. "That goddamn woman. I don't want you thinking about either right now."

He sits up and pulls his shirt over his head, makes a V with his forefinger and middle and points them in his eyes. "Focus on me."

My gaze drifts down his perfect, tattooed body.

God, if he insists.

He pulls off my T-shirt and his jeans and then we're naked together, pressed against each other tightly with our legs tangled together.

I capture Laz's face in my hands and whimper, "Fuck me like I'm yours."

He drives his thumb into me, and then draws it out, spreading my wetness all around. Then he takes his cock in his hand, lines himself up at my entrance, and thrusts deep inside me.

"You *are* mine."

I feel the truth of those words at my very core and all the way to the tips of my fingers and toes.

His.

Chapter Eleven

LAZ

I groan as I sink my cock into Mia's pussy. This is all I've been able to think about for days, getting my girl on her back with her legs spread for me while I pound into her tight, pink velvet. So tight she's only letting me in a few inches. She gasps and presses her hands against my belly, telling me to slow down because she can't cope.

I ease up and move slower, giving her a chance to relax so I can go deeper, murmuring softly to her, "Who's my good girl?"

I look around at her bed, her room. It's so cute, and I get to fuck her in here. This is all I've been dreaming about for weeks.

Mia whimpers and clutches my shoulders as I move harder and deeper. After a few more strokes I pull out, turn her onto her stomach and drag her hips up.

Now she's spread open before me, and what a sight she is. I take myself in my hand and plunge back into her.

"Give me that sweet grip of your pussy, Bambi. No one fucks like my angel of a stepdaughter."

She buries her face in the blankets and moans with horror and desire. "Don't say things like that when we're having sex."

"Why not? You love being a little slut for your stepdad. Look at that arch in your back. Only horny girls throw their asses out like this. Should I fuck that pussy like you need it?"

Apparently I should because she moans louder and starts to work her clit with her fingers. She moans faster and faster until her cries reach a peak.

Mia's whole body flushes red as she comes, her face buried in the blankets and her arm scooped tightly around them.

I take that as my cue to finish fast and hard inside of her, groaning and gripping the fleshy part of her ass as I shoot my load deep inside her.

I smile to myself as I draw slowly out of her. "If you don't like me talking dirty to you, you shouldn't come like a horny little girl when I do."

A door opens and closes downstairs. It sounded like the front door.

Mia gasps and jumps out of bed, grabbing for her clothes. "That's Mom."

She yanks her T-shirt and shorts on, gasps something about

having a shower, and races out of the room.

I laugh under my breath and slowly pull my clothes on before remembering her birth control. How annoying that she's hiding it from me when her getting pregnant could solve all our . . .

Problems.

I meet my own gaze in the vanity mirror and a wicked smile spreads over my face, stretching the scar on my lips. Oh, now there's a plan.

Sure, it could create other problems, but think of what it could do for us. Faber told me to get my wife pregnant, but Mia's been more like a wife to me than her mother has. Settling down with a family would be wonderful if it was with her.

Mia, our baby, my auto shop. That sounds like a life worth fighting for.

My gaze strays over Mia's drawers, her bookshelves. Where would she keep the pills? I assume she's hiding them because of Giulia. I try and think like a teenage girl who doesn't want her mom to find something in her room.

Hiding them in a drawer or a box is out, and Giulia would think to look behind the dresser and under the mattress. How about somewhere in plain sight? There are framed prints on the walls, and I lift each one up and check behind it. The third one, I find what I'm looking for. Several packets of birth control pills taped behind the picture.

"Bingo."

I take a photo of the pills with my phone, send it to one of my contacts, and then call him.

Gus picks up on the second ring. "Yo, Laz."

"How much time will it take you to make half a dozen packets of fake birth control pills?" I tell him I've just sent him a picture, and I wait while he checks it out.

"You want knockoff birth control pills? There's no profit in those." Gus makes fake boner pills for a living and sells them on the internet. The man is minted.

"I don't want knockoffs. I want fakes," I explain. "All of them sugar pills. Can you do that?"

"Sure, why not. Aren't you married now? Why is your wife on the pill?"

"Never mind about my wife. Just get me the pills, and fast. And don't tell my brothers about this."

"Wouldn't dream of it. I hope you're a daddy real soon."

I smile as I hang up the phone. Yeah, I hope so, too.

We need to come up with a plan so Mia doesn't have to marry Drago Lastra or any other man. Maybe this isn't the sort of plan she'd envision, but desperate times call for desperate measures.

By Wednesday evening, the fake birth control pills have been taped behind the print in Mia's room for two days. She's fertile right this second and the knowledge is making me crazy. I'm itching to get my hands on my girl and fuck her into next week and back.

But do I have the opportunity? No, because here comes my brother with Drago Lastra.

They arrive promptly at eight in the evening, Lastra holding a bouquet of red roses. He's a tall, somber-looking man with heavy-lidded blue-gray eyes and a suit precisely tailored to his frame. A heavy silver watch glints on his wrist, and he murmurs a polite hello to everyone. He's been elbow deep in men's guts while they scream their dying screams, but you wouldn't know it by looking at him. Under Giulia's expensive lights, Lastra looks domesticated.

Almost, but not quite. There's still something sharklike in those blue-gray eyes, and my hackles are all the way up.

Mia looks stunningly beautiful. She's been worrying at her lips with her teeth, but her matte red lipstick is perfect, and her long lashes are dark and silky. Her hair is pinned up with a few loose strands falling softly around her face. The short, silky red dress rustles across her skin. It's got spaghetti straps, and I know, Lastra knows, Faber knows, everyone fucking knows that Mia's not wearing a bra. The sexy dress clings softly to her body in such a way that she may as well be naked.

"Miss Bianchi," Lastra murmurs, offering her the red roses while he devours her with his gaze.

I roll my eyes. Roses, what a cliché. I want to smack them out of his hands and throw him out of this house.

Though she doesn't want to, Giulia is watching her like a hawk, and Mia has to accept the flowers and say a polite word of thanks. The red roses match Mia's slip dress and lipstick so perfectly I feel like Giulia and Faber coordinated these details over the phone.

While we eat dinner, Faber makes polite conversation with Mia that sets my teeth on edge, but it's nothing to what Drago Lastra makes me feel every time his gaze latches onto my woman. I'm gripping my cutlery like weapons. Yes, Mia *is* beautiful. Congratulations for figuring it out, Lastra. Now stop fucking staring at her.

Giulia talks on and on about Lastra's homes, his cars, his luxurious lifestyle. He's been divorced twice but Giulia laughingly waves that off as "clashes of personalities." I'd put money on the fact that his ex-wives are terrified of him, and they ran from the man as fast as they could.

My wife glosses over his criminal activities and his violence. I haven't been innocent in that department myself. Who at this table hasn't beaten someone with their fists, a blunt weapon, a high-heeled shoe? Even Mia's punched a boy in the face. But Lastra's violence is on a whole other level. The rumors alone should be enough to make any loving mother stop and think before getting carried away with wedding plans, but apparently Giulia just doesn't care.

At the end of the evening, Mia looks overwhelmed and confused, but Giulia is beaming.

"Mia and I will show you out, Drago. Come along, Mia."

Mia gets reluctantly to her feet and follows her mom and Lastra to the front door.

"What do you think of Lastra?" Faber asks me from the other side of the dinner table.

"He's too old and too dangerous for Mia. She'll marry that man over my dead body."

Faber gazes speculatively at me, and I realize he's picked up on my anger and jealousy. It can't be hard, seeing as I'm finding it impossible to rein it in.

"My, my. Aren't you protective all of a sudden. Are those paternal instincts kicking in? Is there some good news you'd like to share with me?"

"Not yet," I say through my teeth, my anger doubling at the thought of screwing my wife. Not in a million years, and especially not after what I've just witnessed tonight, the cold, heartless bitch. "I'm hoping I'll be able to announce some happy news very soon."

"See that you do."

I stand up so fast that my chair shoots out behind me, and I plant my hands on the table. "You're not my boss. You're not my father. I'm in charge of my life, not you."

Faber gazes up at me, unimpressed by my outburst. "I was hoping you'd start to mellow out by now. I'm starting to think my little brother is always going to be the irresponsible one of the family."

"Yeah? I've known for a long time that you're a control freak and an asshole. You claim that family is the most important thing to you, but that's bullshit. The only person who's important to Fabrizio Rosetti is Fabrizio Rosetti. Dad must be turning in his grave witnessing what a little bitch you're being about the money that belongs to me."

"I just don't want to see you drive yourself into an early grave."

"You think fixing muscle cars is going to endanger my health?" Faber knows all about my intention to open a garage with the money that belongs to me. He actually asked to see a business plan so he would know the idea was "viable."

Fuck him.

Fuck him to hell and back.

I happen to have a pretty fucking great business plan, but I don't have to justify my dreams to anyone. Share? Yes. I'll happily share my dreams with people who love me, but I'm not feeling much family love lately.

Faber struggles with this for a moment. "You need to learn the value of money before someone hands you hundreds of thousands of dollars."

"Don't feed me bullshit because I can't stand it. Be a man and just admit that you don't like me."

"You're my brother, Lazzaro—

"For the last time, it's Laz." I push away from the table and straighten up. "When I become a father, it's going to be on my terms."

"What's that supposed to mean?"

"You'll see. Good chat, Faber. Lovely to see you, as always." I stalk from the room and toward the kitchen, pleased that Lastra has finally gone.

Out in the garage, I stand in the cool, dark silence next to my car, wishing I could just drive away and leave everyone behind. But that would mean losing Mia, and that girl has me tethered to her heart. I couldn't walk away from her to save my life.

I pop the hood of my car, and even though it doesn't need an oil change, I prep for an oil change. Anything to keep my hands busy so I don't go back into the house and declare that I'm at war with any man who tries to talk to Mia.

I tinker with my car for a couple of hours, and then wash up and fall into a doze on the sofa. Just past dawn, I see that Giulia is out by the pool, about to swim her morning laps. They take forty minutes. As soon as she dives in, I get up and go upstairs to Mia's bedroom.

She's still fast asleep as I approach the bed, pulling off my clothes. When I slip between the blankets, she barely stirs, and I have the pleasure of kissing her awake.

With tongue.

On her pussy.

Mia breathes in sharply and opens her eyes, eyelashes fluttering, and she gazes down at me between her legs.

"Laz," she moans, wrapping her thighs around my head and plunging her fingers into my hair. "You shouldn't be here."

What I hear is, *Please make me come.*

Anything for my girl.

I give her a messy, hungry licking, and she gives me what I want, which is her coming all over my face. A moment later I sit up with my cock in my hand and plunge into her with a groan. I'll never be over how good it feels to raw this girl.

Staring down at my cock moving in and out of her, I say, "I can't wait until you're mine. I hope you know that I'm imagining being balls deep in you at all times, no matter who we're with and where we are, my pretty little stepdaughter."

"Don't start that again," she moans, her cheeks flushing red.

"You love it when I talk like this."

Mia reaches up and presses her hands against the headboard, keeping herself still for me so I can fuck her harder.

"You love every..." *Thrust.* "Dirty." *Thrust.* "Word." *Thrust.*

I groan and tip my head back as my climax crashes gloriously over me.

I start to draw out of my sweet girl when I see my cum creaming all over my length and her pussy lips.

Oh, damn, that's hot. I shove myself back into her, wondering how soon a woman can get pregnant after coming off the pill. I hope it's now. Right this second. I thrust into her, my dick still hard and as deep as I can go. In there, that's where I need to be. I'll stay right here until I'm sure my boys have had a chance to do their thing to her.

Mia tries to wriggle away but I hold tight to her hips and don't budge.

"Let me up."

I smirk at the way she's struggling to get out from beneath me. "I like it here."

"Laz, what if Mom comes in?" she moans.

God, half of me would welcome it. Still balls deep in her daughter, I'd declare that Mia's mine and there's nothing anyone can do about it.

I picture Mia wearing a wedding dress with a pregnant belly, and my dick gets so hard.

I need to fuck her again.

And so, I do.

I pull back and slam into her again, short, hard thrusts.

"Laz," Mia hisses. "What are you *doing*?"

"Hold still, baby, I'm not done with you." I drag her down the bed, pull one of her legs over my shoulder and the other around my waist.

Mia's breathless with desire and panic. "You shouldn't—we can't—"

All her protests are like a red flag to a bull. I *can* and I *will*.

I drive my cock into her, and she has to smother her gasp. I lick my thumb and swipe it over her clit, rolling the tender little nub around while she almost grows cross-eyed from pleasure.

"Shouldn't what?"

But Mia's got nothing to say. She grabs fistfuls of the covers and holds on for dear life. I can feel my orgasm building alongside hers. I know her well enough by now that I can tell from her expression when she's teetering on the brink, and I let go of all restraint and fuck her hard, slamming into her until she comes in a rush, and I burst inside her again.

As we're both panting and catching our breaths, sweat cooling on our bodies, we hear footsteps climbing the stairs.

I give Mia an evil grin. "Do you think that's your—"

She plasters both her hands over my mouth and shakes her head frantically. The footsteps pass by her door, head into the master bedroom, and then disappear back downstairs again.

With her hands pressed to my mouth, I slowly draw out of her. My cum and her wetness is all over her thighs. This room reeks of sex, and the last thing I want to do is leave her. I want to put her legs over her head to keep my cum inside her, but she'd guess that something is up and it's too soon for that.

I tug her fingers away from my lips. "Don't get up. You just lie there, Bambi."

But Mia's too horrified to move. "This can't happen in my room again. It's like we're trying to get caught."

I press my palm over her belly and kiss her. I know what I'm trying for. I'm trying so hard that there won't be a day that goes by her insides aren't coated with my cum.

"I'll worry about that. Go back to sleep." I cover her with the blankets and give her one last kiss.

Two minutes later, I'm in the shower, grinning to myself as I imagine how beautiful my girl is going to look full of my baby.

I carry that delicious thought with me all day, at the gym, at the used car lot where I stumble across a dusty old 1970s Chevrolet Impala just begging for some love and affection. I buy it, because if I don't get my money I'm going to need a secondary plan, and this is the best way I know how to make money.

In the afternoon, I head out in my car when I know Mia will be walking home. I pull up next to her, giving her a lazy grin as I remember that she's been at school all day with my cum inside her. You pervert, Laz. I guess I'll stop being a pervert when it stops being so fucking hot.

"Hey, Bambi. Want a ride?"

She leans down and gives me a smile. "Where are we going?"

"I want to show you something special to me."

Mia pulls open the car door. "Then of course I'll go with you."

As we drive along, I reach out and hold her hand. I can touch her in here. People can't see that I'm doing something as transgressive as twining my fingers through hers.

"How was your day?"

"Not as good as my morning," she says with a smirk.

"Damn, girl, you're going to make me blush."

I glance at our joined hands, and the sight is just so perfect I have to remind myself to look back at the road. I never do this shit. Simple pleasures like holding a girl's hand, just because I like her.

Ten minutes later, I pull up outside the garage that's for sale. It's a miracle someone hasn't snapped it up yet, but doubtlessly someone will before I get my money. Even if it can never be mine, I want to share it with Mia.

"Here we are."

Mia casts her eyes over the building. "What's this place? Why are we here?"

"You wanted to know what I'm going to do with my money when I get it. It's this, or something like it." I describe to her my dream of owning an auto shop for my favorite kinds of cars. Fast ones with engines like beasts.

A delighted smile breaks over her face. "That's perfect for you." Then her smile dims. "And it's a relief to hear you talk this way. I was worried about you. All that talk of dying while we were up at the lookout was freaking me out."

The lifestyle I was born into isn't great for your health, but if I get my hands on this place or something like it, it will do a lot for my longevity.

Screwing my wife's daughter? Not so much. The moment Mia figures out she's pregnant or starts to show, I'll be public enemy number one for the Bianchis, and those uncles are mean motherfuckers.

I'll figure out what to say to them when the time comes, and Faber will be pissed, but he'll have my back. He wanted me to be a father. He's getting his wish, so he can shove any complaints up his ass. I'm doing things my way.

"Don't you feel even a tiny bit guilty?"

"About what?" I ask, wondering for a moment if Mia's figured out I've been messing with her birth control. I was honest with her about having a plan. It's maybe not the sort of plan she'll be expecting, but if the end result is that we're together, then problem solved.

"Maybe you should come clean to Mom," she says, twisting her hands together.

I grin at her. All I can feel is pleasure over the fact that I'm getting my hands on the right Bianchi woman. "You want me to go back to the house now and tell your mom her least favorite daughter gives a killer blow job? That she makes me burst in my jeans just by riding my lap?"

"That's the last thing I want. Laz, please be serious for one second." She gazes up at me with anguish in her eyes.

My expression grows serious. "If you can't stand it and you want me to go home and end my marriage right now, I will. Without bringing you into it."

"You would do that?"

"My heart bleeds for you, Bambi. You get treated worse by these assholes than my family treats me, which is really saying something. You don't deserve to be dragged through the mud any more than you already have."

Mia strokes her fingers up and down my biceps as she considers my offer. "If you walk now, you'll never get your money, will you?"

I shake my head. "I won't. And I won't be able to see you, either." Not nearly as much as I do right now. And I won't be able to protect her from her mom or any men who come calling for her hand.

Mia chews on her lip as she stares at me. "But at least you won't be . . . she won't be able to . . ." Mia groans and her expression is pained. "Please tell me you don't have sex with Mom. That you've never had sex with Mom."

"I don't have sex with your mom."

"Ever?" she asks hopefully.

I shake my head. "Let's not do this, Bambi."

Mia whimpers and covers her face. "Why can't you lie to me? I was really enjoying lying to myself."

I reach out and take her hand. "I didn't like it, okay? It sucked, actually."

She shudders. "Has it happened recently? Since we . . ." She makes a *you know* gesture with her hand and mumbles, "Since we did the thing."

"You want to know the last time I fucked your m—"

She covers my mouth with her hand and gives me a desperate look. I can't help smiling against her fingers because she's so cute like this. She cares so much about things. It makes me remember how good it feels to care.

I take her hand away. "Mia, baby, I haven't touched your mom since before you came all over my fingers."

She blinks at me in surprise. "Really?"

"Yeah. And I won't. On one condition."

"What?"

I give her a wicked smile. "I entered this house as a married man determined to be faithful to the Bianchi family. If I'm not screwing the mom, I better be fucking the daughter."

She punches my shoulder. "I'm trying to have a serious conversation here. Are you sleeping with other women? Any women at all."

Normally I would be sleeping with two or three, but I haven't even thought about another woman lately. "No one but you, Bambi.

You're the only one I want."

"You went to a stripper bar," she points out.

"Yeah, well, I felt like shit and needed a pretty woman to smile at me. Specifically, you. Guess my fairy godmother was on my side that day because there you were." I thread my fingers through her hair and gently push it back from her face. "I would have gone to a regular bar if I wanted to pick up. I only wanted you, even then. You have me, Bambi. You *have* me. As in, I belong to no one else but you."

"But what about M—"

I cup the back of her neck and draw her lips up to mine.

"You have me," I say again, holding her face between my hands. "Always."

She takes a shuddering breath. "That's even scarier than not having you. I can't predict what's going to happen next."

I settle my arms around her and draw her closer to me. "What if I have a plan for us?"

"What kind of plan?"

"A crazy plan. A delicious plan."

"What is it?"

"I couldn't possibly tell you."

Mia narrows her eyes. "Why? Would I not approve?"

A grin spreads over my face. "Probably not."

"Will it work?"

"Pretty sure it will. Or it might blow up in our faces."

Mia presses her face into my chest and moans.

"But the alternative is I go home and knock your mom up and you marry Drago Lastra."

She sits up quickly. "Your plan. I like your plan better. It can't be worse than that."

I hope she remembers this conversation when she's staring down the barrel of a positive pregnancy test.

I kiss her one last time and start the car, and I drive the long way home, just to give myself more time to hold her hand.

***

The Chevrolet Impala is delivered the next morning, and I get her settled into the garage. With some time, parts, and hard work, I can have this car looking and driving beautifully, and sell it for an excellent profit to a private dealer.

If I don't get the money that's owed me, this will be my life. The same goal, to own my own garage, but I'll have to build it up slowly from scratch, car by car.

I smile as I wipe dust from the hood of the Impala with a damp cloth. With Mia at my side, a baby on the way, and no one to answer to but my new family, I'd be deliriously happy living a humble existence and doing what I love. Life feels hopeful when even plan B is better than anything you've ever known before.

In the afternoon I head to the gym. It's chest and arms day and I'm sweating and exhausted when I finish my workout.

In the changing rooms I pull a T-shirt on over my head. It catches over my pectoral muscles like a crop top before I can pull it all the way down. With my chest bare and my wet hair in my eyes, I snap a selfie and upload it to Instagram.

Obnoxious? Yes.

Eighty percent of my feed is my car and the rest is my muscles. I'm a show-off and I know it.

A moment later my phone buzzes with a notification. Someone has left a comment on my picture.

Put them away, slut.

I burst out laughing when I see the commenter is Mia and shove my phone into my pocket. Stalking my Insta, is she? What a fucking flirt.

As I walk out of the gym and into the sunset, I can't stop grinning to myself. I don't think I've smiled this much in years, and it's all thanks to Mia and the hope I have for our future.

On Saturday night, I wait in the alleyway behind Peppers, my heart pounding. As much as it burns me having other men slobbering all over the girl I'm obsessed with, I'm not here to stop her from working. I'll watch over her in the club. I'll pay for all her dances. It will kill me to see other men leering at the woman who should be my wife, but I'll take it as my penance.

I've been an irresponsible asshole all these years, but I can be a man for Mia.

Then at midnight, I realize she's not coming. I groan with relief and head back to my car.

Soon, Bambi, soon. I'll take you away from all this shit and your mom, Drago Lastra, this whole miserable situation will be a distant memory.

I promise you.

Chapter Twelve

MIA

"Am I a sex addict?" I whimper, pulling off my baby doll T-shirt and panties at lightning speed. I'm already wet. My pussy started tingling the moment Laz picked me up on the way home from school and drove us to this remote spot in the woods.

I'm perched on the edge of the passenger seat of his car, my legs outside the door, aching and whipped up into a frenzy by the sight and smell of my illicit boyfriend, and I won't be satisfied until he's screwed me into a senseless and deliciously sore mess.

Laz has already pulled his T-shirt off and is furiously unbuttoning his jeans, the dappled light of the forest playing over his bare shoulders. His dark hair is falling into his eyes and all the veins are standing out on his forearms.

"If you are, I definitely am," he gasps, spreading me open and kneeling down on the ground to swipe my clit with his tongue.

I yelp with pleasure, and for once I don't bother to smother how much noise I'm making. The trees, the sky, can hear how much I want Laz. I need someone or something to know, otherwise this secret is going to grow so big it will burst out of me.

Laz sits up and puts his knee on the seat, his shoulders just fitting inside the car. He grasps his cock, pulls my legs around his hips, and plunges into me.

I cry out sharply, and half a dozen birds explode from the trees around us in a furious flapping of wings.

There's no space. I cling to him and the headrest of the passenger seat. The car moves as he pounds into me. I've never experienced anything hotter in my life. A cool wind blows in, and the fresh air on my naked body ratchets up the intensity.

We shouldn't be here.

We might get caught.

This is *insane*.

His phone rings, and instead of ignoring the call, he pulls his phone out and glances at the screen.

And then he *answers* it.

I clamp my hand over my mouth before I can ask him what the hell he thinks he's doing.

"Hey, Giulia," he says, as casual as I've ever heard him.

My eyes widen and I nearly scream out loud.

He's talking to Mom?

While he's *inside of me?*

Laz continues to screw me like there's nothing happening that's out of the ordinary. Every now and then, he glances down at his cock disappearing inside me and mouths, *Oh, fuck yes.*

I can just hear Mom's voice, but I can't tell what she's saying. "Sure, I can pick those up. Wait, you got a sec?"

Mom's reply takes a moment, and I imagine she's reciting all the things she has to do that day. She's a devotee to the cult of busy. Meanwhile, Laz is rawing my pussy like he hasn't got a care in the world and my juices are all over him.

"Uh-huh. I just wanted to say that you're driving me crazy, but I think I'm starting to like you." He's speaking to Mom but he's staring right into my eyes the entire time. "You talk back, you're fucking stubborn. I know I drive you crazy as well, but I think you're starting to like me, too."

My eyes widen and I'm so shocked that my hands fall away from my mouth.

"No, I'm not high. You can fight me all you want but you know it's true."

"I—" I start to reply breathlessly before Laz grins at me and I clamp both hands over my mouth again.

Shit.

Mom nearly heard me speaking to her husband in my sex voice.

"I just thought you should know," he says, watching himself drill my pussy. "Hang on, I need to put you on speaker." He taps the screen and throws the phone onto the seat behind my head.

"Where is this coming from, Lazzaro?" asks Mom in a peeved voice.

If I wasn't the biggest slut in the city, I'd push Laz off me, but I'm so addicted to what he's doing to me that even now I can't close my legs and be a lady. Push away the hottest man I've ever seen and give up this thick dick because he's speaking to his wife who also happens to be my mother?

Not happening.

Laz takes my hand and draws it to his lips, pressing a silent kiss to my palm. "I've been thinking about it for a while. I want to do this properly."

He does?

"How close are you?" he asks.

So close, I mouth.

"I'll be home in an hour."

"Cool." Lazily, he reaches down and traces his thumb over my clit, round and around in a devastating motion, and I know I'm going to burst apart at the seams any second.

I start mouthing desperately, *Hang up hang up hang up*—

Laz smirks. "I have to go. I think I hear Mia coming."

He reaches over my head, and I hear a beep. Just in time because I come with a wail, my whole body convulsing from a powerful orgasm.

Laz groans and pounds me harder. "Fuck yes, milk my cock, baby. You're such a horny little slut for me."

"Shut up, you crazy asshole," I whimper raggedly, hating myself already as my orgasm tails off. From bliss to paralyzing self-hatred in a matter of seconds.

"Come again and say *thank you* this time. Do as you're told."

My nails dig into his shoulders as I watch him screw me harder. "Go to hell."

"Say, please cream-pie my pussy."

"I'm not saying that."

"Say it or I'll video call your mother while I fuck you and show her what a cock-hungry girl she raised."

I groan at his coarse words, which are making me want to come again. "You'll lose everything."

He grins wider and reaches for his phone. "You daring me?"

Laz seems like the sort of man to take a dare seriously. I slap the phone away. "No."

"Then say it."

I reach down between my legs and massage my middle finger over my clit. Laz's face goes blank as he watches me, as if he's never seen anything so hot in his life. "Please cream-pie my pussy, Laz."

"Oh, hell yes," he growls, pumping faster into me.

The drag and pull of his cock inside me is making me go insane. My clit is alive with sensation. There's sweat on Laz's chest and his eyes are dilated and dark. Suddenly, he clamps a hand around my throat and squeezes. I'm being pressed down into the seat, completely at his mercy. Trapped between his body and the leather.

Suddenly, everything rushes up, and I fly apart into a thousand shining pieces.

Laz is on the verge of coming when I return to earth. I reach around his cock, grab the skin of his ball sack, and *twist*.

He groans but doesn't stop pounding me, and I feel him come as his rhythm stutters, his body flushes red, and his head tips back.

When he opens his eyes to catch his breath, he grins lazily at me. "You little hellcat."

The sound of birdsong reaches my ears and I realize that we just fucked in the woods.

My hands are pressed against his chest, and I can't move with his big body still pinning me to the seat. "Can you let me up?"

Laz pulls back a little but then shoves himself deep again. "Don't want to. I like my cum inside you."

"Why are you so obsessed with that?"

He looks up at me through his dark fringe of hair and pins me with his eyes. "Because it's you, Bambi."

Suddenly, I can't take a breath. I assumed he did this with every woman he slept with because it's some sort of fetish of his.

"I never know whether to trust anything that comes out of your mouth. All those things you said when Mom was on the phone . . ."

"What things? Remind me."

I fiddle with the seam of the leather seat. "That you want to do this properly."

"This is me, doing things properly."

"What do you mean? There's nothing proper about secretly screwing your stepdaughter in the woods that I can see."

But Laz just shakes his head, a mysterious smile on his lips, and slides his cock even deeper.

The next evening we're all supposed to go to Rieta and Nero's for dinner, but Mom is ashen-faced and her forehead is clammy.

"I have a migraine. You and Mia go," Mom tells Laz as she heads for her bedroom, the tips of her fingers pressed to her forehead.

Laz glances at me and murmurs, "Sure. I'll take Mia."

Mom nods absent-mindedly and disappears upstairs. If she were thinking clearly, would Mom realize how strange it is for her asshole husband to agree to take his stepdaughter to a dinner without argument, knowing it won't be fun for him in any way?

Maybe. Maybe not. And I can't find myself caring too much either way. A whole evening with Laz all to myself? I'm ecstatic. Sure, I have to share him with Rieta and Nero, but Nero doesn't say much, and Rieta will be fun. It might almost feel like a double date.

It's chilly outside, and Laz and I are wearing jackets as we walk side by side down the street, neither of us rushing. Laz is wearing a well-worn leather bomber jacket that looks so good over his white tee.

While I'm daydreaming, Laz reaches out and captures my fingers in his.

I gasp and rip my hand away. "Don't."

His eyes are dark and challenging "Why not?"

"You know why not. I don't have to spell it out for you." The last thing either of us needs is for whispers to get back to Mom that her husband has been seen holding her daughter's hand.

Laz glances around and then shoves me down a side street. A narrow path leads behind a row of garden fences, lined with dandelions, and overshadowed by trees.

He holds out his palm, his eyes burning with anger. "Hold my hand, Bambi."

"Just because we think no one can see us doesn't mean it's safe."

But Laz stays right where he is.

"Fine," I say, putting my hand in his and rolling my eyes. He grips me hard and we start walking together in the dark.

When I glance at him, his lips are twitching, and I can't help the smile that breaks over my face. The next thing I know, he's turned toward me and is kissing me as he walks me up against a fence. Kisses that are full of happiness. Full of sweetness.

I never knew that doing the worst thing in the world could taste so much like heaven.

"We're going to be late," I murmur between kisses.

"Just one more kiss." He captures my lips with his again, his tongue pushing deep into my mouth, a promise for later.

A few minutes later, my heart is beating wildly as we stand on Rieta's front doorstep two feet apart. I ring the doorbell, hoping that my reddened, just-been-kissed lips go unnoticed by my sister.

Rieta opens the door with a smile and kisses both of our cheeks.

"Mom couldn't come," I explain. "Migraine."

"Nero can't be here, either. Never mind, I like small dinner parties better." She smiles at Laz as she takes his jacket. "It will give me a chance to get to know you better."

Laz frowns slightly. "Are you mocking me?"

To her credit, Rieta doesn't pretend she doesn't know what Laz is talking about. "Some of us are friendly in this family. I promise."

Amusement hooks the corner of his mouth. "That's unexpected. Are you sure you have permission to be nice to me?"

"This is my house, and you're welcome here. Come in, I'm just finishing dinner."

We follow Rieta through to the dining room and she tells us to sit down and that we're eating right away. The table is set with five places, so I put two of them away. There's also a bowl of salad, homemade vinaigrette, and a dish of shaved parmesan.

"Can I do anything to help?" Laz calls after her.

Rieta sticks her head around the door and points at a bottle sitting on the dining table. "You could open the wine. Thank you, Lazzaro."

"He prefers Laz, actually," I tell her.

Rieta glances from Laz to me in surprise. "Oh, I didn't realize. Why didn't you say anything?"

"It doesn't matter," Laz mutters, reaching for the wine.

"It does matter," I say firmly. "Rieta will remember, won't you?"

Even if it's just Rieta and I who call him by the name he prefers, it's something. It's important that he feels like himself.

"Of course, if that's what you prefer." Rieta smiles at Laz before disappearing into the kitchen.

Laz is winding the screw into the cork. "Why did you do that? I don't care if you're the only one who calls me Laz."

"Because it's the man you are. I like the man you are."

He pulls the cork from the bottle with a pop. "Don't say shit like that when I can't kiss you. Wine?"

I'm not old enough, but wine is sacred in my family, and I've been allowed to have a little with dinner since I was sixteen if I want it. Usually I don't, but I feel happy tonight. I feel relaxed. In Rieta's house, I can almost pretend that Laz is mine.

I hold my fingers up and measure three-quarters of an inch in the air. "This much, please."

Laz pours it out and hands it to me, and then pours a bigger glass for himself.

The two of us end up standing in front of a picture of Rieta and Nero on their wedding day, my sister radiantly beautiful in her lace wedding dress and Nero handsome in his suit. It's a candid photo that's full of chemistry between the couple. A surprising amount of chemistry when you consider that it was an arranged marriage. Things have cooled between husband and wife since the photo was taken. When I see Nero, which I rarely do these days, he's never affectionate with his wife. Trying and failing so many times to have a baby is driving a wedge between them.

But in this photo? He's gazing at the beautiful, smiling woman in his arms with eyes filled with adoration. What happened to all that love? Did it drain away? Burn up and blow away like ashes?

I'm hyperaware of Laz standing by my side, his arm pressing into mine. What if I fall in love with Laz and that happens to us? We could sacrifice everything for each other and be left with nothing to show for it.

"They look really happy," he murmurs.

"Yeah, they sure look that way," I say sadly.

Laz glances at me sharply. "You okay, Bambi?"

I'm saved from answering by Rieta coming in holding an enormous dish of pasta, her hands covered in oven gloves. "I hope you're both hungry. I made enough for six because I thought more people were coming."

The pasta looks and tastes delicious. Chunks of ricotta cheese, toasted pine nuts, roasted cauliflower, cumin, and olive oil. Best of all, dinner is relaxed for once, the three of us chatting away about TV shows, the upcoming mayoral election, the places we've been on holiday. I keep sneaking looks at Laz and smiling to myself as he chats with Rieta. He's an entirely different man when he's not got a snarky wall up or he's not expecting someone's words to knife him in the guts. His smiles are so beautiful that they take my breath away.

I like this man.

I like him a lot.

When Rieta's plate is almost empty, she turns to me, wine in hand. "I heard about your dinner with Drago Lastra. Is Mom insisting that you marry him?"

Instantly, a chill wind sweeps through the room.

"Mom's not insisting yet, but she keeps bringing him up. I didn't like him, and I've told her that, but she can't seem to accept it."

Every time I've walked into a room and Mom is there, it's taken her less than three minutes to bring up marriage, engagements, or so-called suitable men.

Laz puts his water glass down hard and savagely cuts into a piece of cauliflower with the edge of his fork. "Mia's marrying that piece of shit over my dead body."

A thrill goes through me at how angry and possessive he sounds. Rieta must pick up on it too as she watches him with a slight frown on her face. I distract her by pouring her more wine.

"Thank you, Mia. I don't think it's a good idea for you to get married, either. You're so young, and it doesn't seem like a good match for you. Do you even like him?"

Laz raises his head quickly to stare at me.

I feel a flush creep up my neck. Be more subtle, Laz.

And he already knows the answer to that question.

"God, no. He gave me the creeps."

"Then that settles it," Rieta says with a little nod. "I'll talk to Mom and tell her it's not happening."

After that, Laz starts to relax.

When the meal is over, I help Rieta take the dirty dishes to the kitchen, box up the leftovers, and scrape the plates into the bin. I lose myself in the memory of Laz laughing at Rieta's stories about the two of us getting up to mischief when we were kids. I can't remember the last time I enjoyed myself at a family dinner so much.

And it's with Laz. Despite all the sneaking around, despite the fact that what we're doing with each other is sordid and wrong on so many levels, I can't help but feel like I'm in the right place for the first time in my life.

As Rieta rinses the serving spoons, she asks, "What's up with Laz? He's been staring at you all night."

"What do you mean what's up with Laz?" Even before the words are out of my mouth I can hear how defensive I sound. I feel myself start to blush and I whirl away from my sister.

"Just what I said. Mia, why have you turned around?"

I reach for a dirty plate, panic slamming through me. I thought that if anyone questioned me about the tension between me and Laz, I would play it cool. Shrug it off and pretend not to know what they were talking about. I practiced it so many times in the shower, but now that it's really happening, my palms are sweating, and my heart is pounding.

To my surprise, Rieta gives my shoulder an affectionate punch. "Mia Viviana Bianchi. You've got a crush on Laz."

I turn to face her, clutching the dirty plate like a shield. "No—I don't—I—"

Rieta waves me off and turns back to the sink. "Don't worry about it. You have to live with him, and it must be very strange and intense. And I get it. He's young and pretty sexy, and when he loosens up he's fun to be around. More like a big brother than a stepfather, right?"

I shove the dirty plate into the dishwasher. I don't know what to say to that, so I reach for a half-full water glass, intending to empty it into the sink. Water sloshes over my hand and onto the floor. My foot skids on the wet patch and the glass starts to slip from my fingers.

"Oh sh—"

A large hand appears out of nowhere, catching the glass before it can hit the tile floor and shatter. Laz moved so fast across the room that it's like he has superpowers. He's grabbed me before I can fall, too, and he sets the glass down on the counter before helping me straighten up.

"Careful, Bambi." He strokes his hands through my hair, gazing down at my face in a way that makes my heart zoom madly around my rib cage. Dimly, I'm aware that Rieta is staring at us.

"I hope you didn't hurt yourself. Are you okay?"

I nod, still gazing up at him like a deer caught in headlights.

He tweaks my nose and in an even softer tone, he says, "Good girl."

Then he releases me and steps back. In a normal voice he announces to Rieta, "I'll say goodnight. Thank you for dinner."

"You're leaving?" I ask, as he heads into the hall and pulls on his jacket.

"Yep. You stay and have fun. Call me when you're done here, and I'll walk back and get you."

"You don't need to—"

"I said I'll come back and get you." Laz gives me a final lingering look before opening the front door and seeing himself out.

When I turn around, Rieta is staring at the door, wide-eyed with shock.

"Oh, shit," she whispers. "It's the other way around. *He* has a crush on *you*."

I want to sink through the floor.

Disappear like melting ice.

Laz, what the hell have you done?

Rieta turns to me. "I'm right, aren't I?"

"You've got the wrong idea," I say desperately, shaking my head. I can feel the red flush that's giving away all my secrets.

"Mia, he called you Bambi. That's the cutest nickname I've ever heard! Has he tried to kiss you? He *has* kissed you, hasn't he?"

Fuck.

Fuck.

Fuck.

My face is doing all kinds of crazy things out of my control. I whirl around and pick up a stack of dirty dishes. Then I put them down again as my phone buzzes in my pocket. I take it out and see it's a text from Laz.

Tell her. Someone should know about us, and she loves you.

That's *insane*. He's insane. We agreed we wouldn't tell anyone. What am I supposed to do if Rieta freaks out and tells Mom? Rieta is the only one who even talks to me, and I won't be able to bear it if she starts to hate me too.

I try to come up with a reasonable explanation for why Laz would call me Bambi and touch my face like I'm his girlfriend, but it's too late. Rieta's already figured out everything.

I cover my eyes and hold out my phone to my sister, showing her the text from Laz.

She gasps and grabs my phone from me. "Is this from Laz? Tell me what?"

It's out now. I haven't got a choice. "That we're together."

I peek through my fingers at my sister. Her mouth is hanging open as she stares from me to my phone and back again.

"Why is he in your contacts as a knife emoji?"

Because he's dangerous for me, and I'm deadly for him.

"It's a reminder that one of us or both of us are going to get killed if anyone finds out about us. You won't tell Mom, will you? Our uncles will kill him. Literally kill him." I grab Rieta's wet hand, pleading with her.

Her mouth is open as she struggles for words. Grapples with this secret that she no doubt wishes she didn't know. I've put her in a terrible position, trapped between me and Mom.

Finally, she passes my phone back, grabs a dishcloth, and wipes her hands. "Come on. Laz left us alone so we could talk. So, let's talk."

Rieta leads me back into the dining room and pours us both fresh glasses of red wine. We take them through to the living room and sit down on the sofas together.

"Tell me everything," Rieta says.

I take a deep breath.

And I do.

I don't sugarcoat anything. I make sure Rieta knows about all the things that Laz did those first few weeks he lived with us and how much I hated him. As I continue my story, my face softens, and so does my voice. I tell her how Laz stood up to the boys who took compromising pictures of me—though I don't say where, because I'm not ready to share Tasha with anyone else—and defended me to Mom. I tell Rieta how he infuriates me and makes me laugh, and that I can't stop thinking about him.

"What does it feel like?" Rieta asks.

"What does what feel like?"

My sister plays with the edge of a cushion, her expression wistful. "For a man to have a crush on you? To feel his eyes follow you across the room and know that he's thinking about you and only you. Burning for you."

It's a question that an inexperienced little sister might ask her older sister, but Rieta is older than me and she's married. "But you know how it feels. You have Nero."

Rieta shakes her head, misery bleeding into her eyes. "Nero never looked and acted around me the way Laz does around you. At least, he hasn't for a long, long time."

I don't know what to say. Rieta's usually so cheerful and positive, but I can see what an effort that's been for her lately.

Rieta takes a sip of wine and shakes her head. "Never mind. Let's not talk about me right now. Tell me how it feels."

"It feels dangerous," I say truthfully.

"What if Mom divorced him? Would you two be together?"

I let out a burst of scandalized laughter. "Whose side are you on?"

"I'm on the side of love."

"This isn't a fairy tale. This is real life."

"I'm serious. He makes you happy. No matter what Mom says, happiness is actually important for—" She breaks off, a sob in her voice and tears swimming in her eyes.

"Oh, Rieta," I murmur, taking her wine glass from her and putting both of them down. I pull her into a hug. "Are things really that bad between you and Nero?"

Rieta lets herself cry for exactly one and a half seconds, and then she sits up and shakes her head. "Trying for a baby is messing with my head. I'm sorry, I didn't mean to make this about me."

I don't think it's just the frustration of trying for a baby, but I watch as Rieta visibly shuts down her emotions and changes the subject.

"I like him," Rieta says, wiping her face.

"Who?"

"Laz, silly. He's weird and intense and it's ten kinds of fucked up . . . but he cares about you."

I imagined that if anyone found out about Laz and me, I would have to endure a long lecture about what a stupid little girl I've been, heaping even more shame on our family name.

"Do you really think so?"

"Mia, he didn't touch your face and call you Bambi in front of me because he was being careless. He wanted me to know so that you would have someone to confide in. Even though it could get him killed. Not many men would do that."

My heart squeezes in my chest. They wouldn't, would they? But it doesn't matter how selfless and honorable it was if we're still stuck creeping around behind Mom's back.

"What am I going to do?" I whisper.

"What does Laz want to do?"

"He says he has a plan. He wants us to be together."

Rieta's face creases like she's about to cry again. If she's getting mopey over Laz, the least romantic man ever, things must be really bad between her and Nero. "Did he say what the plan is?"

I shake my head. "I haven't asked. It's probably something crazy." If I had to guess, Laz is refusing to give Mom a baby or do anything that a husband should, and he's biding his time before she kicks him out and divorces him. That way he can tell his brothers it wasn't his fault, and he tried his best. As far as plans go, it's not a great one, but it's probably all we have.

"If the shit hits the fan, you're always welcome here," Rieta offers.

"What about Nero?"

"I'll worry about Nero. You think about yourself and Laz, and don't let anyone stand in your way if you believe in your heart that Laz is the man for you."

I throw my arms around Rieta, my heart filled with love for my sister. "I don't deserve you."

"If you've found love, then hold on tight, no matter what," she whispers fiercely.

Twenty minutes later, I send Laz a text message that I'm ready to go, and he replies that he'll be right there. Before I close my phone, I edit Laz's contact name and add a heart next to the knife emoji. The sparkly pink heart.

A few minutes later my phone buzzes.

I'm outside.

I kiss Rieta goodnight and promise to call her if I need anything, day or night, no judgment from her. I hug her fiercely, overwhelmed by gratitude that I don't have to carry this secret alone anymore.

A surreal feeling sweeps over me as I close the front door and see Laz standing out in the street, leaning against a lamppost with his hands in his jeans pockets. The pose is relaxed, but I sense the tension in his body. His eyes don't leave my face as I walk toward him and stop two feet away.

This is as close as I dare approach him when anyone might be watching.

We stare at each other for a long time. Our secret's not just ours anymore. We've given up control and now someone else knows, and we can't predict what happens next.

"We feel real now," I whisper. "You and me."

A smile hooks the corner of his mouth. "You've always been real to me, Bambi." His glimmering gaze drops to my mouth, and in a husky voice he says, "Fuck, I really want to kiss you right now."

"Me, too."

He squeezes his eyes shut and groans. "This is torture."

"Rieta won't tell anyone. She's on our side. But, Laz, please don't . . ."

He frowns. "Don't what?"

I reach out and tug the zipper of his jacket, pleading with him.

"Don't get hurt because of me."

Laz gazes at me from beneath his lashes. "I want to be with you. Always. What do you think about that?"

My stomach erupts in a riot of butterflies and rainbows, but I force myself to stay calm. "Why?"

"Do you need me to spell it out for you?"

I am hungry for every drop of him. Every word he wants to give me. "A girl likes to know."

He pins me with his green gaze. "Because I'm falling in love with you, and with every day that passes, I fall harder still."

I almost throw myself into his arms. "Really? You mean that?"

"I'll say it every day until you believe me. I'll say it every hour if I have to."

"I'm falling in love with you, too," I whisper.

The two feet of space between us feels like an endless chasm.

"How are we going to be together?" I ask.

My lover just blinks slowly. "Would you do anything for us, Bambi? I want to know how far you'd go for us to be together."

The pain of not touching him is throbbing in my chest. "Whatever it takes. Whatever we have to do. But I don't want anyone to die," I add quickly.

He shakes his head. "No one's going to die."

"Especially not you." I know he thinks he's going to die young, but if the Rosetti men are cursed, then we'll break that curse together.

"If my plan works, I'll get my inheritance and you'll be protected from your family. It will be an ordeal when the time comes, but we can get through it together."

"And if it doesn't work?"

"We're tough, you and me. We'll find a way to make it work."

We *are* tough. We're as tough as goddamn nails. "Then I trust you to do whatever it takes."

A dark, triumphant gleam comes into his eyes, and his smile grows cold and a little scary.

Just what is he going to do? Now I'm worried. "Maybe you should tell me what your plan is, after all."

He puts his head on one side, regarding me in silence. "No. I don't think I will. It's best you leave everything up to me. Now come on, let's get going." He nods toward home, and we start walking side by side.

"Are you sure you don't need my help with anything?"

Laz gazes down at me as we walk along, smiling his mysterious smile. "No, Bambi. Not a thing. Just keep being your adorable, beautiful self, and everything will work out perfectly."

As the weeks go by, Laz and I hone our subterfuge. We ignore each other at home whenever anyone else is around, but the second we're alone, we're all over each other. He screws me so many times in my bed that I lose count of how many orgasms I have. It's loving and it's beautiful, but there are no two ways around it.

We don't make love.

We fuck.

Desperately.

Furiously.

The nights I'm meant to be working, we spend together. Sometimes at a hotel. Sometimes just driving around together, listening to the radio, and holding hands. For the first time in my life, I'm happy. Genuinely—complicatedly—happy. I'm being a terrible person by anyone's measure, but I can't bring myself to care.

Being a good girl never brought me anything but misery.

Being Laz's bad girl has set me free.

Not everything's angels and cupcakes, though. Late at night, I hear Mom and Laz fighting. I can't make out the words, but I know what it's about. He won't sleep with her.

He doesn't like to talk about it with me, but he's said enough to make me understand that for a few weeks he was able to make excuses for not having sex, or he pretended to be asleep, but Mom's starting to get frustrated.

When Mom's frustrated, she throws things. Two vases and three wine glasses have bit the dust in the last two weeks.

I lie awake in bed listening to them arguing, but it's worse when they finally go silent because I start to imagine that he's given in and he's having sex with her just to make her shut up. For hours I lie awake imagining them doing it. Picturing him coming to me and confessing what he did. How I'll cry, and he'll beg me to forgive him. It's pure agony, but I can't make myself stop.

One morning, I'm a zombie in the kitchen as I make coffee, and tears keep threatening to spill down my cheeks. I heard them arguing again last night and then they went ominously silent. I'm so tired and overwrought that I've already half accepted that they've had sex, and it's only a matter of time before Laz confirms that my nightmare is real.

He comes into the kitchen, and the sight of him is enough to make a lump rise in my throat.

"Bambi? What's wrong, are you sick?"

I shake my head and open my mouth to beg him to tell me it didn't happen, but then Mom sweeps into the room in her red silk kimono, and I swallow all the words I was going to say. They burn down my throat and make my stomach ache.

Behind her back, he gives me a desperate look and crosses his heart with his forefinger. He didn't.

He wouldn't.

I believe him, but how long can we go on like this?

Over dinner that night, Mom's in an uncharacteristically good mood. We eat braised beef in red wine with fried potatoes, but the food feels so heavy in my stomach that I can only manage a few mouthfuls and spend the rest of the meal picking at my plate.

Laz seems to have tuned out, and answers in monosyllables whenever Mom asks him a question.

I focus on counting the number of baby onions in my stew until Mom draws me out of my reverie by repeatedly saying my name.

I glance up. "Sorry, what?"

"I said I have a question for you both."

My near-empty stomach convulses. For me and Laz? "What question?"

Laz shoots me a glance and I realize how panicked I sound.

"I want to know what you both think of a date I've chosen for an event." Her eyes flash, and there's an edge to her voice. Like I care about any day of the year apart from the anniversary of my father's death.

"What event?" Laz asks.

"Our three-month anniversary. I thought we could invite my family. Yours."

Laz gazes blankly at Mom. "Why?"

"Because it's our three-month anniversary," Mom says, louder, as if Laz is deaf or stupid. "We can celebrate, and a family party will remind us of what our duties are." She glares at him, and my insides shrivel up in horror as I realize what duties she's talking about. Mom will get Laz's brothers on his back about him not sleeping with her.

"I'll ask Fabrizio if he can bring a single man for Mia, seeing as Drago Lastra apparently wasn't suitable," Mom says.

Laz's expression is suddenly murderous. Under the table, I dig my nails into my thigh. How is Mom not picking up on the jealousy that's suddenly a raging tornado spinning around the room? "Don't bother, please."

"I didn't ask for your permission or your opinion. I only want to know if the twenty-third is suitable because that's the date I've chosen." Mom turns to Laz. "Well, darling?"

He drags his eyes away from me and back to her. "What?"

"The *date*. It would be wonderful if we had something to announce, but that's out of my control, apparently," she mutters.

"Something to announce," Laz repeats, glancing speculatively at me, and I think he must be considering telling everyone about us.

I can only imagine what mayhem that will cause with all his brothers and my uncles present. There will probably be blood spilled on the dance floor.

He turns to Mom. "The twenty-third? Sure. Can't wait."

Chapter Thirteen

MIA

Rieta stops dead in my bedroom doorway. "Wow, you're glowing."

"I know," I mutter in annoyance, slapping my cheeks and scowling at my reflection in the dresser mirror. "This is *terrible*."

It's the afternoon of Mom's stupid party, and I'm wearing the oyster chiffon dress Mom picked out for me. I styled my hair plainly and barely applied any makeup. I thought I'd look like shit, considering how badly I've been sleeping, but my complexion seems lit from within.

I swish my hair around my face in an unflattering way, but it's no use. I'm radiant.

Rieta's mouth twitches. "Been, uh, well satisfied lately?"

I shoot her an annoyed look. "Rieta, please."

"That's a yes."

It sure is a yes. Laz has been finding creative ways and places to get me off. If the man Fabrizio brings as my suitor falls to his knees and begs for my hand in marriage at first sight, it will be all my lover's fault.

Laz himself appears behind Rieta in a black shirt and black pants. He absolutely refused to wear a suit, but Mom pestered him into a button-down. He looks absolutely delicious.

My sister gives him a knowing smile and says, "I'll wait downstairs."

She's driving us to the venue as she's decided she's not drinking anymore while she's trying for a baby. Mom's already there, so there's just me and Laz upstairs.

Laz gives a low whistle as he walks slowly toward me. "Bambi, you look drop-dead gorgeous."

"It's ridiculous. I should look how I feel, which is like crap."

His brows draw together in concern. "You feel sick?"

I rub the heel of my hand across my belly and grimace. "Yeah. This party is stressing me out. I haven't been able to eat much all week because I'm nervous."

"You've got nothing to worry about. Just be your beautiful self and I'll handle everything."

"You can't stop Mom from pushing some man at me."

"Oh, yes, I can." His hand drifts up my ribs and he squeezes my breast. I gasp in pain and pull away.

"Shit, sorry. Bambi. Are you sore? Are you getting your period?"

Short of punching my suitor in the face and marching him out of the party, I don't know what Laz can do about him. "I guess. I think I'm late, actually."

"You are? How late?"

I grab a lipstick and shove it in my clutch. Why does my head feel so cloudy? I wish I could crawl back in bed for a nap. "A few days, I guess. I didn't even get my period last month. I heard that you can miss your period if you're stressed and I've not been sleeping well lately. Even when I do sleep, I'm so tired the next day."

I should go to the doctor in case my prescription is messing with me and I need a different one. I expect Laz to berate me for not taking care of myself, but for some reason he cups my face with both hands and kisses me with passion.

A craving for this man sweeps over me. I didn't realize how badly I needed a kiss like this. When he pulls away, I ask, "What was that for?"

Laz smooths my hair back, panting slightly as he gazes down at me. "Because you're beautiful. Now, come on. Let's get this stupid party over with."

We arrive at the venue twenty minutes later and park. Mom's rented a room with an enormous terrace, and a long table is set for fifty people. Everyone important in the Bianchi and Rosetti families is here.

I glance at the trays of champagne, wondering if I can get away with swiping one. I probably could, but my stomach threatens to rebel, so I ask at the bar for a sparkling water and lemon instead.

One of my uncle's wives corners me and begins aggressively singing the praises of the man I'm going to meet today. Meanwhile, across the room, Laz appears relaxed as he lounges against a pillar chatting with Mom's eldest nephew.

Mom appears at his side and takes his hand, and calls to the guests that it's time to eat.

Laz stares at her hand holding his. Suddenly, he lifts his head and raises his voice. "Actually, I have an announcement to make before we eat."

Mom looks at him in surprise.

My guts suddenly knot.

Everyone in the room turns their attention to Laz and the room falls silent.

My lover gazes slowly around at the crowd. "When I married Giulia, my brothers hoped it would mean their wild baby brother would finally settle down."

There's a smattering of polite laughter, but none of it's from Laz's brothers. Fabrizio narrows his eyes. He clearly wasn't expecting or desiring Laz to make a speech.

"All my brothers, especially Faber, have been hoping that I'll become a father. Okay, I'll admit it didn't appeal to me at first." Laz smiles disarmingly at the crowd, and there's more polite laughter. "But I've come around to the idea, thanks to one special woman, and I want everyone to know that I'm ready. I want a family of my own."

Rieta shoots me a confused look and edges closer to whisper, "He's planning on staying with Mom? Mom's having his baby?"

The sick feeling in my stomach quadruples and my hands start to sweat. My soul feels like it's being crushed beneath an unrelenting weight. Laz swore all this time that they weren't having sex. He promised.

Mom smiles up at him, confused but pleased. She's seeing her husband in a whole new light. He's attentive. He's taking charge. She practically purrs, "Darling, I'm so pleased to hear you talking this way."

Heartbroken tears sting my eyes.

A handful of people step forward and start congratulating the happy couple.

Mom laughs and waves them off. "Don't congratulate us. There's no baby on the way just yet."

Laz's eyebrows lift in surprise. "What are you talking about, Giulia? The baby will be here soon. In about eight months, in fact."

The smile drops from Mom's face. "But I'm not pregnant yet."

"No, you're not." Laz's gaze swings to me, trying to disappear on the other side of the room. "But Mia is. Mia's having my baby."

My world contracts to a shocking pinpoint.

Confused heads turn to stare at me.

I'm *what*?

I stare at Laz across a sea of people. His handsome face is calm and his expression steady. My stomach is pitching back and forth like a ship on high seas, and the sparkling water and lemon has turned sour in my mouth.

Come to think of it, everything's tasted weird lately, and my stomach has been so upset, but that's because of nerves. It couldn't possibly be because I'm . . .

Sore breasts.

Missed periods.

Tired.

Nauseated.

And yet I'm glowing.

I start shaking my head and backing away, but I run into a pillar.

It's not true.

It can't be true.

The silence is broken when Mom rips her hand from Laz's and screams. No words, just a long, angry shriek.

Uncle Tomaso appears at my side and grabs my wrist, squeezing painfully. "Is this true? What have you got to say for yourself, you shameful whore?"

"Don't you dare talk to the mother of my child that way," Laz growls, pushing through the crowd toward us. "You have anything to say, you say it to me."

Suddenly everyone is talking. Exclaiming. Gesticulating.

I'm trapped in a nightmare.

"I have a question," Laz shouts over the din, and everyone slowly falls silent. "My brothers were so desperate for me to marry into the Bianchi family. What I want to know is, why I wasn't offered Mia in the first place."

Uncle Marzio and Uncle Roberto exchange glances. Marzio frowns and replies, "We didn't think of Mia."

Laz stares around at everyone, his eyes glittering. "That's the problem with this family. No one ever thinks of Mia. I don't understand why none of you even considered her when she's closer to my age. Did you know she's funny as well? That she's clever? She's got a witty comeback for everything. She drives like a goddamn demon, and you know what else? She's beautiful, and I'm in love with her."

Laz turns slowly on the spot, gazing into the astonished faces of his family and mine.

"Is it such a shock that anyone could love Mia?"

No one replies.

"You can all tell yourselves that this is some scandal or mistake, but it's not going to change anything. Mia's mine, and she's having my baby. You can all drink your wine, eat your canapés, and go to hell."

He stalks over to me and takes my hand, and the anger melts from his face. With a tender expression in his eyes, he murmurs softly, "You okay, Bambi?"

I stare at my hand in his, hyperaware that everyone's watching us. "I'm not pregnant."

"I'm pretty sure you are," he replies.

"I can't be. I'm on birth control."

"Yeah, about that." Laz pushes his tongue into his cheek like he's ashamed about something, but he ruins it by smiling. There's not a trace of honest regret in his handsome face. Actually, he seems pretty damn pleased with himself.

"I may have messed with your birth control."

I remember how Laz reacted when he found out I was on the pill. He immediately started hunting through my things in search of the prescription, and he wanted me to give it up right there and then. Ever since, he's been obsessed with coming inside me every time we have sex. He actually stops blow jobs so he can finish in my pussy, and then he *stays* there. Keeping his cum inside me. It's not a fetish.

It's a goddamn *tactic*.

"You did what?" I say in a low and deadly voice.

Laz has been watching me like a hawk for weeks and repeatedly asking how I'm feeling. It didn't strike me as odd at the time.

"The packets are fake. All sugar pills."

"You sabotaged my birth control and didn't tell me? I'm pregnant, and I didn't even know it?" I shove his chest with both hands. "I might have gotten drunk. I could have done cocaine."

Laz reaches for me, but I shrug out of his grip. "Bambi, you don't do coke—"

I clench both my hands into fists and scream at the top of my lungs, "That's not the point. The point is you did this behind my back. You are unbelievable, Lazzaro Rosetti!"

"Take it easy, Bambi. It's not good for the baby."

I scream again.

His baby.

I'm carrying his goddamn *baby*.

This was the plan he was hinting about these past few months. I cover my face with my hands, wishing I could disappear. Laz reaches for me once more, but I pull myself out of his grip.

"We are not okay, asshole. Don't follow me."

"Bambi, please—"

He tries to take my hand again, but Rieta steps in front of him, an angry lioness staring him down. "She said don't follow her."

Over her shoulder, Mom is staring at me, white-faced and her hands clenched. Actually, everyone is staring at me, and I want to shrivel up and die.

Rieta grabs my hand. "Come on, let's get out of here."

I keep my head down and let her lead the way. As soon as we burst out into fresh air, I gasp, "I need a pregnancy test."

"I've got plenty. I'll take us to my place."

On the drive there, I keep picturing the way Mom looked just now. "Did you see Mom's expression? She looked like she wanted to kill me."

Rieta shakes her head. "That's not fair. You obviously didn't know he was going to announce it like that."

"I didn't even know there was a possibility I could be pregnant. I'm on birth control! Or I thought I was. Laz messed with my pills."

"He did *what?*" Rieta looks as outraged as I feel. "You're eighteen years old. You're still his stepdaughter. What was he thinking?"

"What was he thinking? What was *I* thinking? I was screwing my stepfather."

Rieta is silent a moment while she drives. "I thought the two of you were kind of romantic, like Romeo and Juliet. I knew it would be a load of drama when the time came for everyone to find out about the two of you, but I didn't think Laz would go out of his way to make it as hurtful and dramatic as possible. Why did he do it that way?"

I scrub both my hands over my face. "I can guess. If I'm pregnant, Mom can't drive a wedge between the two of us. He's fulfilling his promise to his brothers to settle down and have a family. They'll put pressure on Mom to divorce Laz so we can make this Rosetti baby legitimate and then they'll finally hand over his inheritance."

It's a good plan.

The only problem is that I hate it.

At Rieta's house, she leads me upstairs to the bathroom and hands me a pregnancy test and explains how to use it.

I close the door behind me and take the test, and then leave it on the vanity, face down, to develop. "You can come back in."

Rieta opens the door, and we stand side by side waiting for the results.

"If you are pregnant . . ." she begins.

I tip my head back and moan. "I'll kill him."

"I know you're angry, but if you think about it, this could actually be wonderful. You love him. He loves you."

There's so much hope in my sister's face. I can tell she's already half in love with the idea of me having Laz's baby. "But he tricked me. This isn't how it was meant to be."

Her face falls, and she nods. "I understand. Sorry, I'm baby crazy right now. I'm not thinking straight."

I reach out and take her hand. I wish with all my heart it was her test we were waiting on. That these were her pregnancy symptoms and her loving husband who was possibly going to be a father.

"Shall we look?" Rieta asks, and even though she's trying not to hope, she's practically crossing her fingers and bouncing on her toes.

I take a deep breath.

And flip over the test.

Chapter Fourteen

LAZ

Faber and Firenze grab me as I try to follow Mia out of the party. My eldest brother's expression is filled with cold fury, while Firenze looks like he's swallowed a lemon and a couple of rusty nails.

"Get your hands off me," I growl, but they drag me into a side room and throw me onto a sofa, standing over me like I'm a disobedient child.

"Are you serious? Did you get your stepdaughter pregnant?" Faber seethes.

"I don't know yet. That's what I'm on my way to find out."

I try to stand up, but Firenze pushes me back. "Screwing your wife's daughter. You are unbelievable, Lazzaro."

"Hey, I was only doing as I was instructed. Settle down, Lazzaro. Start a family, Lazzaro. You two are never fucking satisfied."

I haven't got time for this. Mia needs me, so I duck under Firenze's arms and stalk toward the door.

"Where are you going?" calls Firenze.

"To find my woman and ask if she's having my baby."

"What about your *wife*?" Faber replies.

"You like her so much? You talk to her. I have nothing to say to that snake. The next time I hear her name, I'll be signing divorce papers."

Faber growls in frustration. "I'm not helping you. You are on your own with this shit. You've made your bed, now you lie in it."

Bitterness floods my mouth, and I turn back to glare at him. "What about my inheritance?"

"You can kiss that goodbye."

My hands curl into fists, and I consider throwing a punch at my brother's handsome face. I can feel him wanting me to hit him and justify all his bullshit. "You know what? I don't care. As long as I have Mia and our baby, nothing else matters."

Faber's expression goes slack with shock as I stride out of the room.

That's right, asshole. I'm not going to let you control me anymore. I'll find a way to make my ambitions come true on my own.

Everyone's crowded around a sobbing Giulia as I pass by the party guests and head out the door. I don't have my car, so I guess I'll walk until I can flag a taxi down. Rieta will have taken Mia to her house, so that's where I'll go.

I make it three blocks before I hear someone behind me.

"Hey, asshole."

I roll my eyes and don't bother turning around. I recognize the voice of Marzio Bianchi, and I can guess what he wants. "Not now. Fight me after I've talked to Mia. I'll even let you take the first swing."

"You're a dead man, Rosetti," Marzio growls, and footsteps pound on the sidewalk.

I dodge to one side, and he goes flying past me, but before I can pat myself on the back for getting the better of him, someone else grabs me and shoves me into an alley.

Tomaso Bianchi, with Roberto behind him. Tomaso snatches up a piece of two-by-four and brandishes it like a baseball bat. Marzio blocks my exit.

I look from one brother to the next and then glance behind me. Dead end. I'm penned in. These men aren't wannabe kick-fighting himbos. They're grade-A murderous assholes, and this situation is too sticky for my taste.

I guess I'll make them so angry they can't think.

"I'm on my way to find out whether Mia's pregnant or not. Don't you want to know how much I've shamed your family before you beat me to a pulp?"

"I always hated your fucking face," Marzio sneers. "It's about time we rearranged it for you."

"Like I rearranged your niece's guts?" I ask with a smirk.

All three men turn shades of red and purple.

Roberto lunges at me, and I plaster my back against the alley wall. He stumbles past me, and I duck as Marzio tries to grab me.

I'm about to push past them all and make a break for freedom when Tomaso smashes the two-by-four into my temple. Pain erupts through my skull, and black spots rage before my eyes.

Jesus *fuck*.

It would be too easy to pass out right now.

But I'm not going down like this.

I'm getting to Mia before these gargoyles do.

I fight my way through the men, just clinging to consciousness with my arm raised above my head to protect myself from more blows.

But I'm not thinking about my legs.

Marzio kicks me sharply in the knee, and my leg crumples uselessly under me.

I try to crawl toward the alley entrance, but they all start kicking me in the guts and kidneys. They're not going to just hurt me. These men are going to murder me and bury my body in a shallow grave.

Mia.

I have to get to Mia.

Tomaso raises the plank of wood above his head, malice burning in his eyes, and I know I'm finished.

Just another dead Rosetti with his blood running over the dirty, wet streets of this godforsaken city.

I'm so sorry, Bambi.

I wanted more than anything to stay. I . . .

. . . love you.

Shards of glass are driving their way through my skull. Strobe lights are pulsing in the darkness behind my closed eyes.

If this is death, it sucks.

I slowly drag my eyelids open and see the world from a strange angle. I'm lying on a cold concrete floor. There's not a lot of light wherever I am, but I can see a grille in front of my face like I'm in a cage.

I lift my head and take a look around, groaning as my heartbeat pounds in my ear, my temple, and the back of my skull. Everywhere those assholes beat me.

Yeah. It's a cage. A storage cage where you might lock up valuable things like wine, but a cage just the same.

"Look who's awake. Hello, Sleeping Beauty." Marzio gets up from a chair and strolls across the cellar toward me, a gloating smile on his face.

I push my fingers through the metal grille and drag myself up to sitting. The world spins and my stomach threatens to turn itself inside out. I haven't taken a beating like this in years. My face must be red and purple, and I probably have a concussion.

I cautiously move my limbs and extremities. No broken ribs, legs, or fingers that I can tell. All I have to do it break out of here, get a weapon in my hands, and beat Giulia's brothers to death with it.

I glance up and around. Easier said than done. The cage goes all the way to the ceiling and is bolted into the floor. There's one door with a massive padlock. Everything looks shiny, new, and strong.

I turn my attention to the piece of shit in front of me. "Either kill me or stop wasting my time. I need to talk to Mia."

"That girl is none of your business, and she doesn't want to speak to you."

I haul myself to my feet and rattle the bars of the cage as hard as I can. "That's a lie!"

Marzio pulls a baseball bat from behind his back and slams it over my fingers. I gasp in pain and yank them back through the grille, lose my balance, and fall painfully to one knee.

"Listen up, you piece of shit. You're never laying eyes on that girl again. You're never seeing daylight again. You're going to rot down here."

We'll see about that. I wonder why they haven't killed me, but I suppose they can't murder a Rosetti without bringing Faber's wrath down on their heads. They're stuck with me until they can figure out what to do with me.

Which gives me time to figure out an escape.

Marzio flashes a nasty smile and heads toward the door.

"Wait. I need to take a piss," I call after him.

"What do you think the bucket is for?"

There's one empty bucket in my cell, and one with some scummy-looking water. Great. Just great.

I splash water on my face to get the blood off and take a drink, then lie down on the cold floor. The world spins around me, and I close my eyes, vowing to make every Bianchi but Mia pay for what they're doing to me.

Mia.

I've left her at the center of a clusterfuck and she's all alone.

I must pass out again because the next thing I hear are high-heeled footsteps approaching. There's an ominous ring to the sound.

I crack open an eye and see a dark-haired woman dressed in a red pantsuit, heavy gold jewelry around her neck and in her ears. I wonder how angry she is with me.

My wife lays a stack of papers on the table near the door and folds her arms across her chest, gazing down at me like I'm a worm. "You just keep on digging that grave for yourself, don't you, Lazzaro? Look at you down there. Almost six feet under already. Soon it will be time to shovel dirt over your rotting corpse."

I'd say her anger is about a ten.

Too bad I don't give two fucks. I haul myself upright, my head spinning. "I need to speak to Mia."

Giulia examines her manicure. She's got fresh red polish, I notice. My wife has entered her supervillain era.

She's trying to appear casual, but she's burning up from the inside. "Mia this. Mia that. It's been like that ever since you entered my house. Why are you so obsessed with my daughter? Why is it that every time she's in the room, all you can look at is *her*?"

"Because I love her."

Giulia sneers and rolls her eyes. "Please. Stop making up stupid stories. You're a lowlife piece of shit who fucked around in my house, and you're finding out what happens to unfaithful men."

Like she's so perfect. "I love her. You do remember what love feels like, don't you, Giulia?"

She pinches her brow. "I don't care what—"

"Mia's father. You were in love with that kitchenhand."

"Restaurant owner," she says through her teeth.

I think I've touched a nerve. "If I'd had the chance to meet Mia and get to know her before I married you, I would have—"

Giulia slams her palm against my cage. "You would have what? Passed over me for that little slut?"

This poisonous bitch. There's no telling what she calls Mia to her face while I'm stuck in here. I stand up, my chest heaving with fury. "Don't talk about Mia that way."

She rolls her eyes. "Please. Like you care how I talk about Mia. All you care about is tainting my family with your shame."

"I don't know how I'm going to get this through your thick skull. Let me break it down into tiny fucking sentences. I love Mia. Mia's the one I want. Not you. Not revenge. Not anything else. Just Mia and my baby."

Giulia stares at me like I've gone crazy. "You really expect me to believe that? Fabrizio has told me everything. You live to cause trouble, and you always have."

She didn't deny that there's a baby.

Mia's pregnant.

I want to shout with joy and jump around my cage, but now is not the time.

I growl in frustration and push my fingers through my hair. "For fuck's sake, Giulia. Is someone loving Mia so impossible to you? If you'd paid one scrap of attention to your youngest daughter you would have seen that not only is she beautiful, but she's sensitive, sweet, and funny as well. How could I not fall for her?"

Giulia's shaking her head, but she's turning pale.

"Mia is ten times the woman you are. Maybe she's the black

sheep of your family, but I'm going to make her the queen of mine. When I get out of here, I'm divorcing you, marrying her, and getting the hell out of here with my wife and baby."

"Your baby? We'll see about that," she seethes.

"What?"

Giulia recovers from her shock and her eyes glow with malice. "Mia is not going to make the same mistake as her mother. She'll make the sensible decision, and then forget all about you. In fact, we've already talked it over this afternoon when I showed her my divorce papers. We're both washing our hands of you."

My blood runs cold. "What do you mean?"

"The world doesn't need any more Lazzaro Rosettis."

I start breathing faster. "Mia would never do that to our baby. She knows this is all part of the plan for us to be together. She trusted me to make this happen for us."

Giulia smiles wider, glee etched in every line of her face. "Mia's been crying on my shoulder night and morning about how you tricked her into getting pregnant. What a cruel and stupid man you are, Lazzaro. Do you suppose that any woman on the planet could forgive you for such an appalling thing?"

I expected Mia to be angry with me. I knew she'd shout and call me names, but I thought once we got through that, she'd see that it solved all our problems.

I'm locked in a cage, and I can't remind her she's loved. Our baby is loved. She's not alone because she has me.

"Mia, darling," Giulia says in an affected voice. "I'm so sorry that your twisted, disgusting stepfather was sleeping with both of us, trying to get us both pregnant. You got caught up in his sick plan to humiliate the Bianchis. And now where is he? He's run away."

My chest heaves. "You lying bitch. I haven't laid a finger on you in months."

Giulia gives an eloquent shrug, smiling from ear to ear. "That's not what she thinks now, and who's going to tell her otherwise? Who's going to tell Mia that she's loved and she should keep the baby?" She glances up and down my black-and-blue body, scorn filling her eyes. "You?"

I slam my fists against the bars, trying to smash my way through them and get to her. "Why are you doing this, Giulia? Why can't you let us be happy? You don't care about me, and you never have."

"You humiliated me in front of my friends and family. I'm the laughingstock of this city, and you're going to pay for my humiliation. First, I'm going to make you suffer, and then every trace of you is going to be wiped off this planet. It will be like you never existed. It's not like you achieved anything in your worthless life. No one is going to mourn you. Not me. Not your brothers. Not your precious Mia."

This bitch really knows how to go in for the kill. "My brothers will wage war on your family if you murder me in cold blood. They hate me most of the time, but blood is blood."

"Maybe. Maybe not. I guess we'll find out." Giulia turns on her heel and strolls out with the confidence of a woman who's getting everything she wants.

Rage boils over in my chest, and I shout after her, "You don't know your daughter very well if you think she believed anything you said to her about me."

My wife turns back to me. "I've known my daughter for eighteen years. I know every single one of her weaknesses. Her fears. Do you really think that you learned all there is to know about my daughter while she was giving you a lap dance in a lilac wig?"

I wasn't expecting that, and Giulia smirks as she witnesses my shock. There's no way that Mia told her mom about working as a stripper. There's no *way*.

Giulia gives me a pitying smile. "Don't fool yourself that you know Mia better than I do, Lazzaro."

I beat my fist against the bars. "I want to talk to Mia."

"In your dreams. Enjoy your little holiday down here. While it lasts."

I stick my fingers through the bars of the cage and rattle them. "Then I want to talk to Rieta. Send Rieta down here."

Rieta is the only other reasonable member of this family, and she knows how much Mia and I care for each other. She'll be mad at me for the trick I pulled with the birth control pills, but she'll listen to me. I'll explain that it was the only way for Mia and me to marry and become a family.

She starts walking again. "What you want doesn't matter anymore."

"Screw you, Giulia." I pull the wedding ring off my finger and throw it through the bars. It bounces twice, rolls across the concrete, and comes to rest at her feet.

My wife glances at it, and just keeps on walking.

As Giulia disappears through the door, I hear her say, "You can go in now. I'm finished with him. Get the papers signed before you break all his fingers."

A moment later, Marzio, Tomaso, and Roberto step into the basement. All three of them are carrying baseball bats and are wearing protective gear.

I sneer at them. Three against one, and they're still terrified I'm going kill them with my bare hands. "You three stink of fear."

Roberto unlocks the cage and steps back. "Come on then, dickhead. Fight your way out of here if you can."

All three are hitting their palms with their bats. I stare past them to freedom. Mia's out there.

I pull open the door and step out of the cage, unarmed and unprotected, and spread my arms, the hunger to get to my girl fueling my appetite to fight.

"Bring it on, assholes."

Chapter Fifteen

MIA

"Here."

Rieta puts a mug of milky tea into my hands and sits down beside me on the sofa. Her expression is creased with sympathy as she asks, "How are you feeling?"

It's been three days since Rieta and I stood side by side in her bathroom, staring at the positive pregnancy test. People talk about time standing still when you receive a shock, but it didn't happen that way for me.

Everything started rushing too fast. Out of my control.

I don't remember it, but apparently I was screaming, *I am going to kill you, Lazzaro Rosetti.*

When I came back into myself, I was holding two pieces of the broken test in each hand.

Now, I don't feel anything. I stare into my cup of tea, wishing for a way to make everything make sense.

"Still not heard anything from Laz?" Rieta asks, glancing at my blank phone screen.

"Nothing," I whisper bleakly.

Not a goddamn word from the man who knocked me up without my consent.

After Rieta and I left the party, Laz ran out as well. My uncles tried to chase him down, but Laz lost them in some alleyways, and no one's heard from him since. Rieta told me that Fabrizio Rosetti has been around at Mom's practically on his knees apologizing for what his baby brother has done. Apparently, Laz isn't as unreliable, irresponsible, and reckless as we were led to believe.

He's worse.

But that's no surprise to me. Anyone who can mess with someone's birth control while he's married to someone else must be out of his goddamn mind.

"Mom called again," Rieta says, almost apologetically.

I flinch as I'm speared with guilt. I've received several voicemails from Mom and a dozen messages.

I don't blame you, darling.
It's not your fault, it's mine.
I should never have trusted him in our home.

Lazzaro is a master manipulator.
A cruel man who wanted to humiliate us all for fun.
I'll never forgive him for what he's done to you.
I'm so, so sorry.

I've been at Rieta's for three days, too eaten up with shame to face Mom. It would be easier if she were furious with me and screaming for my blood. Her understanding and sympathy are only making me feel worse.

Rieta's phone vibrates, and then the front doorbell rings. She glances at her phone and sighs. "It's Mom. I told her to stay away until you were ready."

"Maybe I should talk to her. I have to face her eventually." I put down my tea, grab a cushion, and thrust it against my belly. "Oh, God," I moan.

"Are you feeling sick?"

"Yes, but not because I'm pregnant." I take a deep breath. "Let her in. I should get this over with."

"If you're sure," Rieta says doubtfully, and goes to open the door.

I'm sitting on the edge of the sofa with my hands clamped on either side of me when Mom comes into the room. Her cheeks are streaked with mascara tears, and she looks pallid without her usual bright lipstick.

"Oh, my poor baby," she cries, and goes down on her knees before me, capturing my hands in hers. "You dear, sweet child. How could he do this to you?"

It's hard to look at her like this. She should be yelling and screaming, not being sympathetic toward me. "Mom, please get up off the floor."

"To be abandoned by a man in your time of need. He's too cruel. I can't imagine what you must be feeling."

"Mom, I'm begging you. Sit down, please."

Rieta comes to my rescue, helping Mom up and onto the sofa while Mom wails about Laz.

Suddenly, she clenches my hands even tighter, her eyes wild with grief and anger. "Tell me the truth. Did he force you? Did that animal abuse my daughter under my nose?"

I yank my hands from hers. "No! It wasn't like that."

But there's a nagging voice in the back of my mind.

Laz didn't always ask before he touched you. That first night you found him in your bed, he got his hands all over you and then held you down and forced more orgasms from you.

And when he took your virginity on the hood of his car, he didn't listen when you tried to tell him to slow down.

He replaced your birth control pills with sugar pills.

Only an abuser would do that.

I made excuses for the things Laz did, but did I overlook his sinister behavior because he's so handsome and charming?

Mom strokes my hair, her touch loving. "You look scared, darling. Whatever you say about him, I'll believe you, no questions asked. I'll hold your hand at the police station and back you up no matter what."

Over her shoulder, Rieta is chewing her lip, her eyes huge.

It's what I've always wanted, Mom's unconditional love and support. I see suddenly how I could find my way back into my family's good graces after my terrible behavior.

Point the finger of accusation at Laz.

Blame everything on the man they are already primed to hate.

Laz was far from an angel, but in my heart I know what I did, and I'm not going to pretend otherwise.

I shake my head. "It wasn't like that. We're both to blame for what happened. I knew sleeping with Laz was wrong, but I did it anyway."

Mom reaches into her oversized handbag and draws out a handful of garments that I recognize with a jolt. "Are you sure? Because I found these in your room."

Tasha's lilac wig. Tasha's see-through high-heeled stripper shoes. Tasha's white G-string. Seeing those gaudy items in the light of day in my mother's hands makes me break out in a cold sweat.

"Darling, tell the truth. What did he make you do?"

"Laz didn't do anything. I bought these ages ago. I was stripping for weeks before you even met him."

"You were stripping? But why?" Mom's expression is horrified.

I wish I didn't have to go into this right now. There's nothing else to say but the unvarnished truth, so I go ahead and tell her that I took the job because I hated being at home. I wanted to leave as soon as I could.

Mom's expression turns sour as she listens to me. "You're protecting Lazzaro. I know you are."

I take my stripper clothes from her hands and shove them to the other end of the couch behind me. "If you don't believe me, you can call Peppers. The bouncer Jimmy will tell you everything you want to know."

"Lazzaro knew about this, though, didn't he?"

"Mom, you're a broken record. Not everything is about Laz."

"Did he ever come to the club?"

That's private. That's just between me and Laz. But he stripped all my defenses away when he disappeared, and even though I want to tell Mom it's none of her business, she can see the truth as clear as day on my face. "Just once, but—"

Mom shoots to her feet and cries in outrage, "Did he pay you to dance for him?"

"He . . . I . . ." Tears are brimming on my lashes. Furious tears of hurt and pain.

How could you leave me behind to face this on my own, Laz?

Where *are* you?

Rieta pulls Mom back from me so I have space to breathe again. "That's enough, Mom. Leave Mia alone."

"I'm just trying to talk to my own daughter about—"

But Rieta's not having it. "Give her a break. She's pregnant, remember? Everyone, just take a moment to calm down. Would you like some coffee, Mom?"

Mom says yes, but she doesn't go with Rieta. She stands over me, staring at me in cold, furious silence.

Laz promised me that no one would die because of his plan, but if I ever get my hands on him, I think I'm going to kill him.

Once Rieta hands Mom her coffee and sits down with us, Mom opens her handbag and pulls out a sheaf of documents.

"What are those?" Rieta asks.

"My divorce papers."

"They're not much use if you can't find Laz," Rieta points out.

"I'll sign them, and then I'll hand them over to a private detective who'll track Lazzaro down. I can't wait to have that man completely out of my life forever. It's going to feel wonderful." She toys with the papers and then glances at me. "What about you, Mia?"

"What about me?"

"Don't you think we should do something about getting rid of Lazzaro from your life?"

"He's very much not in my life, if you haven't noticed," I snap. If I did see him, what would I say to him?

Probably just scream at him.

Then a lot more screaming.

But after that?

I have no idea.

"No, darling. I mean . . ." Mom glances at my belly.

"The baby? What about the baby?"

"Don't you think you should . . ." She delicately raises an eyebrow.

My confusion clears, and realizing what she means, I reply coldly, "I'm keeping my baby."

"Shouldn't you think about this?" Mom asks.

I don't need to think. It doesn't matter what Laz did or how he tricked me, this baby is here, and it's mine.

Mom glances at Rieta, hoping for an ally, but Rieta looks on the verge of tears. Mom should know better than to have this conversation in front of her.

"Mia, this isn't a decision you should make too quickly."

"I've made up my mind. If you have anything else to say, let's talk about it later." I glance at my sister, who's wiping tears from her cheeks.

"It's okay, Mia. Promise." Rieta gives me a quick, unhappy smile.

It's not okay. Poor Rieta wants more than anything to have a baby, and now I'm sitting in her house, pregnant without even trying, while Mom tries to convince me to get rid of it. Why is the universe so cruel?

"You're going to let that man go on manipulating you even after he's disappeared?" Mom asks. "He's punishing both of us. He found out my greatest mistake and he's forcing you to repeat it."

My hands clench in my lap. "I'm your greatest mistake?"

Mom presses her lips together. "Don't be dramatic, darling. You know what I mean."

I know exactly what she means. She regretted having me, and I just have to live with that pain because she won't let me forget.

I'm not my mother. I'm me. I want this baby, and I'll never regret this child or make him or her think for one second—for one *fraction* of a second—that they're unwanted or unloved.

I wrap my arms around my stomach and hold on tight. There's only one thing I'm certain about in this shitty situation. This is my baby, and no one's taking them away from me.

"Stop being so selfish, Mia," Mom scolds. "A baby is supposed to be a cause for joy, not something conceived furtively while one of the parents is having an affair. You were born out of wedlock and my shameful behavior has been a stain on your existence ever since. Look me in the eye and tell me that's not true."

I turn and face her, meeting her gaze without flinching. "I'm perfectly aware that's true. You could have done so much to protect me from that pain, and you chose not to. Actually, you're the one who inflicted most of it."

We glare at each other in silence.

"I know you don't like me very much, Mia. I haven't been the most loving mother over the years, but please think carefully about what you're going to do next. Do you really want to turn into me?"

I can't help the fact that my child will be born into a family that will despise their existence. To them, this child will always be second class and hated.

But not to me.

"I'll never be like you," I whisper.

Mom stands up and puts her divorce papers back in her handbag, but she has to have the final word.

"You're young, Mia. You have your whole life ahead of you. Think very carefully about what happens next, because once this is done, it can never be undone."

Chapter Sixteen

LAZ

"Wakey, wakey, Lazzaro. Today's the day you get out of here."

I groan and roll painfully onto my side. Another night sleeping on the cold concrete floor hasn't done a thing for my aching bones.

I've occupied myself over the days . . . weeks? Could it have been a month already? I've spent my time doing press-ups, sits-ups, lunges, and throwing punches, when I have the strength. They've been giving me enough food and water to keep me alive, but no more. If an opportunity presents itself to escape, I'm pretty sure I'm going to need to fight my way out of here.

Marzio unlocks the door and stands back, a nasty light in his eyes. "Out you come."

"Oh, yeah? Where am I going next? I hope it's to your mom's place." I make myself sound as bored and disinterested as possible, but my heart is pounding as I get to my feet and saunter out of the cage. "Let's make it a trifecta. Mother, daughter, and grandmother."

Tomaso and Roberto are there, and from the looks of it, they didn't enjoy my crack about their mom. There's another man in the room, one I don't recognize, who's bigger than me, heavier than me, and from his beady eyes and the nasty twist to his mouth, a lot meaner than me, too. He's dressed in shorts and a black polo with its neck emblazoned with a sportswear brand. The way he's cracking his knuckles together sends an ominous feeling through me.

"This is your lucky day," Tomaso tells me with a grin, and holds a hand out to the strange man. "You're going to fight Rocco, and if you win, you get to go free."

I gaze around the dank basement, certain that I've never felt less lucky in my life. I'm fighting in here?

"What's wrong, Rosetti? Not interested in earning the glory you so clearly deserve?" Roberto asks, hatred twisting his face into something uglier than usual.

I stretch my arms lazily over my head, playing for time. Trying to figure out what's really going on. "Glory? Please. I need more witnesses to my glory than you fucks."

"Would we do you dirty like that?" Marzio asks. "We've got a fighting ring ready for you upstairs in the gym, and all our friends are invited to watch you get the shit beaten out of you."

So that's how it is. These brothers want to turn my demise into a spectacle.

Now that I'm out of that cage, even with dozens of these numbskulls' friends around, I might see an opportunity to escape. It's probably going to be my only chance.

"Fine. Let's do this." I shrug and head for the door, but Marzio stops me.

"Housekeeping first. I've got some forms for you to sign so we have proof that you willingly consent to this fight."

"I willingly consent to screwing your mom."

Tomaso sinks his fist into my stomach, and I double over coughing.

Eyes watering, I straighten up and say through my teeth, "Can no one take a joke? What forms? Fucking get on with it."

"Sign these and you can go." Marzio slaps a stack of papers and a pen onto a nearby table.

I take a look at them. They're covered in legalese. "What are they?"

"Divorce papers for Giulia. She wants to be able to say she got rid of you before you got your stupid ass killed. The release forms are for the fight. So your family won't come for us when we send them your dead body. Baby brother Rosetti died in a fair fight."

So, this is how they plan on getting rid of me. It's a good story, claiming my own pride got me killed. That tracks with the way I've lived my life.

Only, I don't plan on dying just yet. I glance at the other fighter. Rocco looks like a walking root canal, but that doesn't mean he's a better fighter than I am.

I snatch up the pen and sign all the forms.

Marzio collects the papers, examines them, and puts them away. "Good. Hold his arms."

Tomaso and Roberto suddenly grab me from behind while Marzio reaches for a baseball bat.

"Wait, what—"

He swings the bat in a vicious arc at my chest. It sinks into my ribs on the right-hand side, and I hear the bones crack. Pain explodes through me, and when my knees give out, I fall to the floor.

Marzio leans down, a gloating expression on his face. "Mia's getting rid of your baby right at this moment. If you win this fight, you'll be just in time to wake her up from the anesthetic."

Every breath causes stabbing pains in my ribs. "You're lying."

"Honor Memorial Hospital. Two o'clock. Booked her the appointment myself, and Mia can't wait."

It's not true.

She wouldn't do that. Not without talking to me.

It's not *true*.

But with her family pouring hate and poison in her ear and me gone, just disappeared like I never cared about her, what choice does she have?

Marzio leans down close to me and speaks in a hideous baby voice. "What's wrong, princess? Are you going to cry? Are you going to wet your widdle pants—"

I pull my head back and slam my forehead into the bridge of his nose with all my strength. He screams and reels back in pain, blood shooting from his nostrils.

"You piece of shit!" he shrieks, and wildly lashes out, slamming his fist into my face.

I reel back and get painfully to my feet. I don't have time to beat another man to death. I have to get out of here now.

They let me get too close to the door. Rocco is too stupid to realize what I'm about to do, but Roberto and Tomaso shout at him to grab me.

Too late.

I lunge out of the door and slam and bolt it behind me.

Then I hurry upstairs, find an emergency exit, and burst out into the sunshine. Where the hell am I? It looks like somewhere downtown, and I run toward the main road to get my bearings.

A bodybuilder comes out of the gym and heads for his car.

I limp after him, clutching my ribs and breathing hard through the pain. "Where's Honor Memorial?"

The man turns and stares at me. From the looks of him, he looks like he enjoys cage fighting so he only seems mildly surprised by the state I'm in. "Lose a fight?"

"Nah, I won."

He grins. "Good for you. But you should probably get yourself to a hospital."

"That's where I'm trying to go." I pull one of my rings from my fingers. "Give me a lift to Honor Memorial and you can keep this. It's white gold. I'm in a hurry."

"You'll get blood all over my . . ." He sighs and shakes his head. "Whatever. Get in and keep your ring. It's only ten blocks."

I get into the car, gritting my teeth against the pain and squeezing my eyes shut as black spots dance in my vision. I can't pass out. Mia needs me.

"What time is it?" I ask as I feel the car start to move.

"Five to two."

Fuck. Only five minutes before Mia's appointment. She's probably already inside, signing forms and doing God knows what.

What feels like an age later, the man pulls up outside an enormous building with Honor Memorial Hospital in foot-high silver letters over the main entrance. I push open the door and get out of the car.

"Thank you. I appreciate it."

"Good luck, man. Come train with me at the gym sometime."

His voice disappears behind me as I limp up the path to the entrance. There are people everywhere, arriving at the door from various parking lots.

Then I spot her.

Mia.

Walking arm in arm with Rieta like her sister is giving her strength for what she's about to do. My woman looks so pale. So forlorn. Even with her sister at her side, she has the devastated air of someone who's all alone in this world.

The agony in my body is nothing compared to the pain that erupts in my heart. My poor Bambi.

I limp toward her, blood dripping from my nose onto the concrete. She catches sight of me and stops dead. Every footstep is agony, and it takes a thousand light-years, but I finally close the gap between us.

I drop to my knees before her and reach for her hand. "I'm begging you not to do this. Please, Bambi."

Mia stares at my bruised and battered body, her eyes huge. Then she lifts her gaze to mine. "Laz?"

My split lip screams in protest, but I smile at her. "I'm so happy I found you in time."

Mia touches my face, her fingers gently skimming my bruises. "What happened to you? Where the hell have you been?"

I swallow hard, trying to catch my breath. "It doesn't matter. Just swear that you won't go into that hospital. We can figure this out, you and me. Just listen to what I have to say, I'm begging you."

She and Rieta exchange confused glances. "Okay, but it's normal to get a checkup when you're pregnant. If you want I can wait until next week, I guess?"

I stare from the building to Mia. "A checkup?"

"Please get up, Laz. People are staring."

"*No*. Not until you swear you won't get rid of our baby."

Mia's eyes grow huge, and she yanks her hands from mine. "What the hell, Laz? You disappear for weeks and then reappear all frantic and covered in blood because you think I'm about to have an abortion?"

I get slowly to my feet, hope slowly unfurling in my chest. "You're . . . you're not?"

"No!" Anger burns hot in her cheeks. "You think I would do that without talking to you first?"

I groan in relief, pick her up in my arms, and spin her around. My ribs scream in protest, but I don't care. Everything I want is here in my arms. Mia and our baby.

"Your uncles—never mind. Oh, Bambi, I thought I was too late. I'm the luckiest man on earth."

"Really? You look like mincemeat, and you smell like an open sewer," Rieta points out.

Mia takes my face between her hands. "They told me you ran away. They said . . . Laz, please put me down so I can talk to you."

I set Mia carefully on her feet and she examines me closely. "You've been beaten up. That's the shirt you were wearing when you disappeared. Where have you been all this time?"

"It doesn't matter anymore."

"It matters to me. Please tell me my uncles haven't been holding you prisoner all this time." When I don't reply, she becomes anguished. "Are you kidding me? They told me you ran away."

"I would never run from you. All I thought about the whole time I was locked up was you."

Mia's expression softens, but a moment later she's severe again. "Do you think I have amnesia just because I'm pregnant? My life was upended *before* you went missing, and that was because of you, Lazzaro Rosetti."

Damn, why does her saying my full name like that make my dick hard?

"Sugar pills. Goddamn *sugar pills*. I've never heard of such a dirty trick."

I can't help but smile at her like a fool. There's fight in my girl yet. I take both of her hands, pleading with her with my eyes. "Bambi, I understand that you're mad at me. After all I've done, I deserve that, but please let me go in there with you."

"Why should I?" she snaps.

"Because I want to be a part of what happens next with all my black and sordid heart."

Chapter Seventeen

MIA

The nurse at the front desk takes one look at Laz and says, "I'm sorry, but we don't have any emergency facilities at this clinic."

"Oh, we're not here for me." Laz wraps an arm around me and beams at the woman. As he smiles, a cut on his lip splits open and blood oozes down his chin. "This is my girlfriend, Mia. She's pregnant."

I shrug out of his embrace and give him a pert look. "Less of the *my girlfriend* business. You're still married, remember?"

"I signed the divorce papers today. I'm a free man." He grins wider, showing me the empty space on his ring finger, and even more blood trickles down his chin.

Mom claimed she was going to give the papers to a private investigator, but something tells me she's known exactly where Laz has been all this time.

I dig in my handbag for a clean tissue and dab carefully at the blood on his face. It's difficult to find a spot on his face that's not bruised or bleeding. "How are you feeling?"

"Ten million times better since I laid eyes on you." He reaches out, his hand hovering over my belly. "Can I?"

I glance down at myself. "There's nothing to feel. I'm only a few weeks along."

Laz's green eyes have grown soft, and he whispers, "I know. But can I please touch you there?"

Slowly, gazing into his eyes, I nod. He presses his large, warm hand against my lower stomach, and closes his eyes and groans.

"I can't believe I'm standing here touching you and our baby like this. Are you sure this isn't a dream? If I wake up and I'm still in that cellar, I'll shatter into a million pieces."

My heart squeezes painfully. I can't imagine what he must have been through, locked up for weeks without light, without hope.

"If this is a dream, it's pretty rancid," Rieta says. "Laz, you really do stink."

Does he? I haven't noticed.

"Excuse me, which one of you has an appointment?" the receptionist asks.

"Oh! Sorry, I do." I turn to her, feeling flustered and hot. I'd completely forgotten she was there. Laz keeps his hand right where it is on my belly, and I blush even harder. "My name is Mia Bianchi. I have an appointment at two o'clock."

We're directed to a room down a corridor and Laz limps along beside us.

"Laz, you really should go to the hospital," Rieta tells him.

"Not until Mia's finished here. I'll do anything she wants as soon as she's had her checkup."

There's only one chair in the room where we wait for the obstetrician, and Laz insists I sit in it even though he seems on the verge of keeling over.

"Are my uncles still alive?" I ask him.

"Unfortunately, yes," he mutters. "How did you know it was them who kept me prisoner?"

"Who else?" I reply, thinking dark and angry thoughts about my uncles. Mom as well, because I'd bet everything I own on her knowing exactly where Laz has been the entire time she was crying about him running away.

A few minutes later, the obstetrician opens the door with a huge smile on her face. As soon as she comes into the room and catches sight of Laz, she gasps in shock. "Do you need a doctor?"

"No," Laz tells her.

"Yes," I say at the same time, and then roll my eyes. "Please go ahead. He refuses to go to the hospital until I've had my checkup."

"I'm the father," he tells her proudly.

"Oh. How . . . lovely." The doctor frowns behind her spectacles as she directs me to take off my clothes from the waist down and get up on the table.

I change behind the curtain and make myself comfortable. The doctor pulls the curtain back and talks me through everything we're going to go over at this appointment. Then she starts asking me questions about my diet, lifestyle, and when I conceived.

Finally, she shoots a look at Laz. "And is everything all right at home?"

I catch her professionally concerned tone and realize that she's not only asking for my sake, but for the baby's sake, too. She wants to know whether I'm bringing a child into an unsafe environment.

"Laz, um," I begin, trying to find a way to explain away Laz's shocking appearance. "Laz is a cage fighter, and he was in one final competition. Things got carried away."

The father of my child comes forward and takes my hand. I consider slapping his fingers away, but the doctor is already watching us like a hawk, so I just smile.

"I'm all about Mia and the baby now," Laz tells her. "Nothing else matters to me anymore."

"Do the two of you live together?"

"No," I say.

"Yes," Laz replies at the same time.

I glare at him and then say to the obstetrician, "He's the father, and while everything's complicated right now, I'm safe and so is the baby. If that ever changes, you'll be the first to know."

The obstetrician casts Laz a searching look, but as he's gazing at me with the goofiest grin on his bloodied face, she seems to decide he's not a threat.

"I've had nervous dads, talkative dads, quiet dads. I've never had a bleeding dad before." She shakes her head and goes to type at her computer. "I'll order a blood test and a urine test for you, and we'll do your first scan now as well."

The doctor inserts the transvaginal ultrasound wand as we all stare at the monitor together.

I really didn't think we'd see anything, but the baby's there. Tiny, but visible on the shadowy monitor.

Laz steps forward and peers at the screen, his mouth open. "Fuck," he breathes. "Would you look at that? Our baby, Bambi. That's our baby."

Suddenly, all the color drains from his face, his knees buckle beneath him, and he falls to the ground in an unconscious heap.

I sigh as I stare at him, totally out cold. "I'm so sorry about him. If we're finished, I should get my boyfriend to the hospital if he wants to survive long enough to hold this baby in his arms."

Rieta looks at me sharply, an amused smile on her lips. "Boyfriend?"

I shake my head at my slipup. "Don't tell Laz I said that."

The obstetrician finishes with the wand and lifts her phone. "I'll order him a medical transfer to the nearby general hospital. I don't think you two can manage him on your own."

"You will? Thank you so much."

A few minutes later, Laz is on a gurney being wheeled out of the room by two paramedics, and Rieta and I say goodbye to the obstetrician.

"Don't let him do any more cage fighting. He's obviously not very good at it."

I promise her that he won't. "See you next time."

At the hospital, Laz is sent for X-rays, given a blood transfusion and a rehydration drip. He has two broken ribs and a hairline fracture in his right wrist. There's not much the nurses can do about his bruises and black eyes, but they put tape on his split lip and make him comfortable in bed.

Laz has stayed passed out the entire time, and it hurts to see this strong, proud man in the throes of exhaustion, pain, and blood loss. Rieta and I sit by his bedside, watching him sleep.

"What do you think, Mia, is this the man for you?" Rieta whispers with a smile on her lips. "This beat-up, black-and-blue, absolute scoundrel of a man is the love of your life, forever and ever, amen?"

I reach out and sweep Laz's dark hair back from his eyes so it's closer to the way he wears it when he's awake. I play with a few strands, gazing down into his handsome face. There's a fierce ache inside me as I wonder how much longer it's going to be before he wakes up.

I've missed him.

I've missed him so much.

"Unfortunately, I love this big dummy with all my heart."

"I thought you did," Rieta replies, grinning. "You want a soda or something?"

"How about a vodka and something?"

"No vodka for you, Mama."

Oh, shit. Of course not.

"Juice, then," I tell her, still gazing at Laz.

The door closes behind Rieta and I'm alone with Laz, perched on the edge of his mattress. I lean down and press a soft kiss to his lips.

"Wake up soon, my troublemaker. You and me? We're having a baby."

Chapter Eighteen

LAZ

I've been waking up on a cold concrete floor for too long, so regaining consciousness in a warm, soft bed makes me wonder what the hell is going on. There's a warm weight on my left shoulder and bicep, and when I open my eyes I see why.

Mia is sitting in a chair next to my bed and she's fallen asleep against me, her cheek pillowed on my shoulder. A sweet ache fills my chest as I look at her beautiful face.

She stayed.

My girl needed to be here when I woke up, and I'm so happy that she is because I've been so lonely locked up in that cage. It felt as if the world had forgotten about me. Like I was already dead.

The hospital room is dark and empty apart from the two of us. It must be the middle of the night.

Moving carefully because my ribs on the right side are aching, I shake her awake and ease back in the bed, making space for her.

"Bambi. Come up here. You're not sleeping in that chair."

Mia lifts her head, the wrinkles of my hospital gown printed on her cheek. "Hm? No, I can't. You're hurt."

"You're pregnant. Get up here, now, or I'll get out of bed and make you."

That persuades her to do as she's told. Mia clambers sleepily into the narrow bed and beneath the covers with me. I wrap them around her and pull her against my chest, gritting my teeth and swallowing a groan of pain as I squeeze her too tightly.

My girl mumbles sleepily, and then falls asleep again. I stroke my fingers through her hair, her warmth and softness seeping into my hard, aching bones. I don't know what I did to deserve her and our baby. Probably nothing. I'll just have to make sure I deserve them from now on.

I wake hours later to sunlight filtering around the closed blinds, and Mia still asleep in my arms. She rouses slowly, rubbing her face and stretching her toes. When she finally looks up at me, I'm smiling at her.

She doesn't return my smile. "I see you're feeling better."

"So much better. Give your man a kiss."

When I lean down to press my lips against her, she turns her face away. "I'm still mad at you."

But she's cuddled close against my chest, her fingers clenched on my hospital gown and her foot rubbing against my calf.

"Kiss me, Bambi, and say you'll be mine. Forever."

"After what you've done you deserve a slap, not a kiss."

I capture her hand in mine and press it over my heart. "I wouldn't have done it if I didn't mean forever."

I've never thought I'd say those words to a girl. I didn't believe I was built that way, or that I'd live long enough for anyone to fall in love with me. Mia's expression softens as she gazes up at me. I must look a sight with my bruised and beaten face, but she gazes at me like I'm what she's been craving most in the whole world.

"Will you be my forever?" I ask.

"You didn't leave me much choice. That was a dirty trick with the birth control."

A smile spreads over my face. "It was, wasn't it? Worked like a charm."

"Stop grinning like that."

"Why?"

Her mouth twitches and she struggles to keep a straight face. "Because it's really hard to stay mad at you when you smile at me like that."

"Bambi?"

"What?"

"Will you marry me?"

Her mouth opens and closes in outrage. "You can't... I'm not... this is... *you are unbelievable, Lazzaro Rosetti.*"

"I hope you always say my name just like that whenever you're mad at me."

"Do you plan on making me mad a habit?"

I grin unapologetically. "Probably. It's just the way I'm wired."

She shakes her head. "I'm having your baby. There are going to be *more* of you running around, raising hell." She touches my lips. "With your wicked smile." Her finger strokes along my jaw. "Your good looks." She brushes down my chest. "This scoundrel heart."

"Don't forget they will have their mother's stubborn streak. And her temper. And her big brown eyes that will make anyone fall to their knees and promise them the world."

"My temper?" she exclaims. "What about your—"

I wrap my arms around her and haul her onto my chest, cradling the back of her head and kissing her hard. I'm vaguely aware of my ribs screaming in protest, but I ignore them, and kiss my girl like I've been wandering in the desert, lost and alone, and she's my rescue team.

"You were made for me, Bambi," I murmur in a husky whisper, squeezing her tight. "If I had to live a hundred lives, I'd choose you every time."

Mia takes my face in her hands and presses another kiss to my mouth. "I'd choose you too, Laz Rosetti. No matter what people think, I'll always choose you."

I want to go on kissing her, but the pain in my chest turns into agony, and I can't stop the moan that escapes my lips.

Mia gasps and pulls back. "I'm so sorry. I'm leaning right on your broken ribs. I should get out of this bed before the nurses see me."

But I don't want her to go just yet. There are still some things I have to say.

I pull her back and wrap my pinkie around the ring finger on her left hand. "What do you think about this? The moment I get out of here, we put a ring on your finger? For real this time."

It should have been Mia wearing my ring from the beginning. I can only hope that the rocky start we've had means there's happiness waiting for us just around the corner. Right now, with my girl in my arms, I'm feeling pretty good about it.

Mia smiles and melts against me, bestowing on me a look so angelic that I think I really have gone to heaven. "I think that sounds wonderful."

Mia steps out of the bedroom dressed in a short, white satin dress with spaghetti straps, clutching a bouquet of pink roses. Her four-month baby bump is showing.

My heart is in my mouth.

"Mia," I breathe. "You . . ." I reach for her and trail off. I have no words for how radiant my bride is. "You're the most beautiful woman I've ever seen."

She smiles and goes up on her toes and kisses me. "And you're the most handsome man I've ever seen."

I straighten the cuffs of my gray suit and adjust my black tie. "Better than my usual outfit of ripped jeans and engine grease, right?"

Lately, that's the only way my bride has seen me. I'm working on engines morning until night, buying, restoring, and selling cars. Mia graduated last month, and she's been learning how to do the accounts, handle the day-to-day running of the business, and scout for new cars and customers. She's been incredible. I couldn't ask for a better partner in crime.

We've rented a small auto shop in a cheap part of town, and we're living above it in an apartment. It's not much, especially considering what Mia's used to, but she hasn't complained once.

We decided on a simple wedding, just us, some of our close friends and Rieta. We had no choice about that, seeing as most of our families aren't speaking to us and every cent we have is tied up in the car business.

As I squeeze her hand, our fingers intertwine, and I notice the plain band she's wearing on her third finger. "I'm sorry it's not a better ring. Or a bigger wedding."

She puts her fingers over my lips. "Stop that. You know a big wedding doesn't matter to me. Being married to you is what I want."

I take her face between my hands and whisper, "No one has ever believed in me the way you do. Want to marry me?"

She pretends to think about it. "Yes, Lazzaro Rosetti. I will marry you. Come on, let's go."

Rieta is waiting for us on the steps of the Town Hall, practically bouncing with excitement. When she sees us, tears fill her eyes. "Look at you, Mia. My baby sister is getting married."

A handful of people are waiting for us in the registry office. My friends and some of hers from school. She's made up with the girls she pushed away because she was afraid of her family hurting them.

It's wonderful to watch her hugging them and laughing.

The ceremony is short and sweet. Just like the first time I got married, I'm looking only at Mia.

She's looking only at me, and the smile that lights her face as she says, "I do," takes my breath away.

As we walk out of Town Hall, I spot a familiar figure standing at the bottom of the steps.

The smile vanishes from my lips. What's my brother doing here? I give Mia a kiss and leave her with her sister, and I walk down the steps to where Faber is standing by his car.

"It's bad manners, crashing a wedding," I tell him, not bothering to smile.

"I'm not here to interfere with your wedding. Congratulations to you and—"

"What do you want?"

He presses his lips together in annoyance. Screw his well wishes. He couldn't have made it any clearer what he thinks.

"To give you your wedding present." Faber passes me an envelope that's thick with sheets of paper.

I open it warily, wondering if I'm being sued by the Bianchis for breach of promise or some other nonsense. When I unfold the papers, I see that it is a legal document.

Not suing me.

Faber is signing over the inheritance that's owed to me.

I stare at them, my teeth grinding together. I thought I'd be deliriously happy the day Faber finally gave me what was rightfully mine.

"I've seen how you've pulled your life together in the past few months, and I've been impressed. Well done, Lazzaro."

I'm being patted on the head for being a *good boy*.

"You're such a pompous dickhead, Faber." I hold the envelope up, glaring at him. "Just so we're clear, this was never your gift to bestow, and I'm not saying thank you. You held what was rightfully mine hostage and made me jump through your hoops. I didn't marry Mia in order to get this money. I married her because she's my reason to go on living and being a better man."

"The fact that you—"

"I'll be able to hold my head up around my son or daughter knowing I've never compromised my own code or been a flaming hemorrhoid to my family."

"You've been a flaming hemorrhoid plenty of times," Faber reminds me.

"For fun? Sure. But the difference between you and me is that I don't destroy anyone's dreams."

I turn around and walk back to Mia, shoving the envelope inside my jacket and greeting my bride with a kiss. For a moment, I think I've had the last word with my brother.

I should have known better.

"Lazzaro."

For fuck's sake. Can't I have any peace on my own damn wedding day? When I turn around, Faber is looking supremely uncomfortable, shifting on his feet with an expression of both irritation and regret on his face.

"About withholding your inheritance. I . . . may have been wrong to do that."

I wait, brows lifted.

Faber takes a deep breath. "I was wrong. I'm sorry."

I watch him with narrowed eyes. "What do you know, my big brother knows what an apology is, after all. I'll think about forgiving you when that money is in my account."

"I would like us to be brothers once more."

"We are brothers. There's not much we can do about that. Can I enjoy my wedding day now?"

He turns to my bride. "Congratulations, Mia. I'll leave you and Lazzaro to your celebrations, but I came for a reason other than to give my brother those papers. I have a message from your mother."

Mia immediately stiffens.

"No," I say sharply. "You're going too far. Get lost before I throw you off these goddamn steps."

Mia puts a soothing hand on my chest. "It's all right, Laz. What does my mother want, Fabrizio?"

Faber casts a wary look at me and then back at Mia. "She'd like to see you. That's all."

Mia hasn't spoken one word to her mother since I busted out of the prison that her uncles made for me.

"Thank you for passing the message on, Fabrizio."

"Will you see her? Ms. Bianchi will ask me for your reply."

"Quite the lap dog, aren't you, Faber?" I growl. Can't he take the hint that this is none of his damn business?

Mia firmly shakes her head. "Not right now. I want my life with Laz to have a chance to blossom before I even think about inviting anyone in who doesn't want the best for me."

"Your mom does want the best for you."

"Then she can show me that herself when I'm ready. Thank you for passing the message on. I've got nothing else to say about it."

When he opens his mouth again, I hold a finger in his face. "Not one more word. I'm not above a fistfight on my wedding day."

He closes his mouth and nods. "Goodbye, and congratulations again."

I turn to Mia when he's gone. "Are you all right? I'm sorry about that. Faber doesn't know when to shut his goddamn mouth."

Mia gives me a smile. "Nothing could shatter my good mood today. Come on, let's go celebrate."

We have our wedding dinner in a restaurant, then our friends see us off as we drive into the mountains. Our wedding present is a weekend in a remote cabin with a big bed and a Jacuzzi.

Mia drinks a glass of non-alcoholic champagne, and we lie in the tub together. Both of us are covered in bubbles. I scoop water over Mia's belly and watch the suds slide down her bump as I cup her from behind with both hands.

There's a mirror off to one side, and as she puts her champagne down, our eyes meet in the glass.

"We're starting a new life together, you and me," I murmur, gazing at our reflections.

I remember that time all those months ago when I crept into her bed and woke her up in the middle of the night. I was behind Mia, and she saw me in the mirror by her bed. She asked me what I was doing in her room, and I told some stupid lie. That I was bored. That

I was angry.

The truth is, deep down, I've only ever wanted to be with Mia.

Ever since I first laid eyes on her, it's always been her.

I plant a kiss on her neck, smiling into her beautiful Bambi eyes. "You and me. And our baby."

Epilogue

MIA

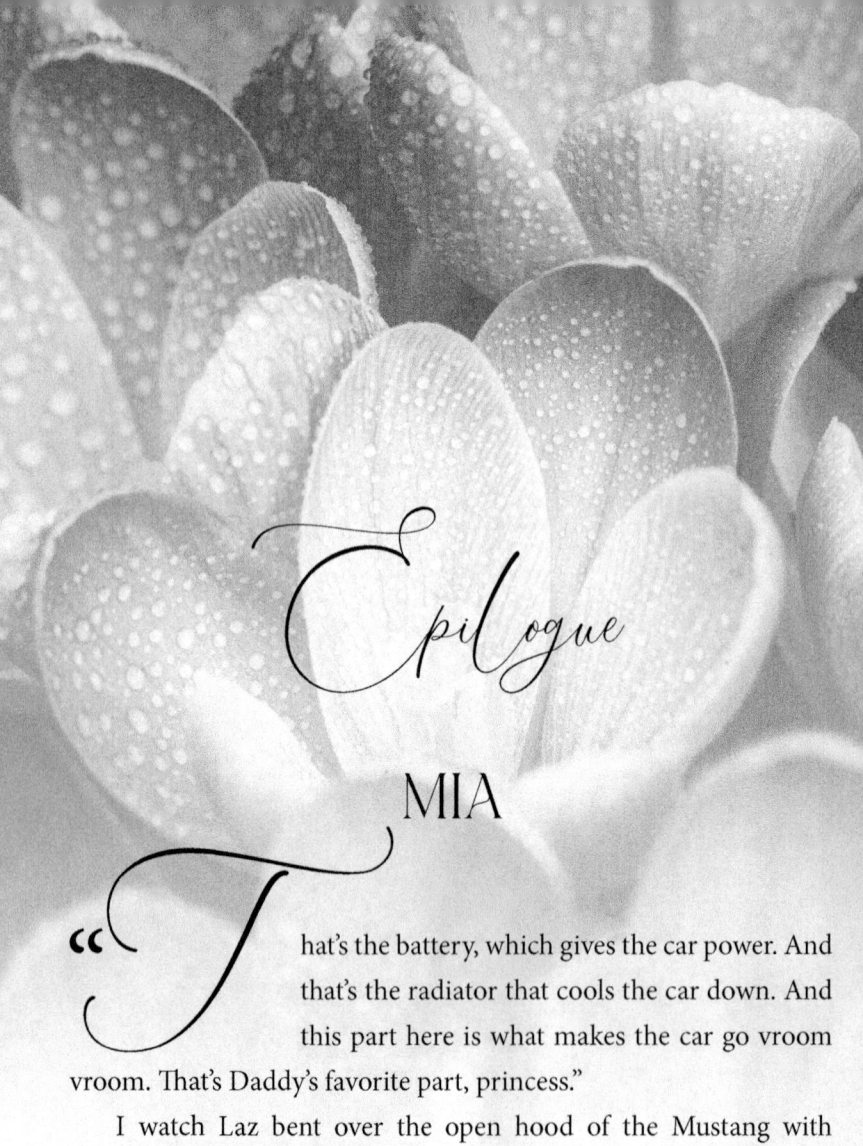

"That's the battery, which gives the car power. And that's the radiator that cools the car down. And this part here is what makes the car go vroom vroom. That's Daddy's favorite part, princess."

I watch Laz bent over the open hood of the Mustang with Mirabella in his arms, her chubby arm reaching for the shiny engine parts and black tubes.

"She's going to be fixing cars before she can talk," I tell him with a smile, pressing a kiss to his lips and then another to Mirabella's cheek. She has her dad's green eyes and his sense of mischief, too.

"That's the plan," Laz tells me with a grin. "I'll have her driving a stick shift by the time she's five."

God, I hope he's joking. I have a sneaking suspicion he's not, but all I can do is smile as I gaze at my handsome husband holding our ten-month-old daughter.

I cast my eyes around the showroom and the half a dozen classic cars on display, each one restored by Laz and his team. He's got two assistants, a young man and a woman in her fifties who knows even more about cars than Laz does. While they repair, I run the showroom and the office with an assistant of my own, and I'm studying business management part-time as well.

Life is very full, in the best possible way.

The first thing Laz did after our honeymoon was put an offer on this place. Well, the second thing. The first thing he did was to go out and buy me a big "fuck-off rock" for my ring finger. And boy is it. He wants it known from space that I'm taken.

I was so happy in our little rented place with Laz working lovingly on a handful of cars by himself. I was reluctant to leave our little nest and move into this sparkling new auto shop. What if the new place somehow spoiled things for us and sucked away all the joy? I'm so used to being miserable while living in luxury.

I should have known that nothing could spoil the magic of our relationship. Laz was happy in the rented place, and he's happy in his own, bigger place. His love for me could never change with our geography, nor my love for him.

"Come on, let's get this angel to bed, and then I'm having the longest shower known to man." He yawns noisily as he takes my hand and leads me out of the showroom.

I switch off the lights and lock up behind us, and we walk the short distance back to our house.

Once Mirabella has settled for the night, Laz takes my hand and pulls me through to the bathroom.

"Come get naked with me. I want to wash your hair."

I can tell from the gleam in his eyes that he wants more than to wash my hair. As I shimmy out of my denim dress and take off my earrings and lay them on the vanity, I watch my husband undress behind me in the mirror's reflection. The sight of his naked body still takes my breath away like it did the first time. All long limbs, lean muscle, and broad shoulders.

He catches me staring at him in the mirror and comes up behind me to help pull off my bra and panties. A moment later, his hard-on presses into my ass.

Laz kisses my throat and breathes in my ear, "Bambi, I want another baby."

I smile at his reflection, raising one ironic eyebrow. "Oh, do you? Thank you for letting me know this time."

I wondered if he'd been thinking about getting me pregnant again. He's been dropping hints about Mirabella getting older and just how beautiful I looked while I was pregnant. The thought may have crossed my mind, too. I'd love a little boy who was just like his daddy. Handsome and strong and who could protect his big sister.

Laz's hand dives down my stomach and he strokes his fingers against my clit. "What do you think, shall we have another baby?"

"I'm still breastfeeding." My head tips back against his shoulder as pleasure rolls through me. Just in case, I've been telling him to pull out when we have sex. It's hardly foolproof, but it's the easiest way to manage things. I reasoned that if I did get pregnant then it would be a wonderful surprise.

But are we ready to actually try for a baby and put one hundred percent into it?

"Not as much as you were breastfeeding. How about I stop pulling out? What do you think about that?"

I smile and open my eyes. "Why don't you find out?"

He growls and nips my neck, his eyes turning feral. "You tease, Bambi. All right. I will."

Laz goes down on his knees, pushes my legs apart, and thrusts his tongue into my pussy. He licks me all over, and I gasp and grab the edge of the vanity.

Just when I think he's going to tip me over the edge, he stands up and thrusts into me, and then grips me by the hair to keep me in place while he fucks me. Like I want to go anywhere.

The swift, deep strokes of his cock tell me just how turned on he is by the thought of getting me pregnant.

With my free hand, I reach down between my legs and roll my fingers over my clit, losing myself in the twin sensations of his thrusts and my urgently rubbing fingers.

"I'm going to come," I moan. "Please don't stop, I'm going to come."

"Well, Bambi? Am I pulling out? Or are we doing this?" His voice is roughed by desire. He's teetering on the brink of coming and he wants to hear me say it.

"Don't pull out. Fill me up with your cum." I manage to say right before my head tips back with a wail and my orgasm rips through me.

"Fuck, yes," he growls through his teeth. He strokes a handful more times and groans, and I feel his rhythm stutter. He pounds me even deeper and then slows to a halt.

But doesn't pull out. He pats my ass. "Stay right there, Bambi. Got to make sure my boys have time to work their magic."

"Your boys are tenacious already. Don't worry about them." But I go down on my elbows and relax, letting him admire the sight of his cock thrust deep into my pussy.

"This is my favorite place in the world," he murmurs, running his fingers around the place where we're joined. He hums softy to himself for a few minutes, and then slowly pulls out. "Yep, that'll do it. You're pregnant."

I push his shoulder, smiling. "You can't possibly know that."

"If you're not, I'll just have to try again. And again. You know how much I love trying with you, Bambi."

"Oh, boy, do I."

He takes my hand and tugs me toward the shower. "Come on. I promised to wash your hair."

"Happy birthday, angel!" I set a cake covered in rainbow sprinkles down in front of Mirabella's highchair. There's a fat number one candle burning on top of the cake.

Laz is wearing a paper party hat with his usual ensemble of ripped jeans and a black T-shirt, and I feel a delicious pang of love as

I watch him fitting our daughter with her party hat.

"Shall Mommy and Daddy blow the candle out with you?" Laz asks her.

Mirabella has no idea what's going on, but she's delighted by all the colors and attention and slaps her pudgy hands together.

We blow the candle out and help Mirabella open her presents. A wooden xylophone and a ride-on car from me and Laz. A wooden jigsaw puzzle with farm animals from my friends. A picture book about cars from Laz's friends. A princess Duplo castle from Auntie Rieta.

Laz reads the book about cars to Mirabella while she sucks her sticky cake fingers.

I reach into my pocket, butterflies in my belly and trying not to vibrate out of my chair in excitement. "I've got a present for Daddy, too."

I slide a pregnancy test across the table toward him.

Laz stares at it and I can see how his mind grinds to a halt, unable to believe what he's staring at. It's been two months since we started trying to get pregnant and it happened already.

He stands up with a shout, staring at the test in his hands. "You're pregnant? Oh, my God, you're pregnant!"

"I am. It was so nice for *me* to tell *you* this time."

I'm grinning as I say it because nothing could pop my happy bubble today. I'm not mad about what he did all those months ago when he secretly messed with my birth control. We've been through so much together since then, and he's been scrupulously honest about everything.

All my troublemaker wanted was for someone to love him just

as he is.

If anyone tries to hurt us, I know he'll defend us no matter what and then move heaven and earth to make things right again.

I stand up and wipe birthday cake crumbs from his mouth and give him a kiss.

"I love you, Laz Rosetti."

"I love you, Mia Rosetti," he murmurs, returning my kiss. "The mother of my children is so beautiful."

The father of my children is clever and strong, and I can't wait to see our family grow. The meaning of the word family has changed so much for me since I fell in love with Laz. It's not enough to just have one.

I reach out and stroke Mirabella's curls, wrapped tight in Laz's embrace.

Now I have a family I love, and who loves me in return, which makes me the luckiest woman in the world.

THANK YOU FOR READING BRUTAL INTENTIONS. IF YOU ENJOYED THIS BOOK, PLEASE CONSIDER LEAVING A REVIEW ON AMAZON AND GOODREADS.

ACKNOWLEDGMENTS

I wrote *Brutal Intentions* in between chapters of *Crowned*. Laz and Mia were my happy, carefree escape from some of the darker, more emotional parts of Lilia, Konstantin, Elyah, and Kirill's story. I don't love one or the other book more, but they each fed a different part of my soul.

Laz makes me laugh so much. He says whatever prim and proper people don't want to hear and he doesn't give a damn. The only person he cares about is Mia, and I love that for her.

Laz was inspired by Christian Locke and his ridiculously sexy Reels and TikToks with his guitar. Instead of giving him a music obsession, I made his about cars. I also gave him Toji's lip scar from *Jujutsu Kaisen* because I remarked to a friend once, "Toji has fucks-his-stepdaughter energy" and I couldn't get that thought out of my head.

Thank you to my beta readers Arabella, Claris, Darlene, Evva, Jesi, Liz, and Sam. When I first told you guys about *Brutal Intentions*, I knew it was going to be a challenging read for some of you. "You want me to read a cheating book?? Oh my God. Only for you, Lilith." I hoped that Laz would win you all over! Thankfully he did *phew*

Thank you to my wonderful editor Heather Fox for your support and insight. You're always a pleasure and bouncing ideas and solutions around with you is so much fun.

Thank you to my proofreader and all-round amazing person Rumi Khan.

And thank you to you for reading *Brutal Intentions*. It's been an amazing one year and two months publishing Lilith Vincent books. I'm so thankful that you've all embraced my bad boys, mafia men, and the sweet heroines who bring them to their knees. I'm excited for what's next, and I hope you are, too.

Also by Lilith Vincent

Steamy Reverse Harem

THE PROMISED IN BLOOD SERIES (complete)
First Comes Blood
Second Comes War
Third Comes Vengeance

THE PAGEANT DUET (complete)
Pageant
Crowned

FAIRYTALES WITH A TWIST (group series)
Beauty So Golden

ABOUT THE AUTHOR

Lilith Vincent is a steamy romance author who believes in living on the wild side! Whether it's reverse harem or M/F romance, mafia men and bad boys with tattoos are her weakness, and the heroines who bring them to their knees.

Printed in Great Britain
by Amazon